ROCK REJECT

A NOVEL BY
JIM WILLIAMS

ROCK REJECT

Roseway Publishing
an imprint of Fernwood Publishing
Halifax & Winnipeg

Editing: Sandra McIntyre
Cover design: John van der Woude
Printed and bound in Canada by Hignell Book Printing

This book is a work of fiction. Any resemblance to actual events or persons, either
living or dead, is entirely coincidental.

Published in Canada by Roseway Publishing
an imprint of Fernwood Publishing
32 Oceanvista Lane, Black Point, Nova Scotia, B0J 1B0
and 748 Broadway Avenue, Winnipeg, Manitoba, R3G 0X3
www.fernwoodpublishing.ca/roseway

Fernwood Publishing Company Limited gratefully acknowledges the financial support of
the Government of Canada through the Canada Book Fund, the Canada Council for the
Arts, the Nova Scotia Department of Tourism and Culture and the Province of Manitoba,
through the Book Publishing Tax Credit, for our publishing program.

Library and Archives Canada Cataloguing in Publication

Williams, Jim, 1949-

Rock reject / Jim Williams.

ISBN 978-1-55266-516-9

I. Title.

PS8645.I44494R62 2012   C813'.6   C2012-903166-6

Dedicated to Ellen Hurley (1949 – 1977), who died from meningitis,
contracted while working on an oil drilling rig in northern Alberta.
Your memory was with me as I wrote this book, and will be with me always.

ONE

Peter stepped out of the plane and descended the long flight of steps to the wet tarmac. He drew his coat tight, leaning into the wind and rain as he made his way to the terminal. Piles of snow lay against the log building, and a weathered sign beside its doors bid him Welcome to Watson Lake, Yukon Territories. With a look back at the Canadian Pacific jet that had brought him from Edmonton, he went inside.

The terminal was like any of the small-town bus depots he had been in since Toronto, florescent-lit and drab. A few locals leaned against the counter of a small canteen, drinking coffee and watching the newcomers. Peter joined the other passengers standing at the baggage conveyor. After several silent minutes it began to move and a duffle bag emerged from behind a wall, followed by cardboard boxes and two bulging green garbage bags. Then came his leather suitcase and guitar, which he carried outside to wait for the ride he had been promised at the hiring office in Edmonton.

Water dripped from the awning that covered the entrance to the terminal building. A potholed gravel road curved away a hundred yards to where it joined a highway, beyond which rose a round hill, covered in forest and touched by heavy grey cloud. Rain blew on his suitcase and he pulled it back under the shelter, then took a package of cigarettes from the pocket of his London Fog coat. As he lit one, the doors opened behind him and two men came out of the terminal. The first carried a duffel bag on one shoulder and wore a Montreal Canadiens sweater under an open jacket. A wispy moustache drooped around his mouth. Behind him the green garbage bags from the baggage conveyor

1

pushed through the doors and were dropped on the cement landing. Their owner grinned, revealing empty spaces on the sides of his mouth. His thinning hair descended into Elvis sideburns.

"Could you spare one of those, buddy?" He nodded towards Peter's cigarettes. He smiled his thanks and his thin cheeks sucked in to take a deep drag.

"That's better now," he said, blowing the smoke out the side of his mouth. "Warms you to the core, right?" He offered a large, bony hand. "George S. MacDonald. From Sydney, Cape Breton."

"Peter. Peter Stevens." His hand felt weak in George's.

"Good to meet you, Pete. This here's Claude." He gestured to the other man.

"Claude Savard." He shook Peter's hand and smiled.

"He comes from Rivière du Loup in Quebec," George continued. "I got stuck in that jeezly town hitching home from Ontario a few years back." He nudged Peter with his elbow and smiled. "Couldn't find anybody who spoke English."

"You couldn't have looked too hard," Claude said.

"I suppose not. I get freaked out trying to speak French. I hate not being able to talk to people." George sucked on his cigarette and let the smoke flow out his nose. "So where're you from, Pete?"

"Toronto."

"The Big Smoke, I figured so. I got relatives up your way. It's where the jobs are. I don't suppose you know Byron MacDonald in Oshawa."

Peter shook his head. "No, I'm afraid I don't."

"Thought I'd take a shot," George said. "You never know." He nodded his head sideways towards Claude. "So Claude and me were sittin' together on the plane and it turns out we're headin' to the same place. What are the chances of that?"

Peter shrugged and gave a small smile.

"I saw you there in Edmonton when we got on the plane," George said. "You really had your nose in a book. Where're you off to?"

"Stikine," Peter said. "A mining operation."

"No shit? That's where we're goin'. You doin' some business there?"

"Labourer. I'm hired on as a labourer in the Mine."

"Really? I would've figured you as a professional. A teacher maybe. Isn't that what you'd think, Claude?"

Claude shrugged. "How someone looks doesn't tell you what they're about."

"Christ, that's true enough. No offence meant Pete," George said. "But I do like the look of your guitar case. You're a player?"

"Yes. Well, not much recently." Peter stared for a moment at the case. "I wasn't going to bring it."

"Good thing you did, buddy. I can see we'll be havin' some good times this winter. I play a bit myself. I bet between us we know a shit-load of tunes."

Peter nodded. "We probably do." He turned away to flick his cigarette into a puddle, then stared through the rain to the grey horizon.

A station wagon turned off the highway and fishtailed on the muddy gravel, then straightened and sped to the entrance, skidding to a stop. A mud-streaked logo on the passenger door said Stikine Asbestos Corporation. The driver got out and blew out his nose on the road, then opened the rear door of the Chevy Suburban.

"Stikine, ladies and gents. Load your gear in the back."

Claude flopped his worn duffel bag inside and George tossed in his plastic bags. Peter cleared away bits of stone and gravel before carefully putting in his guitar and suitcase, bracing them steady with George's bags. He turned to see the driver watching him.

"You've got no fucking idea where you're going, do you?" He laughed as he slammed shut the rear door, then went inside the terminal building.

Peter lowered his eyes to the wet gravel. From the back seat of the wagon he heard George and Claude laughing, and for a moment he imagined taking his luggage and getting on the next plane to anywhere. Turning to step back under the awning to wait for the driver to return, he collided with a man coming out of the terminal. He looked like he hadn't shaved in a week and matted hair hung in clumps over his forehead. A smell of alcohol drifted off him.

"Sorry," Peter said automatically.

The man grunted and stumbled to the vehicle. He stood for a

moment staring at the logo on the passenger-side door then swung his leg back and kicked it hard with his heavy boots, leaving a dent, then he got in, dragging a canvas bag after him.

The driver returned and walked past Peter with a styrofoam cup of coffee. "What're you waiting for, city boy, get in the wagon. That nice coat's gotta get dirty sometime."

Peter followed him around to the driver's side of the Suburban and opened the back door. The floor was strewn with garbage, the seat greasy and covered in dust. He hesitated, then took off his coat and stepped in, folding the coat on his lap. George nudged him with his elbow and grinned. Peter couldn't help looking at the gaps where his teeth were missing.

"Looks like buddy here's been partying hard," he said, nodding to the front where the passenger was slumped against the door, already asleep, his mouth hanging open.

"Fucking idiot's like this every time he comes back from leave," the driver said as he pulled away and accelerated towards the highway. "Throws his money away on booze and women, the fool." He shook his head, swaying the oily tufts of black hair that hung over his jacket collar, sending off a sickly sweet smell of hair oil that mingled with the rank odour of whiskey breath.

Peter remembered the same smells from the hiring office in Edmonton, two days before, when the agent came out of a back room and eyed him across a sticky counter. A Hank Snow tune came out of a little transistor radio on a shelf.

"You want labourer? Order just came in for three in Stikine."

"What kind of a place is it?"

"It's a fucking mine, kid." His face was twisted by a scar on his cheek, his nose pockmarked. "Open pit, asbestos. Six ten an hour."

"Isn't asbestos supposed to be harmful?"

"I don't know and I don't fucking care."

"Can I have some time to think about it?"

"Listen kid, don't dick me around. You don't look like you're up to the job, but I'll take a chance on you. If you don't want it, then get out of here and quit wasting my time."

Peter felt his cheeks burn. "I'll take it."

Two fingers were missing from the hand that passed the forms to fill out. Peter looked for a moment at the blunt stumps protruding from the knuckles before the agent covered them with his other hand and pointed with his chin to a table across the room. Peter was sifting through his wallet for his social insurance number when another man came in the office.

"Do you have anything for labourers? I've got experience."

"Nope," the agent said, barely looking up from the papers he shuffled on the counter. "Nobody's hiring."

"Should I check again tomorrow?"

"You can check as often as you want."

The man remained standing at the counter, looking at the agent. His mouth tightened, then he turned and left the office.

The agent watched him leave, his lip curled in a sneer. "But you'll sooner find work back in Africa as you will here," he muttered.

The radio began a whining country song. The tinny sound of steel guitar grated in Peter's ears. His teeth clenched as he looked at the agent, then he swallowed and bent to finish filling the forms.

The station wagon stopped at a junction. Across the road was a vast collection of signs nailed to tall posts, announcing towns, streets, distances, populations of many countries, in many languages. Through the dirty window Peter scanned the hundreds of signs, searching for a reference to home. One post with signs pointing in all directions gave the mileage to various cities. Peter saw "Toronto" but the distance was obscured by mud.

They turned onto a wide two-lane highway. George pointed to a roadsign.

"The Alaska Highway. Learned all about it in school."

"This your first time north?" the driver asked.

"That's right. I'm gonna work a year, head home and build a house with my savings."

"Most guys last three weeks in Stikine," the driver said.

"Not me," George said. "I've got a plan and I'll stick to it."

"I've heard that one before. We'll see if you're still here after Christmas."

It began to rain again as they drove west, the Suburban rattling on the wet gravel surface and rocking in the wake of transports heading in the other direction. The driver pushed a cassette tape into the player in the dashboard. Freddie Fender began singing about wasted days and wasted nights. Through the side window Peter could see only the ditch filled with muddy snow and the dark branches of the spruce forest. They approached a bridge and passed a sign that said, "Liard River," but the rain and mist hid the water from view as they crossed over. At the far end of the bridge they hit a pothole and the wagon swerved. The sleeping passenger in the front swayed to the side and back again, his head cracking against the side window. Slowly, he pushed himself upright.

"Jesus Christ, Reinhard. Give me a fucking break." He rubbed the side of his head, then his eyes, then grimaced and hit the eject button on the cassette player.

"It's bad enough having to ride with you without having to hear that twangy hick crap."

"Fuck off, Koopman," Reinhard said, reaching to push the cassette back in, but Koopman took the tape and threw it into the glove compartment. He turned to the three in the backseat.

"This asshole is mostly harmless except when he's behind the wheel." He nodded his head sideways towards the driver. "He backed two Haul Pacs off the mountain last year."

"Up yours. It happened once."

Koopman laughed, his small teeth looked dirty. "Pardon me. You just forgot to set the fucking brake when you got out of that other one."

"What's a Haul Pac?" George asked.

"Ore haul dump truck," Koopman said. "They were both eighty-five ton, right, Reinhard? You like to smash up the big ones."

"One was a seventy-five, and quit fucking reminding me." He cranked the wheel hard and the station wagon turned at a junction in the highway, skidding sideways before straightening on the adjoining road. A sign said they were heading south into British Columbia.

"A case in point," Koopman said. "You can't talk and drive at the same time." He rummaged in his bag for a pint bottle of whiskey. "Who do you go down on, Reinhard? There's gotta be a reason they let you operate this piece of shit, and Christ knows it's not your driving skill."

"Quit buggin' my ass, Koopman. I'm trying to drive. Drink your fucking booze and go back to sleep."

"If you insist." Koopman took a drink and let out a belch. He turned to the backseat. "You guys labourers?"

"That's right," George said. "It'll do for starters. What's your job?"

"I run a blast hole drill in the pit. At least I did before I went on leave. Reinhard, what the fuck's happening with the contract negotiations?"

"How the fuck should I know? Nobody's saying anything."

"What's that all about?" George asked.

"The contract expires soon and we want a big wage hike to keep up with the mines in the Yukon. They were supposed to start talking when I went out on leave."

"What do you think will happen?" Claude asked.

"It all depends. There's still a shitload of high-grade ore in the Mine but the Company's profits are way down. If they don't think we're worth it then you guys'll either be walking a fucking picket line or riding back to Watson Lake in a month." Koopman took another drink, then offered the bottle to Claude. "You might as well be drunk when we get there. The place might not look so bad then."

Claude took a drink, then George. Peter put it to his lips and let a bit burn into his throat, then handed it back to Koopman. The taste of the cheap rye turned his stomach and he opened the window to chase away its smell. Drops of cold rain hit his face. For a moment he saw a river through an opening in the trees, then the forest closed in again and all he could see was a blur of spruce branches. He thought of Toronto on a warm September evening, of walking with Rose, of how her body felt against his. He rolled up the window, feeling suddenly cold. Wrapping his arms around himself, he closed his eyes and let his head fall back against the seat.

The taste of rye was in his mouth ten days before when he drank the remains of a bottle he found under the kitchen sink on the last walk-through of his empty apartment. Standing in the entrance to the living room, his eyes roamed the bare walls and curtain-less windows. All that remained was a music stand in the centre of the dirty parquet floor. Heat from the whiskey rose into his chest and throat, and his eyes stung with tears as he picked up his suitcase and guitar and left the apartment.

The gravel highway wound south for an hour and a half through forest and rising mountains. It was six o'clock and getting dark when they passed a large mud-splattered sign that said Stikine, Home of the World's Finest Asbestos. A few minutes later, buildings came into view.

"That's the Administration Building," Reinhard said, nodding towards a wide, two-storey log structure. "You need to be there at nine tomorrow morning for intake."

They passed a massive building on the left. Directly behind it loomed a hill, twice the height of the building itself.

"That's the Mill," Koopman said. "Working in there is dusty and dead boring, but it's fucking warm in the winter."

"What's that behind it?" Peter asked, twisting around to get a better look.

"The tailings pile. It's the waste from the Mill and a lot of it's asbestos fibre."

A long structure extended from the Mill up the side of the pile, ending a distance above the top. A steady stream of waste fell off the end of it onto the pile, sending up a cloud of dust that floated away. Peter wondered if anyone lived near the dust. Or if he was going to live near it.

The Suburban splashed through mud and potholes, passing men walking along the road towards a large log building. Steam poured out of exhaust vents on its roof.

"Dinnertime," Koopman said. "Reinhard, you're a prince. An asshole, but a prince."

They came to a row of long, low buildings and stopped in front of one of them. Its front door banged open and shut as men went in and out, crossing the muddy porch on their way to eat.

"This is your bunkhouse," Reinhard said, handing each of them in the backseat a key. "Your room numbers are on the key tags. Get your stuff and go to the cookhouse for dinner."

"Good luck," Koopman said as he headed off to his bunkhouse.

Peter waved after him but Koopman didn't turn around. Reinhard drove away, spinning the tires and throwing mud on Peter's bags. He stared for a moment at his splattered belongings, then bent down and tried to wipe off the worst of it with his hand.

In the growing gloom, he looked around at the muddy road, at the row of bunkhouses with paint peeling, at the dark forest and darker mountains that squeezed the narrow valley. A huge front-end loader rumbled along the road followed by a pickup truck carrying some kind of machinery. A group of men in grimy coveralls and hard hats walked by, laughing loudly through their ragged beards and moustaches.

George was on the porch of the bunkhouse introducing himself to men coming out the door, heading for dinner. Claude stood on the stairs, his duffle bag on his shoulder, smiling comfortably. Peter felt hollow. The voices, the footsteps, the engines all echoed inside him. He pretended to tie his boots, waiting for the porch to clear, then picked up his bags and went inside to find his room.

He closed the door and leaned back against it, savouring the solitude. The room reminded him of a university dorm: a small single bed, a counter under the window, a chair. A sink, shelves and cupboard by the door. He listened to the voices of men walking on the road, the sound of the bunkhouse door opening and closing, footsteps along the hallway, keys turning locks, the hissing of steam heat in the radiator. He sat on the bed and struggled with a desire to lie down, sleep the night and get a ride back to Watson Lake in the morning. Staring at the floor, at a crack running across the dingy vinyl tiles, he thought of his journey to this place, of the long, numbing days on the bus to Edmonton, of the strained goodbyes in Toronto. Of riding in an elevator to the top floor of the Park Plaza Hotel, watching himself in the mirrored wall as he put on his suit jacket, noticing the stained underarms of his white shirt, wet from the mid-day heat and from his nerves. He noticed too the looseness of his collar as he tightened his tie, how it slid from side to side as he centred the knot. Wishing he could simply press the button to retreat downwards, when the doors slid open and he stepped out and entered the restaurant.

His father was finishing his soup as the maître 'd brought Peter to the table. He made a show of taking a pocket watch from his vest to check the time, his mouth twisting in a familiar critical curl.

"You realize you're late. I have patients at one thirty."

"I'm sorry, Dad. I was delayed."

His lips pressed tight, he signalled to the waiter, then forced a smile towards his son. "I've ordered for you, to save time."

"I'm not very hungry."

"Nonsense. You're thin. Your clothes are hanging off of you."

Peter shrugged. "I'm fine, really." A bowl of soup appeared in front of him. He picked up his heavy soup spoon and toyed with the thick vichyssoise.

His father took an envelope from the pocket of his suit coat and laid it on the table. "Here are the post-dated cheques for your rent. They will see you through your next term, and when you begin your residency we can discuss what you will need then."

Glancing at the envelope, Peter picked up his water glass. His shaking hand spilled some on his shirt as he took a sip. "Actually, Dad." He dabbed at the wet spot with his linen napkin, avoiding his father's eyes. "I won't be needing your help. I'm giving up the apartment at the end of the month."

"Why in god's name would you do that?"

Peter let his spoon drop and nudged the bowl aside. "I've decided to go away, Dad. I can't just carry on as if nothing's happened."

His father laid his hands on the table, his face assuming its look of certainty. "Of course not. You must carry on knowing full well what has happened. You have a responsibility, Peter."

"To whom? You?"

His father's eyes narrowed. Peter turned from them, leaning his head onto his hand, the elbow propped on the table. "I'm sorry, Dad. Maybe I'll finish school sometime, but not now." He looked at his father. "Please try and understand."

His father's hand went to his chin, stroking it as he studied his son.

"This is hardly what I had hoped for, but that goes without saying." He leaned back in his chair, his eyes softer. "Where is it you want to go?"

"I don't know. Somewhere to work. And to think."

His father nodded. "I suppose it might do you good to be out in the working world. The summers I spent in the logging camp…"

"I know, Dad. You've told me about that before."

They looked briefly at each other, then his father consulted his pocket watch.

"Duty calls." He picked up the envelope and slipped it in his pocket, then stood beside Peter and laid a hand on his shoulder, looking down intently into his son's face, searching into him in a way Peter hadn't known before. "When your plans are clear, let your mother and me know." He hesitated, and Peter wondered for a moment if he would see his father cry, then he gave Peter's shoulder a squeeze, turned and left.

A waiter placed a plate of poached salmon in front of him, silently removing the untouched soup. Peter looked at the artful arrangement of fish and vegetables, their aroma turning his stomach, and pushed back his chair. He felt like he was floating as he made his way out of the restaurant into the stairwell beside the elevators, and slowly down fourteen floors to the heat of Bloor Street.

TWO

Peter arrived at the Administration Building just before nine and the receptionist waved him over into a chair beside her desk.

"New employee?"

"Yes, I just arrived yesterday."

"Name?"

"Stevens."

She sifted through file folders and found his. He watched a long blonde braid roll over her shoulder as she scanned his application form.

"Toronto. I took a summer course there two years ago. It's a big change to land here, eh?" She smiled at him; he dropped his eyes.

"It is, yes."

"A few items aren't filled out, though. Let's see, next-of-kin?"

He saw her glance at his wedding ring. He slid his hands off the desk onto his lap, twisting the ring around on his finger.

"In case there's an emergency."

"Oh, sorry. My parents." He gave her the details.

"Previous employer and occupation."

"I've been a student."

"Really?" She looked at the top of his form. "You're what? Twenty-five? You've been in graduate school?"

He glanced at her, surprised at the question. Her face was open, interested.

"Sort of," he replied.

"What were you studying?"

He looked back down at his hands. "Things that I'll never use."

"If you say so," she said after a moment passed. "You'll be starting work tomorrow, day shift up in the Mine. Be at the Mine Dry at eight. Go to the Board Room now for the safety lecture." She pointed to a door across from her desk.

"Is there a washroom I can use first?"

"Down the hall, on the left." She looked at a clock on the wall that said one minute to nine. "But you'd better be quick. He starts at nine sharp."

Peter stood at the sink in the men's room washing his hands. His fingers paused on his ring, then slid it over the soapy knuckle. He looked at it sitting in the palm of his hand and remembered the moment Rose slipped it on his finger, her smile as she held his hand in both of hers. He closed his eyes to the memory and put the ring in his pocket.

His looked into the mirror, into his face ten inches away. His unshaved cheeks were drawn in, his brown eyes rimmed with darkness. Less than an inch of hair showed above his high forehead. He rinsed the soap from his hands, then flicked his wet fingers at his face in the mirror and watched as the drops rolled down the glass, fragmenting his reflection.

The instructor stopped in mid-sentence and looked at his watch when Peter entered the Board Room.

"We run on time here. Lateness costs you demerit points. Don't let it happen again."

"Sorry sir," Peter mumbled, taking a seat at the back.

Seven men sat around the table. The instructor stood in front of a blackboard across which was printed: IGNATIUS "IGGY" BENEDETTI—SAFETY SUPERVISOR. His shirt was starched, and tight curly hair matched his tight mouth. He glared for a moment at Peter, then slowly swung his gaze around the table, pausing on each face in turn.

"Punctuality, obedience and responsibility are the cornerstones of safety. Be on time for everything. Obey management personnel immediately for your safety and well-being. They wear white hard hats, like mine here."

He held it up high. Safety Supervisor was on the front, in tall red letters.

"Management is there to protect you, just like your safety boots, hard hats and safety glasses. Wear your safety glasses at all times. Even walking down the road, something could fly up and hit you in the eye. Two demerit points for not wearing safety glasses on the job."

He paused to look at the new employees. "Any questions?"

George MacDonald raised his hand. Peter saw him nudge Claude with his other elbow. "Suppose it's really cold, sir. And suppose I'm outside and having a coffee break. Maybe the steam'd fog up my safety glasses. They might even freeze over. Would we get demerit points if we take them off then?" He winked at Claude, who twirled the end of his moustache.

"That's a stupid question," Iggy said. Clean safety glasses are a must, but you have to take them off and clean them at a safe and responsible time." He looked at Claude. "And long hair is a safety hazard. Keep it short and it won't get caught in machinery."

He gave them both a severe look, then looked down to make a note on his clipboard. George gave him the finger. Peter watched, fascinated.

"And that goes for all of you," Iggy said. "Carelessness and irresponsible behaviour can cause serious injury or death and I won't put up with it. Any more questions?"

Claude's hand went up. Iggy frowned.

"What?"

"A couple of my cousins work in the asbestos mills in Quebec and they wear dust masks. Are we going to wear them here?"

"That's a good question and I'm glad you brought it up so I can set the record straight." Iggy folded his arms across his chest. "We mine chrysotile asbestos here and it doesn't harm you. That's what they mine in Quebec too, so you should tell your cousins they don't have to worry. Ours is white asbestos. It's the blue that's harmful and they mine it in Russia and South Africa."

"But why would his cousins need to wear masks if it's not harmful?" George asked.

"Perhaps they are working in extremely dusty conditions," Iggy replied, irritation creeping into his voice. "Look, anything can be hazardous to your health if there's too much of it. Alcohol, overeating, medicines, sunshine. I could go on and on, but my point is that our asbestos is no different from anything else. So if you feel that you're sensitive to a little dust, then you can ask your foreman to get you a mask." He checked his watch. "That's all. Go for your medical exams in the infirmary now, and I wish you all safe and happy working."

George looked at Peter and rolled his eyes. Peter forced a smile and shrugged.

A cigarette hung from the mouth of the company doctor as he tested Peter's reflexes. The unbuttoned collar of his once-white shirt was stained. His tie was loose and off to one side.

"Where did you study?" Peter asked.

"What's that?"

"Where did you get your degree?"

He looked at Peter suspiciously, one eye closed against the cigarette smoke.

"Ontario."

"Oh. U of T?"

"No." He looked into Peter's eyes and ears.

"How do you like practising way up here?"

"Nobody bothers me. Take off your shirt." He listened to Peter's lungs.

"Is it true that the asbestos dust here isn't harmful?" Peter asked as he buttoned up his shirt. "That's what the safety supervisor just told us."

The doctor made entries in a file, then looked across his desk at Peter. "I'd wear a mask." He closed the file and put it on the side of his desk. "You're fine. Send in the next guy."

Just before noon Peter stood at the bottom of the wide wooden steps in front of the Administration Building, looking north across the road at a wall of mountains a quarter of a mile away, their upper halves covered in snow that dazzled in the sun. One of the mountain peaks looked like a broken tooth, a jagged piece missing from its top. A road zigzagged up the slope to this gap and as he looked closely Peter saw a dump truck, tiny in the distance, climb to the top and disappear behind a long building that seemed to cling vertically to the side of the mountain. From the building's lower end what looked like a ski chairlift emerged. Peter followed it down the mountain and across the valley and saw that it carried huge buckets that crossed high over the road and disappeared into a massive shed connected to the Mill. A bucket came out of the shed and began the ride in the other direction. He looked more closely along the length of the cable and saw dozens of buckets on their way up and down the mountain, the sun throwing their moving shadows across the spruce forest.

Footsteps thumped down the stairs behind him.

"Pete, where've they put you?"

Peter turned and looked at George. "Put me?"

"What job you got, man? What department?"

"Oh, sorry. Up there, in the Mine." He looked again to the jagged top of the mountain peak and felt nervous. "I start tomorrow day shift."

"Claude and me are in the Mill. It'll be a warm, cushy winter." He clapped a hand on Peter's shoulder. "Let's get some lunch and hit the bar."

Peter made himself not recoil from George's hand. He forced a smile and walked alongside them to the cookhouse for lunch. Afterwards, George and Claude turned towards the bar, but Peter hung back.

"I want to pick up my work gear from the Company Store."

"Shit, Pete. You got all afternoon for that. Come on for a few first."

"No. I just want to get it all done. I'll see you later."

"You know where to find us," George said.

He put his new coveralls, miner's boots, hardhat and safety glasses on his bed. The curtain fluttered in front of the window he had left open in the morning to purge the stale smell left by the last resident. He closed the window and picked up the paperback novel he had brought with him. The book's outline remained on the desktop. He ran his hand across the Formica surface and looked at the fine dust that coated his palm, then at the desktop with the swipe across its dusty surface. He looked around the room, at his blankets and pillow, at his clothes hanging and at the floor, wondering if everything was as dusty as the desktop. He took a dirty t-shirt and wiped the surfaces mostly clean, then sat in the one chair and lit a cigarette.

He watched the slow movement of the curtain waving in the heat rising from the radiator. Through the window was another bunkhouse, thirty feet away. Snow covered the ground in between. A light was on in a room opposite his, and he watched as its occupant paced back and forth, talking to someone, maybe himself. Peter stubbed out his cigarette and sat as daylight faded to dark in the room.

Someone switched on the light in the corridor and it reflected into the room from under his door. He thought of blocking it with a towel to give himself darkness, but couldn't bring himself to move. He heard men coming through the front door and going into rooms. Back from dinner, he guessed. He looked at his watch. Not yet. Another half hour. He stayed motionless in his chair in the gloom, listening, feeling his heart beating. At ten to seven, ten minutes until they stopped serving, he forced himself to stand, put on his boots and coat, and go to the cookhouse.

He pushed through the door as Claude and George were leaving. George grinned as he walked unsteadily, awkwardly trying to pull on his jacket.

"Pete, old buddy," he slurred. His eyes were glassy. "You gotta get your arse over to the bar. We're havin' a hell of a time."

"After I eat." Peter backed into the dining hall. "I'd better get in here before they close up."

The steam counter server turned and looked at the clock as Peter stood with an empty tray. It was two minutes past seven.

"The rule is if you're late you don't get served." He pushed a plate of mashed potatoes and pork chops at Peter.

"I'm sorry. It won't happen again."

The potatoes were cold. A woman in dirty kitchen whites washed the floor while a few men smoked and laughed loudly at a table in the corner. The laughter, the buzz of the overhead fluorescent lights, and the clatter and banging of dishes in the kitchen all grated in his ears. He took his tray to the dishwashing counter, put on his coat, and went outside.

He stood on the muddy road in the damp freezing air, listening to the thump of a jukebox coming from the bar fifty yards away and he moved towards the music. Someone came out of the bar, nearly fell as he stumbled down the steps, then weaved erratically along the road. He gave a drunken salute as he passed Peter. The cookhouse door opened and two men came out. The drunk stumbled into one of them, who grabbed him by the front of his open jacket.

"Don't fuckin' bump into me, you little shit, or I'll break your arm," he said, and shoved him against the cookhouse wall. His friend stood smoking a cigarette, watching the drunk slide down the wall onto a pile of dirty snow. The two men walked away laughing. The drunk leaned to one side and vomited. Peter crossed the road and put an arm around his shoulders to help him up, but the man shook him off.

"Leave me alone," he said. He sat on the snow with his head between his legs, alongside a puddle with a skim of ice on top. Peter stepped back and watched him for a minute, the stench of alcohol and puke filling his nose.

"Are you okay?" he asked. "You sure you don't need any help?"

There was no response. Peter waited for a minute, then walked slowly back to his bunkhouse.

THREE

In the morning Peter opened the curtain to six inches of snow piled up on the window ledge. He felt empty as he remembered how it had been the year before in Toronto. Mid October, warm sun, red and yellow leaves falling. He and Rose with their guitars, on a bench by the playground in Christie Pits. Children watching as they made music together. Without thinking his hand came up and slapped the side of his face, startling him away from the memory. He turned from the window and began to dress for work.

His miner's boots looked huge with their thick felt liners and bulbous steel toes. They're like clown's shoes, he thought as he clumped through the snow to the cookhouse for breakfast, anxiety knotting his insides. He made himself eat, hoping the food would settle his stomach, then followed a group of men to the Mine Dry. A toe of his boot caught the edge of the stairs up into the wood frame building and he fell on his outstretched hand, sending a stab of pain through his wrist and his hard hat into the snow. Three men passed him as he got up and brushed himself off. He avoided their eyes, nothing was said, and he entered the building behind them.

Inside was a large room that smelled of sweat and machine oil. Men stood by rows of benches lowering grimy coveralls and heavy jackets that hung from baskets suspended by pulleys attached to the high ceiling. They were changing out of their clean clothes which they put into the basket, then hauled on a rope to hoist the basket back up. Peter pulled a tag from his pocket with the number of his basket on it, but as he had unknowingly changed into his work clothes in his bunkhouse room, he edged to the wall by the entrance and leaned against it to wait.

Beyond the benches an opening revealed a tiled shower room. A door to Peter's left said "Management Personnel Only," and a window next to it looked into a room where men in white hardhats leaned over a table covered with charts. A few men stood waiting in front of the window and others joined them as they finished dressing for work. The window swung open.

"Alright, listen up."

Peter wondered about the accent. English? Australian? He edged closer to see. "Mine Superintendent" was on the front of the man's white hat, a sharp nose, clipped moustache and starched brown shirt underneath. He flipped through pages on a clipboard.

"We're falling behind on our production targets for the month, and things better pick up this week. There's too much goddamn lag time between drilling, blasting and mucking-out. I want to see the machines moving in quicker between each operation and I especially want to see you goddamn truck drivers haul ass up out of the pit to the crusher. I want things moving up there. Understand?"

There were muttered obscenities from the crowd of miners. A strong voice boomed from behind Peter's shoulder.

"Piss off, De Vleit. I know the mine regulations as well as you do, and we move at the speed that's allowed."

Peter glanced behind him and saw a man a head taller than himself. His moustache was long and ragged, and it looked like he hadn't shaved in days. He wore rimless glasses and a red hard hat with a Union logo on the front, above the words Shop Steward. He pointed a thick finger at the superintendent.

"You're telling us to risk our fucking lives up there while the Company negotiators are telling us to go screw ourselves over a wage increase."

The superintendent's face hardened. "You and your goddamn Union aren't running this mine, McGuinness. I'm running this mine and you do what I tell you to do." He paused and his fingers went to the collar of his shirt, then smoothed across his moustache. "And that goes for every goddamn one of you. Now, here's today's assignments, and let's get mining."

He called each man's name with their orders. Peter's was last.

"It'll be Rock Reject for you, Stevens." He looked Peter up and down. "See how you like swinging a shovel. Look for Clarkson, the foreman, he'll show you what to do. Get going, the man-haul bus is here."

Peter hurried out of the building. Men were filing out of what looked like an old school bus and they passed him going into the Mine Dry, their faces dirty and bleary-eyed after working the night shift. Peter's shift began boarding the bus and he joined the line. A few steps away he saw Koopman looking his way and he half-raised a hand in hello but Koopman ignored him. Peter dropped his eyes to the beaten-down snow on the ground, stuck his hand into the pocket of his new work coat and waited for his turn to climb onto the bus. He found an empty double seat in the back, sat and stared out the window.

The bus bounced along the potholed road to the foot of the mountain then began to climb, slowing to a crawl at each sharp switchback where muddy snow was piled high. As they gained altitude he could see all of Stikine: the Administration Building, the Mill and a dozen other buildings clustered at one end, all dwarfed by the massive bulk of the tailings pile, and all partly obscured by the haze of dust drifting from it. A strip of forest stood between the plant and the townsite, with the bunkhouses, the cookhouse, the store, the bar, and then rows of streets with single houses. They climbed higher and soon he could see far down the valley and the mountains stretching to the horizon, their peaks glowing in the low morning sun. He remembered a family trip to the Rockies, sitting in the backseat looking out at a wilderness valley, the hum of the road running through his twelve-year-old body. The smell of his mother's perfume and his father's aftershave filling the car. Wanting the trip never to end. He was startled when McGuinness sat down beside him.

"Dave McGuinness, your Union president." He offered a hand that dwarfed Peter's.

"I'm Peter," his voice cracked. He cleared his throat and tried again. "Peter Stevens."

"Good to meet you. Where are you working?"

"He told me to go to Rock Reject to shovel."

McGuinness shook his head. "There's a futile fucking job. I did my share of it before I started driving truck." He glanced down at Peter's hands resting on his legs, at his long thin fingers. "I hope you've got good gloves with you. Shovelling that shit all day will tear up your hands pretty quick."

Peter curled his hands into fists and slipped them into his coat pockets. "I got a pair in the store yesterday."

McGuinness smiled and his moustache draped over his top teeth. "Most guys do fuck all in Rock Reject, so don't bust a gut trying to get much done."

"Won't that piss off the superintendent?" Peter asked.

"De Vleit. Don't get me started on that asshole. The Company brought him here from their operation in South Africa, and he's been trying to treat us like he treated the miners there. I think it drives him crazy that he can't have us whipped."

Peter smiled. He felt like laughing out loud to release the tension he felt, but he stayed quiet. The bus pulled to a stop in front of a battered plywood building.

"We're here," McGuinness said. "That's the Mine office. There's a heater in there if you need to get out of the cold." He handed Peter a booklet. "Here's the contract with the Company, the collective agreement. It's got all your rights in it. We're bargaining for a new one with a wage increase but the Company's taking a hard line. Come to the meeting next Wednesday and you'll hear a report on the negotiations. The more we've got the membership behind us, the stronger we'll be."

Peter followed him off the bus. McGuinness pointed to a white pickup truck parked across the road. The driver wore a white hardhat and was talking on a radio. "There's Clarkson. He'll show you what to do. If you've got any problems with your job, come find me."

Peter tried to think of something to say, a question to ask that would keep McGuinness with him longer but nothing came into his mind. He stood for a moment watching him head towards a line of immense dump trucks parked along the edge of the rock-strewn roadway with their engines running, then he turned and walked over to Clarkson's pickup. The foreman was still talking on his radio so Peter stood to the side and waited while snow swirled around him. A horn blared behind him and he turned to see one of the dump trucks bearing down on him, its tires far taller than he was. The truck thundered past as he ran to the edge of the roadway, then two more followed behind, the roar of the engines and the crashing of the empty boxes on the truck beds vibrating through him. He watched as the trucks disappeared down a steeply sloping road, then took a deep breath to try and calm his shaking insides.

A mound of earth and snow four feet high ran along the edge of the road. He put one foot on the mound to brace himself and looked over it across a pit, the far side two hundred yards away and just visible through the blowing snow. The top of the mountain had been sliced off and its centre hollowed out. He leaned forward to look down, staring in amazement into the massive hole in the earth. The pit narrowed as it deepened, with five huge benches ringing the inside. A steep roadway went from bench to bench and he saw the dump trucks banging their way down the hundreds of feet to the bottom level, where a giant shovel sat facing a wall of earth. The bottom of the pit slowly faded from his view as snow began to fall harder.

A door opened and shut behind him and he turned to see Clarkson standing in front of his pickup.

"You the new labourer?" He looked at a sheet of paper from his pocket. "Stevens?"

Peter liked his voice. It had an easiness that made him relax. "That's right. I'm supposed to go to Rock Reject."

"Into the dungeon." He gave Peter a quick smile as he stuck the paper in the back pocket of his jeans, then gestured with his head, "Follow me."

He was tall, his strides long, and Peter hurried to keep up. Fifty yards along they came to a battered plywood building perched on the edge of the road opposite the pit. Its front was mostly open to the road, and it extended several hundred feet down the side of the mountain in the direction of the townsite, somehow clinging to the steep slope. Out of the bottom emerged the tramline of buckets that he had seen from below the day before. A dump truck drove past, then stopped and backed up to the edge of the open front of the building and tilted up its box, sending a cloud of dust into the air as the load fell inside. Clarkson waved to the driver and climbed up the ladder on the side of the truck to speak to him while Peter waited, looking up the twelve or more feet to where the two men were talking. The wind gusted a heavy flurry of snow against his back and he shivered as it melted on his neck. A few feet away a battered door hung crookedly on the side of the building, and he went through it to get out of the wind.

The door led directly onto a steel grate walkway that skirted the edge of an undulating, v-shaped pit that was chewing the load of rock from the truck. One side of the pit was a huge, rotating steel plate, and the boulders were being methodically crushed into pieces small enough to fall out of the narrow opening at the bottom. A wooden railing separated Peter from the pit. A sudden rush of vertigo made him lean away, back against the plywood wall. He covered his ears against the noise and stared in fascination as the last of the load was crushed small and dropped onto a moving conveyor underneath. Through the open front wall he saw the dump truck pull away, and a moment later Clarkson was beside him.

"This is the jaw crusher," he shouted. "It's the first step in the concentration process for the ore. You'd better get yourself some hearing protection from the store since you'll be spending time in here."

Peter followed Clarkson down the walkway that extended thirty feet along the edge of the crusher pit. At the far end was a dust-coated booth with a window that overlooked the pit, and Clarkson slid open its door to speak to the man sitting inside. He wore two coats over his coveralls, and earmuffs clamped his hard hat to his thin, bearded face. A heater glowed red inside the cramped compartment, where the surfaces looked as dust-covered as the outside. An open paperback novel sat alongside a control panel, and Clarkson pointed to it.

"Keep that out of sight, Paul. You know the rules."

Clarkson turned and started down a flight of steel stairs. The crusher operator closed his door. Through a side window Peter saw him pick up the book and settle back in his chair to read.

Peter awkwardly descended the steep stairs in his heavy miner's boots to where a wide conveyor belt came from under the jaw crusher and sped along a dimly lit corridor that sloped steeply down the side of the mountain. Bare bulbs hung from the ceiling, lighting the dust that floated in the cold air, so thick that the view beyond fifty feet was obscured in the haze. Peter felt the back of his throat tighten with each breath he took.

He followed the foreman down the corridor to a door that led into a warm fluorescent-lit room. Koopman sat at a table with a book in his hands while two other men played cards. A water cooler sat next to a filthy sink.

"Shit, you guys," Clarkson said. "If De Vleit shows up and sees you all fucking the dog in here, my ass is on the line."

"De Vleit can go fuck himself, Ian," Koopman said. "And I'll say that to his face, too. If he's so concerned about us not working, then he can get us some goddamn machinery that runs. If my drill is down then I should be sent home with pay and screw this 'go to Rock Reject' bullshit."

Clarkson took off his hardhat and wiped his forehead. "I know what you're saying, Michael, and six months ago I was saying the same thing. But I'm wearing this white hat now and I need you guys to at least look like you've been out shovelling spills back onto the conveyors, or else I can get canned. De Vleit's going to be through here sometime this morning, so give me a break and don't be hanging around in here."

He turned to leave and saw Peter by the door. He turned back to Koopman.

"Show this new guy what to do, will you, Michael?"

Clarkson left. Koopman went to the water cooler and took a drink, then looked at Peter. "He was a shovel operator until a few months ago, then he took the foreman's job. They just had a second kid and he wanted better benefits."

"He seems like a nice guy," Peter said.

"That's right. A lot of the management guys are pricks. Power trippers. But Ian's a good shit." He crumpled his paper cup and threw it on the dirt floor.

"I was in the car with you the other day, coming from Watson Lake," Peter said.

"That so? I was pretty hungover, can't say I remember much of the trip."

"So what should I be doing in here?"

Koopman laughed. "What you should be doing is getting another job. What you're supposed to be doing is a fucking waste of time. Leave your lunch here, grab that pick and shovel and follow me."

They stepped out of the lunch room just as a deafening roar rolled over them. Peter covered his ears against the noise.

"That's a truck load dumped into the crusher," Koopman shouted. "Happens every few minutes if the digging in the pit is good." Hearing protectors were attached to the side of his hardhat and he flipped them down over his ears, then started down the corridor.

Jagged lumps of broken rock the size of grapefruit began to speed by on the conveyor belt. The light grew dimmer as they walked downwards along the packed earth floor. Dust coated the unpainted plywood walls and ceiling and Peter tasted it in his mouth. He turned and looked back and saw their footprints like they were in new fallen snow.

They climbed down a flight of wooden stairs beside a ten-foot-high, funnel-shaped machine. The conveyor they had been following dumped ore into its open top and another one led away from the bottom, moving the rock that had been crushed smaller further down the building and out of sight into the murky haze of dust. The machine made a piercing noise—like a nail being driven through his ears. At the bottom of the stairs the corridor was smaller, the ceiling lower. Koopman leaned close to Peter to shout.

"There are three of these cone crushers down the line from the jaw crusher and where the ore drops out of them is where the spills usually happen. We're standing on spilt ore, so you can shovel away to your heart's content. Dig the stuff off the walkway and throw it onto the belt."

Peter looked up at the ceiling timbers that were caked in dust. He raised his hand and touched them. "How come the ceiling's so low here? It'll be hard to swing the pick."

Koopman laughed. "They say this place was built with fifteen-foot ceilings so that means there's over seven feet of ore spill under our feet. Like I said, it's a futile fucking job. Coffee break's at ten, lunch at noon. Have fun."

Koopman turned and went back up the stairs towards the lunch room. Peter watched him leave, then stared at the machine in front of him that was smashing apart the rock pouring into it and depositing a stream of fist-sized pieces onto a conveyor underneath. It travelled another thirty feet before dumping the ore into the top of another crusher. He searched in his pocket and found a Kleenex, which he tore in half and stuffed into his ears, easing the piercing pain from the noise.

He picked up the shovel, raised it over his head with both hands and rammed it down into the years of compacted spilled rock and dust. The top inch chipped away like it was concrete; the shovel vibrated through his hands and arms. Pain shot through his sore wrist, making him drop the shovel. He took the pick-axe and swung it hard, feeling a satisfying thud as the heavy point sunk in deep. He levered the pick and pried away a chunk the size of his head, then swung again and again. Sweat ran over his face and down his chest and back. His wrist throbbed as he pounded into the waste of the mine.

At ten o'clock Peter stopped digging and wandered down the corridor, past more crushing and screening machines, until he found a door that let him outside. He sat on a boulder next to a pile of discarded machinery and garbage in a truck-turning area that had been cleared of snow. He lit a cigarette. He was on the side of the mountain, where the ore tramline came out of the bottom of Rock Reject, the full buckets swaying from the cable as they floated down the mountainside to the Mill.

The clouds that had brought the snow moved away and the sun lit up snow-covered mountains that stretched endlessly to the southern horizon. He sat motionless, watching the play of light and shadow on the brilliant peaks, the beauty opening a joy inside him. He closed his eyes, clinging to the feeling he hadn't known for so long, only to have it smothered in an instant, pushed back down inside him by remorse. He opened his eyes to the mountains, dull now with the return of the clouds. His numbness returned as well. The wind picked up and he was suddenly cold, shivering in his damp clothes. He threw his cigarette into the snow and went back to Rock Reject. Above the door someone had nailed a hand-lettered sign: Abandon All Hope Ye Who Enter Here. He read it and nodded in agreement, then took a last breath of outside air and returned to his pick and shovel.

At noon, his face plastered with dust and lined with the tracks of sweat, he returned to the lunch room. Koopman looked up from his book and laughed.

"Jesus, you're keen. Did you get to the bottom yet?"

Peter shrugged. He took a drink of water from the cooler and blew his nose. Green mucus covered the tissue. "It makes the time go faster, having something to do."

"That's probably what Sisyphus thought."

Peter gave him a puzzled look.

"Futile and hopeless labour, the ultimate fucking punishment. I'm detecting gaps in your education."

Peter's face reddened. "Education has to be pretty practical for my family." He sat on a bench across from Koopman. "Did you study Classics?"

"Yep. Got a B.A." He sucked on his cigarette and blew a smoke ring into the dusty air. "And you?"

"Oh, I dropped out." Peter looked around for something to clean the dust from the table, and reached for a dirty, balled-up rag that sat on the edge of the sink. "The sign above the door down at the bottom. That's Dante, right?"

"You like that?" Koopman smiled. "I shovelled in here my first couple of months and nailed that up when I got a job on a drill. Pretty fucking appropriate, if I do say so." He dropped his cigarette on the floor and ground it with his boot. "Let me show you something." From his satchel he took out a cube of shiny green rock, three inches on a side. He put it on the table in front of Peter. "That's what it's all about here. Finest ore in the world."

Peter held it, feeling the smooth, ridged sides. Satiny strands of white fibre escaped from the rock, flexible and silky. "It's beautiful," he said.

Koopman extended his hand, and Peter gave him the rock. "They call this crude. They hire students in the summer to hand-pick blocks like this and bigger after a blast, and it gets specially processed for weaving. NASA uses the stuff." He hefted it in his hand. "Watch." His long fingers closed around the shiny green stone and squeezed, grinding it in his fist then opening his hand to reveal a handful of long, white fibers. "Metamorphosis," he said. "Fibres from stone." He teased at the asbestos lying in his palm, then dumped it on the dirt floor by the wall. "Fucking stuff's worth a fortune." He picked up his book and leaned his back against the wall.

Peter looked at the pile of white fibres for a moment, thinking how the strands resembled milkweed, thinking of a late summer walk with Rose on Manitoulin Island. The roar of a load falling into the jaw crusher snapped his attention back to the room, to the layer of dust on the table he was about to eat at. He wiped it with the stiff, dirty rag and watched the dust fall to the floor.

"It's like there's more dust than air in this place," he said. "Does anyone wear a mask?"

"Couple of guys did a while back but they said they were useless. The filters got clogged with the dust and they froze up in the cold. Couldn't hardly suck any air through them." He turned a page in his book. "But it's amazing what you can get used to when the money's good."

Peter opened his lunch bag and unwrapped his sandwiches. Dust floated onto them from the sleeves of his coveralls. More fell from his hands as he tried to wipe the bread clean. He glanced up to see Koopman watching him.

"What the fuck," he said, turning his attention back to his book. "You're hungry, you eat."

Peter looked at his food, half covered with green dust, then ate.

FOUR

The work schedule was seven and one. Seven day shifts and a day off, then seven four-to-midnights, then seven graveyards. Peter's life was Rock Reject, the cookhouse, his room and solitary paths in between. Being first in line for dinner meant finishing while others were still arriving. Glancing sideways after returning his tray to the dishwasher, seeing groups of men talking, laughing, planning their night in the bar, he cast his eyes down and returned to his room.

On the afternoon of a day off, he sat at his desk, a pen in his hand. He had picked up clean sheets from the laundry on his way back from lunch and they sat in a wrapped bundle on his unmade bed. Clothes were strewn on the dusty floor. Used tissues caked with green-flecked mucus surrounded a half-full wastebasket. At the edge of the desk was a small cassette player he bought at the Company Store, and a few music tapes he brought from Toronto. In front of him was a sheet of airmail letter paper with "Dear Dad" written at the top, followed by a comma and nothing more. He stared at the words, then out the window at the grey mist that hung in the air and the steady drip of snow melting from the roof of the next bunkhouse. He looked over at his tapes and put *Dark Side of the Moon* into the player and listened as Pink Floyd told him to, "Breathe, breathe in the air. Don't be afraid to care."

He closed his eyes and swayed slowly in his chair to the song, letting it seep into him. Halfway through he got up and took his guitar case from the cupboard and opened it on his bed. The sight and smell of it sent a rush of grief through him that he fought to control as he joined in the last lines of the song. "Perched upon the highest wave, heading for an early grave." His hand was on the guitar, lifting it out of the case, when he was startled by a knock at the door.

"Who is it?"

"Christ Almighty, open up Pete, it's George and Claude."

Peter opened the door part way. George's grinning face had a week's growth of beard. Claude stood behind him, twirling his moustache between his fingers.

"Come on man," George said. "Grab your coat. We're here to get you out of your room."

Peter looked back into the disorder of his room and the unwritten letter. "I've got things I should be doing." He felt like he could cry.

"No way. You've been a friggin' hermit all week and you need some fun."

"They've got some music happening at the bar later on," Claude added.

Peter turned back to look at the two men, into their faces and eyes. Something gnawed inside him, a question, a feeling, he didn't understand what. Moments passed. Claude and George exchanged glances. The wailing sax in "Money" came shrill from the tiny speakers inside the room.

"Maybe we'll see you later then?" Claude said as they started to move away.

"No. I mean, wait a bit. I'm just… I am going a bit crazy." He stepped back inside his room and reached for his coat. "Fuck it. I'm coming with you."

At three in the afternoon, Eric's bar was two-thirds full and thick with cigarette smoke. Peter's shift was going on four to midnight the next day so they had twenty four hours to drink and sober up. Men crowded the bar, ordering drinks two at a time, hauling money from jeans pockets to toss at Eric, leaving tips sitting in pools of spilt beer. Peter edged away from George and Claude to a spot at the end of the bar, beside jars of pickled eggs and pepperoni, and nursed a beer. A strand of Christmas lights with three bulbs missing hung in front of a long mirror, above the bottles of rye, rum and vodka that flanked a block of asbestos ore. Photos of a shovel, a drill and a D9 bulldozer were screwed to the walls, each with a young Eric standing and smiling beside the machine. Peter watched him bend over to get beer from a fridge under the bar. His pant leg raised just enough to show a glimpse of a steel brace.

A burley man weaved his way to the jukebox, punched in a song and leaned against the machine for support, his head hanging limply between the speakers as he listened to Hank Williams sing, "I'm So Lonesome I Could Cry." The song ended. He dropped in another dime and played it again. A hand landed on Peter's shoulder and he turned to see George cradling three beers. Handing one to Peter, he motioned for him to follow. "Got a table at the back with a bunch of guys," he shouted over the din.

The back section was quieter. Peter nodded to Michael Koopman and three others from his shift in the Mine, and took an empty chair beside a big man with a bushy ponytail hanging down the back of a brown leather coat.

"Pete, say hello to Bob," George directed from across the table.

Peter turned in his seat and offered his hand, then froze in shock. He stared into a bearded face that was equally shocked.

"Holy shit. Peter Stevens. I don't fucking believe it. You're the last person I'd ever expect to see here."

"Bob O'Neil. It's … it's good to see you."

"You guys know each other?" George asked.

"We sure as hell do. Pete and I were in school together. Had a lot of good times back then. Jesus, I haven't seen you since…"

"Since the wedding."

"Christ, that's right. Are you here with Rose?"

Peter shook his head. Bob shrugged his shoulders.

"Don't sweat it man. Shit happens, no explanations needed."

They drank their beers, and Bob turned in his chair and signalled to the waiter for more.

"So are you here to work in the clinic? You must be a doctor by now."

"A doctor?" George said from across the table. "Christ Almighty. You're a doctor, Pete?"

"No. No I'm not." He turned to Bob. "I dropped out this year. I'm up in Rock Reject."

Bob stared in disbelief. "Rock fucking Reject? Jesus, I wouldn't have thought it in a million years. How far did you get in med school?"

Peter shrugged. "Pretty far. Would've started my residency next year."

George nudged Claude with his elbow. "Did you hear that? Pete's practically a doctor."

"Christ, George," Peter half shouted. "I just said I'm not. I'm a drop-out." The waiter arrived with more beer and he reached into his pocket for money. Bob grabbed his hand.

"Put it away, man," he said. "This is my pleasure." He turned to the waiter. "Bring a couple of rounds for the table in honour of my old buddy here."

Peter took a new beer from the table. "How long have you been here?"

"Four years this month," Bob said. "I worked for the Company for two then said screw this, quit and bought my own 'dozer. I've been contracting with Stikine ever since, working my own hours and making twice what they were paying me as an employee." He grinned and drank half a bottle of Black Label, then wiped his moustache with his sleeve.

"What about Mary?" Peter asked. "Did she come with you?"

"No, we split years ago, probably not long after your wedding. I hooked up with her friend Dianne and she was up for getting out of Toronto and heading north." He had another drink of beer then smiled. "Shit, what am I thinking? Of course you know her. That night we dropped mescaline at my folks' place."

Peter felt his face flush red. "Yeah, I remember. Really nice girl."

"We've got a cabin in Crystal Creek, about a ten-minute drive from town. You've gotta come out and visit. Have dinner. Dianne's a great cook."

"Sure. Maybe, yeah."

Peter picked up his beer and dug at the label with a fingernail, peeling a strip down the middle. Bob's hand fell on his shoulder.

"But we gotta get you out of Rock Reject. A man'll go insane in there." He turned to Koopman. "Hey Michael, didn't your oiler quit?"

"Yeah, with the drill down and getting sent to Rock Reject every day he went haywire. Day before yesterday we were halfway to the Mine Dry and he suddenly says I'm outta here, goes into the Admin Building and quits. Left for Watson Lake that morning with half his stuff still in his room."

"Anyone in line for the job?"

"I don't think so. Clarkson told me they'll post the job tomorrow."

Bob looked at Peter. "There you go man, your ticket out of that hellhole. Drill oiler's gotta be the easiest fucking job in the place."

"What's the job involve?" Peter asked Koopman.

"Not much. Working a grease gun, cleaning up the drill, keeping me company. Unless there's someone with more seniority who wants the job, you should get it no problem."

Peter looked away, fumbled for a cigarette and lit it. "Well, I guess I could think about applying," he muttered.

"Don't think about it, man," Bob said. "Just do it tomorrow."

The waiter arrived and laid a tray of beers on the table. Bob flipped a fifty into his hand.

"Keep 'em coming, man. We're celebrating."

Two hours later the table was a garbage heap of empties, overflowed ashtrays, chip and peanut bags. Peter sat sideways in his chair, his elbows planted on its sticky wooden arms, clutching a bottle, long empty. His body swayed as he leaned towards Bob.

"I screwed up, man. I really did, and now Rose is gone."

Bob's eyes were glassy, his hand holding a bottle. He banged it onto his thigh and beer foamed out of it onto his leg. "I told you, man. Don't get fucking married. Shack up with her for a while. Remember me telling you that?"

"Yeah, but that's not it."

"Rose was cool but you needed to play around, get it on with other chicks." Bob belched loudly. "And her parents. They spelled trouble to me."

"Shut up for a goddamn second." Peter shook Bob's shoulder. "Rose is dead."

"You mean she's split, Pete. Not fucking dead."

"No, you don't understand. She's gone. She died."

Bob stared at Peter and shook his head. "That's insane. How the hell could she die?"

Peter's mind spun. "We… no." He brought his fingertips to his forehead and rubbed over his eyes. "I wasn't there. I was at an exam when she went to the hospital and then it was too late."

"But what did she die of?"

Peter shook his head. "She hemorrhaged." His eyes filled, and he looked for a moment into Bob's, then reached for another beer.

Bob looked down into his hands. "Man that's tough. If you were there, you probably could've done something. You've got the training." He ran a hand through his hair and looked at Peter. "You must feel…" He shook his head. "Shit, Pete. I'm sorry."

Peter took out a cigarette and struggled with matches that were wet with beer. He inhaled deeply and rubbed his fingertips over his forehead as he sighed the smoke from his lungs. "I screwed up. That's all I can say."

At quarter to nine Peter pushed himself to his feet and tried to put on his jacket. George helped him get his arms into the sleeves. As he stumbled away from the table Bob leaned back in his chair to shout at him. "You're coming to dinner next fucking day off, Stevens." His chair tipped over backwards and he crashed to the floor.

Peter turned to look, but the room was dense with smoke and his vision a beery blur. He pushed through a crowd of men coming in from the drizzling rain and out the door.

Outside he passed through a line of four men blocking the entrance to the bar. They were faced by two burly men standing at the edge of the road.

"We don't fucking want you in here."

Peter recognized the man speaking, a shovel operator from his shift, an ugly look on his thick face.

"We've got every goddamn right to go in, Spencer. Eric serves us in there."

Spencer folded his arms. "You Indians'll have to go through us to get in." He paused and looked around him. "And I don't see your gimp Eric out here to look after you." He looked at Peter who stood watching ten feet away, swaying on unsteady legs. "Do you, Rock Reject man?"

Peter stared at Spencer, his image blurry. In his head he shouted fuck off into his face, but his mouth wouldn't form the words.

"You assholes can go to hell," one of the men said, then spat on the ground at Spencer's feet. They turned and went to the parking lot, climbed into a pickup and left.

The four men laughed, then went inside the bar.

Peter stood for a minute, his heart pounding and his hands clenched in fists. He turned and stumbled into the centre of the muddy road, then stopped and screamed into the moonless sky.

"Assholes. Fuck you!"

A horn honked behind him and he staggered to the side of the road. The wheels of a passing pickup splashed him with mud. He weaved fifty yards further then stopped to lean against a telephone pole and closed his eyes to the spinning in his head. He leaned over and threw up.

At two in the morning he woke up suddenly, his mouth dry and his head pounding. He took aspirin and drank water, then lay back in bed, staring at the ceiling, listening to the sounds of heat creaking in the pipes, of men snoring or muttering in their sleep, of water dripping off the roof.

"I wish we could just live together." Peter sat on Rose's bed, rolling a joint, wearing only his underpants. His clothes were strewn on the floor. Rose's were folded on her desk. She wore a long t-shirt and nothing else.

"Not an option," she said, reaching to take the joint Peter held to her. "We'd have to declare war with my parents to do that." She took a puff and handed it back to Peter. "And with yours as well."

"Lots of people are just taking off out west. To Vancouver." He took another hit and held it in. "We could go out there and be together all the time," he said through his held breath.

He held out the joint again and Rose shook her head. "One toke's good. I don't like getting too stoned." She took her guitar from its stand in the corner of the room and sat cross-legged on the bed. "I'm content with how things are," she said, strumming chords softly. "Especially with Mum and Dad away as often as they are. It lets us play house."

"Yeah. For one Saturday a month." He took another toke and slid beside her. He traced the line of her ear with a finger, then down her neck and across the collar of her t-shirt. "I'm sick of living at home. I want to live with you."

Rose took his hand and kissed it. "Listen, Peter. I love you, but I love my parents, too. We've got our whole lives ahead of us and I don't want to blow things up because you're impatient. You've got med school to get through, and I've got to finish my education degree. We need our parents until we're done with all that."

Peter fell back on the bed. "I'm just tired. I want things to be different."

Rose put the guitar aside and lay down beside Peter. "Things aren't completely terrible, are they?" Her fingers brushed the few hairs on his chest, then slid down his belly.

He lay still for a moment. "Well, what if we just got married then? I mean, if that's what it'll take for us to be together…"

Rose rolled onto her back and stared at the ceiling. "I don't know. There are a lot of things I want to do."

"But the whole point is to do them together. Our parents will help us and we can see them as often as you like."

"Peter, you're all over the map here. One minute you're desperate to leave town and the next you want to get married. What the hell's going on?"

"I just want to be with you all the time." He lay back down and put his arm across her chest. "And if we have to get married for that to happen, then okay, let's do it."

FIVE

Job postings were on the bulletin board in the Mine Dry, with application forms in a pouch on the wall. Peter read the notice for the drill oiler vacancy, but turned away without taking a form.

Stay where you are, he told himself. At the bottom.

After four days the posting was gone from the board. He saw Koopman as they waited for the man-haul to go up to the Mine and wanted to explain why he didn't apply for the job. He caught his eye, but Koopman didn't acknowledge him. Peter looked down at the frozen mud and said nothing.

He looked for the dark corners of Rock Reject to work in, the back sides of conveyor belts to shovel spills. He took smoke breaks alone outside, beneath where the tramline buckets emerged, sheltering his cigarette in a cupped hand, sucking the comfort deep to dull the ache that never left his chest. The buckets vanished into the snow that fell steadily, that swirled around him as he leaned against the peeling plywood, feeling the sting of snow hitting his face.

Rose arranged a surprise get-away for his birthday a year after they were married. A rented car, her parents' cottage, champagne. They made love in front of the stone fireplace and afterwards walked out onto the frozen lake swept bare of snow by the February winds. They lay on the ice, listening to it groan and snap, looking into each other's eyes, feeling flakes of snow drift down onto their cheeks.

He opened his eyes as an empty tramline bucket rose up out of the gloom to enter the building above him. A full bucket emerged and began its descent. Snow had covered his boots and the legs of his coveralls were soaked through. He shook himself, picked up his shovel and went back into Rock Reject.

Peter ate his dinner quickly and left the dining hall. Inside the front door notices were posted. A permanent one advertised times for mass and confession at the Catholic Church, and next to it a hand-lettered notice announced the monthly Union meeting. He pulled the hood of his parka tight and went out into the swirling snow, raising his hand in a mute hello to his shift-mates on their way in to eat. As he shook snow off himself inside the bunkhouse front door, the door to George's room opened and Claude's head leaned out.

"Pete," he whispered. "Come on in. We've got some stuff."

Peter stepped out of his boots and entered the room. Claude handed him a beer as he sat on the edge of the bed. Tin foil squares lay on the desk and George was crumbling the contents of one into the bowl of a small water pipe. A half empty bottle of wine sat on the windowsill.

"Came in the mail today from my cousin in Montreal. Blonde Lebanese hash. You're cool with it, no?"

"Maybe not. Bad memories." He thought of the last time he was stoned, coming into the apartment, Rose sitting at the kitchen table. He shuddered at the memory.

"You don't mind if we toke?"

"No problem."

"Filtered through wine," George said. "Gives it a great taste."

Peter nodded in agreement, and looked around the room. Photographs and drawings of houses were tacked to the wall, alongside a map of Cape Breton Island. A stack of novels teetered on the edge of the desk. On the bed lay a large magazine, a black and white photo on its back showing an old woman sitting in a tiny wooden wagon in front of a tarpaper shed, her white hair wild, her face amused by the joke of her pose. Peter picked up the magazine.

"*Cape Breton's Magazine*," George said as he took a match from a box. "It came yesterday from my uncle. There's articles about the old-timers and how they did things."

He lit the bowl and inhaled. Peter smelled the familiar aroma as he flipped through the magazine, glancing at the articles on rope-making, gardening and old fiddlers.

"That's for me, Pete," George said as he passed the pipe to Claude. Smoke curled out of his mouth. "Back to the land. Build my own house." He gestured to the drawings on the wall. "Those are my plans. Just sketches so far, but I'll make up ones to scale next. I should have enough in the bank after a year here to get the house up and closed in, then I'll take my time with the insides."

Peter turned a page and looked at a grainy photo of an isolated cove. A few houses behind a headland, a road passing through steep hills, the ocean foaming on the beach. He thought of Rose and felt his chest hollow. He put the magazine back on the bed.

Claude offered the pipe back to George.

"One more," he said. "I just want a light stone tonight, enough to make the meeting more interesting."

"The Union meeting?" Peter asked.

"Of course. My old man'd kill me if he knew I missed one. My whole family's union people." He took a puff and exhaled slowly. "I just like to go on my own terms."

He looked at Peter and offered the pipe with a smile and raised eyebrows. Peter shrugged, then reached over and took it from him.

"What the hell." He sucked hard from the pipe and struggled to keep the smoke in. It streamed out from his mouth and nose as he leaned forward, coughing.

"You got greedy, my friend," George said while banging Peter on the back. "You gotta watch it with a water pipe."

"Sorry," Peter gasped for breath and took a drink of beer. "It's been a while." He recovered, then put a match to the pipe and took another hit. He offered the pipe to Claude who shook his head lazily, then to George.

"No man, that's strong shit. I don't want to space out totally at the meeting."

Peter had one more puff and sat back in his chair. Sweat broke out on his forehead and he closed his eyes to slow down the spinning in his head. "I think I need some air."

George looked at his watch. "We may as well head to the Rec Centre. Won't matter if we're a bit early."

Peter got to his feet and stumbled to the door. "I don't know if I'm up for a meeting."

"Christ yes, Pete. The walk'll straighten you out. Besides, what the hell else will you do? Lie in your bunk and pull your wire? Let's get going."

Peter followed behind, pulled in the wake of George and Claude, the crunch of his boots on the snow vibrating into his teeth. They merged with groups of men talking an incomprehensible babble, all moving towards the Rec Centre. Double doors sucked him inside with a blast of heat from the overhead propane burners, his boots splashing through puddles of slush on the linoleum floor and his eyes squinting against the harsh florescent light buzzing in the gymnasium. The din of a hundred voices echoed off the concrete block walls, a haze of cigarette smoke hung halfway to the ceiling. Peter joined a line of men signing in at a table near the door, and he was handed a Union card to fill out. He bent over the table, staring at the words on the card until a voice from behind startled him into focus.

"For fuck sakes, get a move on. You're holding up the line."

He moved to the end of the table and filled out the card, then looked for Claude and George who had found seats in a full row near the back. He saw an empty chair at the far end of the second row. He found himself in the chair, but couldn't remember crossing the room. He closed his eyes to gain some control of the confusion in his head, to block out the blur of people and noise. Elbows on his knees, his head resting in his hands, his mind floated away to nowhere and then back to his pounding pulse and the vibrations of voices. He wished he hadn't smoked the dope.

He heard the meeting called to order. He lifted his head to watch but the movement made him dizzy so he looked down again and tried to focus on what was being said. Someone was reading the minutes of the last meeting. He stared at his boots, at the water stains on the leather, at the puddle surrounding them on the tile floor. Someone talked about finances, about raising money for a swimming pool. A voice behind Peter complained that the Indians from the reserve would be using it. Someone from the back of the room shouted for him to shut the fuck up. A rush of anger ran through Peter that made him sit up, his head clearer.

Dave McGuinness stood up at the table at the front of the room and shouted for order. "Keep your goddamn racist comments out of the Union meeting, Schneider," he said. "That pool's going to be open to everyone whether you like it or not."

Peter turned and looked behind him. The four men who had blocked the door of the bar sat together, their arms identically folded across their chests. Spencer looked at Peter.

"What do you think, Rock Reject. You want to swim in a pool that Indians have made dirty?"

Peter stared at him, the sudden clarity he had for a moment now lost in a fog. Spencer's voice felt heavy, his blue eyes threatening. Peter shook his head to disagree with him. "That's bullshit," he said.

"You're right," Spencer said, "it is bullshit."

"No, damn it," Peter said. "That's not…" The sharp sound of McGuinness's hand slamming on the table at the front startled him and he turned to the front of the room.

"I said order," McGuinness shouted. "That's enough on that issue. We're moving on to the contract negotiations." He sifted through a pile of papers. "Talks are stalled right now. The Company is saying they can't afford our wage demands plus the environmental improvements we want. They're proposing a pay increase of about half what we're asking and some bullshit about studying the pollution issue. The contract expires in less than a month, so I want everyone to know that we may be looking at a strike if they don't put a lot more on the table."

"We can't afford to have a strike," a worried voice said. Peter recognized a truck driver from his shift. "I've heard that the Company's profits haven't been good. What if they close the Mine?"

"They won't close the goddamn Mine," McGuinness said. "There's too much high grade ore up there."

"He's right about the profits being down." Michael Koopman was standing along the wall, his arms folded. "But that's because market prices for asbestos are down."

"Then why is De Vleit on our backs about low production levels?" the truck driver said.

"Because they're trying to make us think we're the problem," McGuinness said. "Production is slow because equipment is old and breaking down. Management is trying to get by on the cheap."

"Then why are you pushing for this pollution control business, McGuinness?"

The voice came from the back of the room, from a thin, dark-haired man with a goatee and an eastern European accent. "What we need is the wage increase and what the Company needs to spend on is new equipment, not millions on housekeeping. I say drop that demand."

"I say it stays, Bukowski." McGuinness planted his fists on the table and leaned forward. The sleeves of his checked shirt were rolled up, showing his thick forearms. "I want environment and health issues up at the top of the agenda."

"Maybe that's what you want," Bukowski shot back. "But what the membership wants is better wages, benefits and pensions, and that's your mandate."

"The election was six months ago, and you lost. You still want to be president, then run against me next time. Otherwise, get over it."

"But he's got a good point, Dave." Peter didn't recognize the short, stocky man with a thin beard. "It would take a fortune to control the dust in the Mill, and they're always telling us that the asbestos here doesn't cause cancer. So why go to the wall over it?"

"That's easy to say when you only stay here a couple of years and then go back down south." Two men stood at the back of the room, near the doors. "We live in that dust that blows down the valley into the Reserve. We raise our kids in it and we've been after the Company for years to do something about it and they've done fuck all."

"They've given you a job, Grandison," Spencer said with a sneer. "Quit fucking complaining."

"Yeah, I've got a job. After fifteen years of refusing to hire a native, they finally give us a couple of jobs. And as for the dust not being harmful, tell that to my father or my brother-in-law. Come and watch them cough for an hour in the morning."

"Hear hear," someone said. "I agree that we should be demanding that the Company do something about the environmental mess they've made here."

Dave McGuinness banged his hand on the table once more. "Okay, that's enough on this. It's in everybody's interest to get the Company to agree to make this a cleaner place to work and live, and it's going to stay as a demand in the negotiations." He ran a hand through his bushy hair. "This is probably a good time for Gord Evans to give the Safety and Health report. Gord?"

McGuinness sat down and lit a cigarette. A man in front of Peter turned around in his chair but didn't stand. He smoothed the side of his slicked-back hair.

"Well, I went on the safety tour with Iggy a couple of weeks ago…"

"Stand up, Gord. We can't hear you back here."

"Sorry." He stood up and held onto a sheet of paper with both hands, a string tie swaying in front of his cowboy shirt. His voice was thin and nasal, and reminded Peter of a high school teacher he detested. He slouched forward again and stared at the floor.

"Anyway, we saw some conveyor belts that needed guards installed on them. There were places where someone could trip and fall and a few loose railings. Iggy promised that all these problems are going to get fixed."

Gord stopped and cleared his throat. Peter looked at the intricate leatherwork on his pointy cowboy boots. "I guess that's about it," he said.

"Didn't we get some information from the Vancouver office about asbestos dust and disease?" McGuinness asked.

"Yeah. It had to do with shipbuilders spraying asbestos insulation. But they were using the other kind of asbestos. Crocodile or something."

Laughter came from the crowd. "Crocidolite," Dave said.

"That's right, thanks," Gord said. "Anyway, Iggy says that our asbestos here is different and isn't bad for you. But the shipbuilders were getting cancer and asbestosis and something else. Mess something."

"Mesothelioma," Peter blurted out. "It's always fatal and symptoms may not surface for decades." His face reddened as he saw people looking at him. "Sorry," he said to Gord.

"No, that's okay. Do you know more about these diseases?"

Peter shook his head and turned away. He looked for an exit near him, but there was none. He wished he hadn't opened his mouth, hadn't come to the meeting.

"Well, I guess that's it for my report," Gord said.

Peter heard him sitting down. He heard McGuinness's voice talking about something. He heard his father's voice telling him to be quiet. He felt the shame he felt at Rose's funeral.

He stayed in his chair after the meeting ended, waiting until the room cleared before leaving. George appeared and sat beside him.

"Shit man, you're up on this health stuff. Do you think we'll get sick working here?"

Peter shook his head. "I don't know, George. Probably not."

"I hope you're right. You know, Gord could probably use you on his committee."

"Don't make me laugh," Peter said. "I'm the last person in the world to have anything to say about anybody's health."

George shrugged. "If you say so." He stood up and stretched, then started towards the door.

Peter hesitated a moment, then grabbed his coat and hurried after him. "Wait, George. I don't mean to give you a hard time. Let me buy you a beer."

George turned and smiled. "Now you're talking." Peter looked at the toothless space in his mouth and felt somehow comforted.

The chairs at the tables were all taken, so they stood at the end of the bar with their beers, watching the scene. Dave McGuinness was talking to men at a table when one of them stood up suddenly and pointed a finger at him.

"Don't screw with my job over some dust bullshit," he shouted.

The man next to him stood up. "Since when is our health bullshit?

You think you're Superman? You'll never get sick? I got news for you, Lucas."

Lucas pushed the other man in the chest and he fell over his chair. He got to his feet and Lucas stepped menacingly towards him but the waiter moved in and quickly had Lucas's arm in a half nelson. He was out the door in seconds.

"You too, Wilson," Eric said to the man who had fallen. "Out. Take your goddamn hormones to the parking lot."

"Man," Peter said. "People get hot about this."

"Little wonder," George replied. "They're worried about a strike happening. And those guys don't need much of an excuse to go at it anyway."

"That waiter sure moved fast."

"That's Shaun Wilcox," George said. "He was provincial champ in wrestling when he was in high school in Vancouver. Almost went to the last Olympics, but something happened at the last minute and he got left off the team."

"Anyone know why?"

"Eric likely does, but he keeps his mouth closed about most things."

Peter lit a cigarette. "How do you know all this stuff?"

"It's my home away from home in here, Pete. I'm interested. I ask people questions and they give me answers."

McGuinness moved to a table near the bar and sat next to the receptionist from the Administration Building. She put her hand on his.

"What's the deal between the Union president and that guy at the meeting?" Peter asked.

"Bukowski? He's been here for years. I heard that he and Dave went at it in the parking lot last spring. Can't stand each other for some reason."

"I can't imagine that little guy putting up much of a fight against McGuinness."

"They say Dave loses his temper when he drinks hard stuff. A smart little guy can do pretty good against someone like that."

"How fucking smart is he that this is where he's ended up?" Peter finished his beer and shook his head. "The end of the goddamn road."

"Shit, Pete, you sound like you're gonna die here. This place is opportunity. I'm grateful to be here."

Peter looked at George for a moment. He felt envious of his certainty. "What makes you so clear about what you want?"

George put his beer on the bar and from his wallet removed a small school photo of a young boy grinning in a white shirt and bow tie. He looked at it for a moment before handing it to Peter.

"Your son?"

"Yes sir. He's a fine little guy." There was a catch in George's voice. "Alexander. Named after his grandfather. Eight years old next month." He turned his head and wiped his eyes with his sleeve.

"So you're married then?" Peter asked as he handed back the photo.

George's mouth tightened. "Used to be. She's got someone else now." He put the photo into his wallet and took out a five-dollar bill. He flashed two fingers at Eric. "Anyway, I'm going to get back there and build a nice place so Alex can spend time with me. A kid needs his father, right?"

Peter picked at the label of his empty bottle. Eric put two Molsons in front of them. Peter put his empty on the bar and ran his fingers down the cold wet of the fresh one. "You're right," he said at last.

"How's that?" George asked.

"Fathers. Kids need them."

"Goddamn right they do. I just need to get the friggin' judge to say the same." He took a drink of beer. "So what about you, Pete? You got a plan?"

"A plan? Why am I here?" He shrugged. "Because it's the end of the road."

"Jesus, Pete. It can't be as bad as that. I think you're whacked out from that smoke."

Peter looked at George and shook his head. "No, it's not the smoke. It's..." He stopped, words stuck inside him. George waited for him to continue but the moment passed and Peter let his eyes slide away. He took a drink from his beer.

"Mind if I join you two?"

Peter turned to see Dave McGuinness standing behind them.

"Christ, Dave, not a bit," George said, sounding relieved. Peter nodded in agreement.

McGuinness put a stool next to theirs and settled himself on it. He signalled to Eric. "You guys want another?" he asked.

"Twist my arm," George smiled.

"I think I've had enough," Peter said.

Two more beers appeared and McGuinness took one, downed half of it and wiped his moustache with his sleeve. He turned to Peter. "So you know some things about asbestos diseases?"

"No, just… Nothing really."

"Pete's practically a doctor," George said.

"Oh shut up, George."

"That so?" McGuinness asked.

"I'm a drop-out."

"There's a few of those here," McGuinness replied, levelling his eyes into Peter's. "I got halfway through law school and couldn't afford it anymore. Hope I get back there someday. Maybe you will too."

Peter didn't respond. He dug his thumbnail through the label on his beer.

"The membership's really getting split over the health issues and we could use help on that front to bring people around. Gord's a great guy and he does well on the safety tours, but he's not much for digging into things and the dust and cancer stuff freaks him out. Of course the Company keeps telling us that the dust isn't harmful, but even if that's true, there's so goddamn much of it everywhere. It's insane in the Mill and Rock Reject and the stuff that blows off the tailings pile gets everywhere."

"That's where the dust in the bunkhouse comes from?" George asked.

"Yeah. It mostly blows east down the valley, but when the wind shifts it's all over the town."

"Down the valley means over the Reserve?" Peter asked.

"That's right, and they've got a right to be pissed off about it." McGuinness paused to light a cigarette. "Anyway, we could really use someone who can help us get a handle on this issue. Someone who can analyze reports and data." He waited for a response from Peter, which didn't come. "Someone like yourself, maybe?"

"I can think about it," Peter said, without conviction.

McGuinness nodded, then turned when the receptionist came up behind him and put a hand on his shoulder.

"Am I interrupting?"

"No, I'm just working on Pete here. Twisting his arm a bit. George, Pete, this is Susan."

She smiled. Peter saw Rose's smile. Wisps of hair escaping from her braid were almost the same colour as Rose's hair.

"I remember you guys from your intake day. How's it going?"

George beamed at her. "Great. Love it here."

Peter gave her a tight smile. "Fine, thanks."

She turned to McGuinness. "I'm heading to my bunkhouse. See you tomorrow night?" He kissed her cheek and she squeezed his shoulders, then leaned closer to his ear. "Just beer, okay?"

He nodded as her hands stroked across his shoulders, then she left. McGuinness reached forward and put his empty on the bar. Peter glanced at her back as she walked to the door.

Strong hips and shoulders. Rose was thinner.

McGuinness stood up. "Won't keep you guys any longer." He looked at Peter. "It's a long winter here, and having something worthwhile to do can keep you from going crazy."

He left. Peter felt dizzy. He leaned an elbow on the bar and rested his head on his hand. Spilt beer soaked into his shirt sleeve.

"He's right, Pete. Winter goes on forever in Cape Breton, but it's probably nothing compared to here. I might see if I can get on some committee. My dad'd like that."

My dad'd like it if I were someone else, Peter thought.

He sat on the bed in his bunkhouse room, his back against the plywood wall, arms wrapped around his drawn-up knees. Classical guitar music hissed from the cassette player's speaker, the volume low at two in the morning. A poor homemade recording Peter made of Rose two years earlier in their living room as she worked on pieces by Bach. Tears ran unchecked down his face and neck and soaked into his t-shirt. He saw her face in total concentration, her hands moving, creating the weaving, circular patterns of notes floating in the room.

SIX

At one in the afternoon on the first of two days off, Peter sat on the stairs at the back of his bunkhouse smoking a cigarette in the weak November sunshine, looking south across a service road into a strip of spruce forest that hid the river from the town. New snow covered the muddy road and brightened the tree branches. Two crows called to each other and landed on the railing of the next bunkhouse, then flew away as a snowmobile came down the road and stopped. Peter flicked away his smoke and picked up his backpack that clinked with bottles.

"Never been on one of these," he said as he straddled the seat behind Bob O'Neil.

"Welcome to the North. Hang on."

Peter looked for something to hold on to as Bob gunned the motor. He was jerked backwards and yelled in alarm, barely keeping himself from falling off by gripping with his legs. Bob stopped and turned around.

"I mean hang on to me." Peter gave a sheepish smile, then grabbed onto the sides of Bob's leather coat and leaned into him as they drove to the main road, past the Mill and Administration Building and out of town, speeding along in a blur of snow, trees and noise. Through the trees he caught glimpses of the river in the valley, and he watched the sparkling landscape go by until his eyes teared up from the wind, then he closed them and tucked his head behind Bob's back for protection. They slowed for a tight bend in the road.

"There's the Indian Reserve," Bob shouted, gesturing towards houses down the slope to the river. "Our place is just past its boundary. Not far now."

Peter looked for a moment at the village then closed his eyes again. His memory went to a summer during high school, to a night at Bob's parents' house when they were away. Bob's girlfriend Mary and her friend Dianne. Mescaline. Rose waiting for him at the movies. Standing her up while being naked with a girl for the first time, with Dianne, who was now Bob's wife. He wondered if he should have stayed in his room.

They parked next to an old pickup and Bob hopped off the machine and removed his goggles. Peter was stiff from the cold and he climbed off slowly, looking at the scenery while he stretched his back and legs. The land sloped gently thirty yards to the river, through trees that were widely spaced and weighed down with snow. Ice on both banks narrowed the width of the channel, and the water flowed fast and dark in the shadows of the forest and the mountain that rose up steeply on the opposite side of the valley.

"It's beautiful," Peter said. "Peaceful."

"Thanks. I've taken out a lot of trees to get the view of the river. Dianne's got a big garden on the other side of the house and she's done a great job fixing up the inside."

A path through a foot of snow led to a log cabin surrounded by spruce trees, smoke rising from its stone chimney. Peter followed Bob to the house, their boots crunching on the dry snow.

"Welcome, Peter." Dianne stood in the open doorway wearing jeans and a peasant blouse with details of flowers embroidered across the front. Bob bent over to kiss her lips and ran his hand down her back. She stroked the side of his face and turned to Peter.

"It's great to see you again," she smiled, her face open and warm.

"It's good to see you too." He pulled two bottles of wine from his pack and held them out, shielding himself from the hug that she was offering. Bob took the wine and looked at the labels.

"Holy shit. French. Where did you find these?"

"Just some persistence at the liquor store. Wine usually means Baby Duck to them, but they do have some good stuff. They said it's for when the bosses come from Vancouver."

"We're having roast venison for dinner," Dianne said. "The wine will be perfect." She took Peter's coat and hung it near the wood cookstove, then put her hand on his shoulder to guide him through the kitchen to the living room. Her touch felt hot through his three layers of clothing. "I couldn't believe it when Bob told me you were here. I still remember meeting you that one night, what was it, seven, eight years ago?"

"Something like that, I guess," Peter mumbled. His face flushed and he turned away in embarrassment.

"Meeting him?" Bob laughed. "That's one way to put it."

Dianne poked him in the ribs. "I'll have you know that was a very nice evening, Mr. O'Neill. And I seem to recall you having your nasty way that night with Mary."

"True enough." Bob put the wine bottles on the table. "We were young and innocent. Well, at least Pete was innocent."

Peter shook his head. "It seems like that happened a million years ago. It's all pretty vague," he lied. He turned to look out the big window behind the couch. "Your place is great. There's so much light."

"That's 'cause of the snow," Bob said. "The trees keep it darker in the summer and fall."

"It can get gloomy," Dianne said. "But not today. Let's have a coffee and go for a ski. It's just one thirty, we've still got lots of daylight."

Bob turned to Peter. "There's a set of rapids through a canyon down the river. We like to ski there."

Peter nodded. "Fine by me. I haven't exercised in a long time." He looked around at the interior of the cabin. A closed door was on his left. The bedroom, he thought. An open door next to it revealed a bathroom sink. The rest of the house was one large room, all in wood, with a long counter separating the kitchen from the dining and sitting areas. Peter watched as Dianne reached up into a cupboard for mugs. Her blouse rose to reveal her back and side.

"This could be the last chance to see the rapids before it really freezes up," she said, bringing coffee and cake to the table. "The radio said there's more snow tonight coming from the Pacific, then a cold front's moving down from the Arctic after the storm passes. Winter's setting in."

"It was raining like crazy in Toronto when I left," Peter said.

"Was there a big send-off party for you?" Dianne asked.

"No, I can't say there was," Peter replied. Rose's parents would've been happy to tar and feather me, he thought. "My mum dropped me at the bus station on Bay Street, and I rode straight through to Edmonton."

"The bus?" Bob said. "Shit, I imagined you flying, or at least the train."

"No. I wanted to do the bus trip. It felt right."

"Man, that's a long, painful trip."

Peter looked at Bob. He wanted to tell him how painful it really was, that Bob didn't know the half of it. A jumble of words of truth bounced around inside his head, but he couldn't bring himself to let them out.

"Yeah, I guess it was pretty rough. Especially the nights, trying to sleep in those seats. Gives you lots of time to think about things, though."

He looked down at the coffee mug he was cradling and took a sip. Water dripped off the eaves and splashed on the ground outside. Wood sputtered in the stove. He glanced at Dianne, who was looking at him intently over the rim of her mug, but he couldn't meet her eyes and turned away.

A workbench in the corner of the room held tools and pieces of stone.

"Is one of you into crafts?" he asked.

"Yeah," Bob said. "Dianne's been carving local jade. She makes beautiful stuff."

"Can I take a look?" Peter went to the workbench and reached to touch one of the carvings. Dianne got there first and picked it up.

"Sorry," he said. "I just wanted to see what it felt like."

"She's pretty protective about her work," Bob said.

"I sold some pieces at a craft fair in Whitehorse and I was so nervous that they'd get dropped. I couldn't relax until the customers left with them and they were out of my sight."

"What's that going to be?" Peter pointed to a block of stone eight inches wide. The top had been partly carved away.

"An eagle. At least I hope it will." She played her fingertips over the stone's rough chiselled top edge. "I sometimes like to think that there's a figure inside the jade that I'm trying to find."

"Didn't Michelangelo describe his sculptures like that?" Peter asked. "Freeing the figure from the stone?"

Dianne laughed. "Me and Michelangelo."

Peter smiled with her. He looked down at her closed hand. "What's the one you're holding?"

She opened her hand to reveal a polished pendant with an inscription. Peter ran a fingertip over the letters etched into the stone.

"What does it say?"

"Creideas," Dianne said. "It's Gaelic. It means 'have faith.'"

Peter looked at the stone. At her hand and wrist. "Faith." He shook his head. "In what?"

"In whatever you choose, I suppose. God, Nature. In yourself."

Peter turned to the window and the snow-covered trees and the river. "I don't know if I have faith in anything. Certainly not in myself."

They skied along the bank of the river. Peter struggled to keep up and fell twice early on.

"I've only done this a few times before," he had told them when they handed him an old pair of Bob's skis. "My folks always took me south in the winter, not north."

He stopped to catch his breath, letting Bob and Dianne carry on ahead. Taking off his gloves and toque to feel the cold on his hands and head, he lifted his arms and face to the blue sky. The valley was narrow and he imagined stroking the rocky tops of the mountains with his outstretched fingers. He imagined falling backwards into the snow and lying spread-eagled staring at the heavens, or falling forward and having the impact drive the emptiness out of his chest. But he stayed upright, swaying in the sunlight.

He remembered standing at the edge of the grave when Rose's casket was lowered down, her parents at the opposite corner, as far from him as they could get. His parents next to him but feeling a thousand miles away. Black umbrellas sheltering everyone but him from the driving sleet. Water running down his face and neck, soaking up through his shoes.

The casket reached the bottom. The mourners sprinkled sand into the grave, then left and he was alone. He took a handful of sand and stretched out his arm but couldn't bring himself to let it drop. "Domini non sum dignus," he whispered. "Lord I am not worthy." He brought back his hand and emptied the sand into his pocket.

"I'm sorry, Rose," he said. He opened his eyes to see Bob was skiing towards him, ten yards away.

"You okay, Pete? You look like you were crucified there."

He snorted a laugh. Saint Peter, he thought. Died on the cross for his sins.

"Just taking a breather. Stretching. I'm out of shape."

"The rapids are just a bit farther. Dianne's waiting for us with a bottle of rum. You gonna make it?"

"I'll make it there, but will I make it back after the rum?"

"Good point. You're too fucking big to be carried."

"I'd better behave myself then."

Dianne had cleared the snow off a rock ledge overlooking a small canyon, and Peter took off his skis and sat beside her. She handed him a plastic mug, poured a shot of rum into it, and added hot water from a thermos. He sipped and took in the scene.

The river poured through a channel of high rock walls twenty feet wide. Boulders studded the bottom and water flowed around and over their smooth surfaces. Ice coated everything not submerged. On the other side of the river the mountain loomed close, giving Peter a feeling of vertigo when he looked up to its top. Clouds had moved in, and he shivered in his wet undershirt. He lit a cigarette and sucked in the warmth, then offered the pack to Dianne and Bob.

"No thanks," she said. "We both quit. I heard that smoking increases your chances of getting an asbestos disease."

"Where did you hear that?" Peter asked.

"Lynn Benedetti, Iggy's wife. She read it in some industry publication. Now, she said that it referred to people exposed to the other kinds of asbestos, but we decided not to take the chance."

Peter took a drag of his smoke. "Great, the safety and health guy gets information about cancer risks. Meanwhile half the town is smoking its brains out. Me included."

"Well, maybe it is just the blue asbestos that causes disease," Bob said. "But for sure, Iggy toes the company line. End of story."

Peter sucked deeply once more on the cigarette then flicked it into the canyon and watched it fall into the river.

"Where does this water end up?"

"This joins the Dease River," Bob said, "and then it joins the Liard up around the Yukon border. That's all I know."

"The Liard joins the McKenzie," Dianne added, "and it flows north through the Yukon into the Beaufort Sea. The Arctic Ocean." She turned to Bob and smiled. "I loved geography."

Peter stared at the flowing river. "I'd love to travel with the water. Start here, end up in the Arctic Ocean. The path all laid out by the terrain."

"Talk about going with the flow," Bob laughed. "I never thought of you as being so laid back."

Peter smiled. "Just call me Nature Boy from now on. I'll just submit to her will and be carried away."

"You'd better be prepared for some long portages," Dianne said. "There's a lot of rapids along the way." She poured another rum and hot water for each of them, then put away the bottle and thermos. "We'd better start back, unless we want charred venison for dinner."

Snow began falling halfway back from the rapids, and by the time dinner was ready it was coming down hard. Bob stepped outside into the darkness to check on the conditions.

"Looks like about five inches down so far, and more coming fast." He brushed snow off his hair onto the wood stove where it sizzled. "It'll be interesting running you back to town tonight."

"Why doesn't Peter just stay here tonight?" Dianne said. "Save the trouble, and we can all just relax."

"I don't have to work tomorrow," Peter said as he opened a bottle of wine. "I'd be happy to stay as long as it's not a bother."

Dianne looked at Bob, who hesitated a moment. "Yeah, sure. I guess that makes sense. I can't say I'm dying to go out in this storm."

They sat at the table and Dianne served the plates. Peter filled their glasses and raised his.

"Thanks for having me out here."

"Hey, no problem, man," Bob replied. "Glad to give you a rest from the cookhouse."

"That's right." Peter drank down half his glass. "It seems a million miles from Rock Reject here."

"Rock Reject?" Bob said surprised, his mouth full of meat. He washed it down with wine and poured himself more. "I thought you were on a drill. Koopman's oiler."

Peter topped up his glass and Dianne's, then busied himself with opening the other bottle. "No, that didn't happen. I'm still shovelling shit."

"How come? I figured you'd get that job for sure."

"Well I, I couldn't really make up my mind about it, and then the posting was filled."

Bob looked at him and shook his head. "In high school you were always Mr. Action, wanting to make things happen. What was it you would say… seize the day."

"My dad was forever saying that," Peter said.

Bob shrugged. "Whatever. It's just that getting out of Rock Reject seemed like a no-brainer."

"Don't give him a hard time, Bob," Dianne said.

"No, Bob's right. I probably should have just gone after it. I guess I didn't feel ready to leave there yet."

Bob snorted a laugh. "Not ready to leave? Man, that place is Purgatory. You must be atoning for some wicked sins."

Peter forced a smile and turned his attention to his meal. An awkward silence hung over them as they ate.

"The venison is wonderful," Peter said at last. "I've only had it once before, and this is way better."

"Where did you have it?" Dianne asked.

"Some restaurant in Huntsville, near Rose's parents' cottage. She and I spent a long weekend up there last fall." His voice trailed off. He remembered them in her parents' bed, the only double bed in the cottage. They had forgotten to bring condoms.

"I can't imagine how you feel," Dianne said, putting a hand on his.

"Bob told me about Rose's death. I'm so sorry."

The warmth of her hand travelled straight to his chest and Peter feared he might cry. He slid his hand out from under Dianne's and ran it through his hair, shaking his head.

"I feel..." He looked away from the table, across the room to the window. Snow was falling. Big flakes, lit up by the light from inside. He remembered their bed in the apartment, and the stain of blood on the mattress. He felt dread seep through him again.

"I thought she'd be fine," he said quietly. He felt suddenly cold. He drank more wine and looked at Dianne. "I'm sorry, I'm being a real drag here."

"It's okay Peter. It's good to talk about it."

"That's right," Bob said. "Dianne and I had our own losses and I needed to get stuff off my chest."

"What happened?" Peter asked, relieved to shift the conversation.

Dianne and Bob looked at each other. "Two miscarriages," she said. "Both pretty far along." She reached over and squeezed Bob's forearm, then pressed her napkin to her eyes.

"God, I'm sorry," Peter said. "I didn't imagine you'd be into having kids."

"Goddamn right we are," Bob said. "You can't believe what a disappointment it's been." He pushed his plate away. "So we've been trying to adopt this past year and we're getting the runaround from fucking Children's Aid about living here in the Creek. All this bullshit about our home not being suitable."

"We'll head to Vancouver in a few years and try to adopt then," Dianne said bitterly. "I can't risk trying to get pregnant again."

The room fell silent. Peter felt disoriented, his head reeling from the wine. Dianne sat with her hand pressing against the side of her tense face. She let out a long breath, then stood up and gathered the plates.

"You two go sit where it's comfortable and I'll make tea."

Bob finished clearing the table, then took his glass and the rest of the wine to the couch. Peter went to the bathroom where he sat on the edge of the bathtub, leaning forward and resting his head in his hands.

He remembered Rose's face that March morning as she lay in bed.

Pale, almost grey. The bleeding hadn't stopped and he'd told her he'd stay home, miss his exam. There was an edge of anger in her voice as she told him to go, that she'd look after herself, that she didn't need him. He said he was sure she'd be fine, but he was afraid. He left, but he knew he shouldn't have.

Dishes clattered in the kitchen. Bob's heavy footsteps made the wood floor bounce. Peter stood up. Unsteady, he leaned against the sink and looked at himself in the mirror. His hair and beard had grown and though his face was hidden in the dim bathroom light, in his eyes he saw his father's eyes, the accusing eyes that met him when he arrived at the Intensive Care Unit, when his father took him into an empty room and told him that Rose's condition was grave. His hands cramped from gripping the sides of the sink. He shook them out and washed his face, then returned to the living room.

Dianne sat next to Bob on the couch, stroking a sleek black cat on her lap. Peter took a chair and watched the cat stretch under her hands.

"This is Jade," she said.

Peter stared at the animal.

"Are you okay with cats, Peter? I can put her in the bedroom."

He shook his head. "No, it's fine. She just reminds me of someone." He took a mug of tea from a tray on the coffee table. The cat jumped from Dianne's lap, and with a suspicious look at Peter went into bedroom.

Dianne settled back on the couch with her tea. "You were telling us your memories of Rose and then we got sidetracked on our problems. Do you want to talk more about her?"

Peter's mind became so dense with images it felt blank. He would have liked to curl up in the chair and close his eyes, and he struggled to find words to speak.

"I loved her." His throat was tight as the words came out. "She was beautiful, she really cared about people." He looked into the tea that he cradled in his hands. "You remember her, don't you Bob?"

"Of course I do. She was a terrific chick. Great looking, great smile."

Peter sipped his tea, trying to moisten his dry mouth. "She loved the grade twos at St. Raymond's where she was teaching. And they were nuts about her." He paused and shook his head. "I still have a hard time believing she's gone."

He closed his eyes and saw Rose's father standing beside her bed in the hospital, glancing up to see him come into the room, then turning back to his daughter, ignoring Peter as if he was someone who had come to empty the wastebasket.

Dianne's voice brought him back. "How did it happen?"

"She bled to death. She hemorrhaged and didn't recover."

"Jesus Christ," Bob said. "A car accident?"

Peter shook his head. "A miscarriage," he said, his eyes going from Bob to Dianne and then to his reflection in the window behind them. He felt as thin as the image in the glass, as insubstantial. He imagined himself outside the window looking in and wondering what the person in his body on the couch was feeling. Grief? Shame? Anger? Relief? Was he feeling at all?

A heavy sob came from Dianne. Bob put his arm around her shoulders and drew her close as her body shook. He looked at Peter, his eyes wet. "Dianne almost died from the second miscarriage. The first time, two years ago, there wasn't a lot of blood, but last fall it happened again and she just kept bleeding."

Peter saw the blood-smeared towels lying on the bathroom floor of the apartment.

Dianne wiped her eyes with the sleeve of her blouse then took a drink of her tea. "I'm sorry, Peter. I don't want to keep interrupting your story, but I guess it's still so fresh for me and to hear that Rose died of the same thing hits me hard."

"I understand," Peter said. He saw pain in her glistening eyes. Then her image blurred as his own filled with tears and he quickly rubbed them away with the palms of his hands. "What matters is that you're alive."

"I was lucky."

"It was a close call," Bob said. "I was working in my dozer up on the north peak, way above the pit, and she managed to get the message to me."

"It was Simon De Vleit that did it," she said, taking Bob's hand in hers. "I called Susan at the Admin Building and she radioed up to him."

"He had me down the mountain pretty fast," Bob said. "And I think I hit a hundred coming out here to get you."

"And then they had enough of my blood type on hand at the infirmary." She looked at Peter. "Were you able to be there when Rose..."

"When she hemorrhaged?" He shook his head. "I was in exams." He stared into the empty cup in his hands. "By the time I got to the hospital, she was..." He stopped himself, his head shaking side to side. "But De Vleit," he said emphatically a moment later. "I thought he didn't have a decent bone in his body."

Bob shrugged. "Nobody's a hundred percent prick. He was really concerned about Dianne."

"He came to see me in the infirmary the next day." She paused and looked at Peter, encouraging him with a nod to continue his story, but he looked down, staying quiet. "Not all the fetal tissue came out with the miscarriage and that's why I hemorrhaged," she continued a few moments later. Her voice changed, sounded flat. "They did a procedure in the infirmary to take out what was left. Was that what happened to Rose?"

Peter nodded. He saw the tubes in Rose's arm, the look on her face. "She lost too much blood." He sank back in the chair.

"You're exhausted, Peter," Dianne said. "You've been through so much and now you're up here working in Rock Reject. You need to treat yourself gently."

Peter turned again to the window. Snow had blown against the glass and melted, the water slowly making its zigzag way downward, fragmenting the reflection of the room. "You're right," he said. "I feel empty."

"Let's pack it in then," Bob said. "We'll head into town after breakfast. The roads should be cleared by then." He went to the stove and began loading it with wood.

"I'll get you blankets, Peter," Dianne said, going to the bedroom.

Bob adjusted the damper on the wood stove, then took a fire poker and hit the stovepipe several times with it. A soft sound like sand pouring came from inside the pipe.

"What'd you just do?" Peter asked.

"Loosening the creosote in the stovepipe. The last thing we want here is a fire." His tone was terse and his face strained as he turned to Peter. "You need anything?"

"No thanks. I'm okay."

Bob nodded then headed towards the bedroom.

"Goodnight," Peter said.

Bob paused at the bedroom door. "Goodnight," he replied without turning, then went inside and closed the door. A minute later Dianne brought out an armful of bedding and arranged it on the couch.

"This should be enough, but if you're cold you'll find more in the bathroom closet."

"I'm sure I'll be okay."

"I hope you sleep well," she said, then started to turn away. Peter's hand went out, beckoning her to wait.

"I just wondered. How far along were you?"

"Sixteen weeks, the second time."

"Was it ... painful?"

A grimace crossed her face. "A lot. Like how giving birth must feel."

A gust of wind moaned across the top of the chimney.

"How far was Rose?"

"Fourteen weeks."

"Had you two been trying long to get pregnant?"

"It was an accident. We weren't really ready." He looked down at the floor. "You and Bob got cheated."

"And you too, Peter. Our pain is no more real than yours."

In her face he saw compassion, and he imagined leaning down to kiss the side of her mouth. She reached to touch his arm, but the feel of her skin on his made him flinch, and she pulled her hand back and folded her arms across her body.

"Goodnight." She turned and went into the bedroom.

He stood for a minute, listening to the sounds of her moving around on the other side of the door, wishing he hadn't reacted as he did. The bed creaked as she got in beside Bob.

He turned off the light and lay on the couch so he could see out the window. The storm had passed, and with the sky clear the silhouette of the spruce tree swayed across the smear of stars in the Milky Way. In the bedroom a radio was turned on and the voice reading the ten o'clock news came through the wooden door.

Two pubs had been blown up in Birmingham, England. Twenty-one were dead and a hundred eighty-two injured. He imagined being in the midst of the blood and wreckage, trying to patch people, save them. Then he drifted away, back to the trees and the stars and imagined himself floating above the valley, clean and free of the weight of his feelings. A mouse ran across the floor and the sound brought him back. A new voice on the radio read the weather. Overnight lows in Whitehorse minus thirteen, Haines Junction minus fifteen, Watson Lake minus seventeen.

The radio switched off. He heard them shifting in their bed and imagined them holding each other. He covered his swirling head with the pillow and tried to sleep.

"When are we having kids?" Rose asked.

Peter lay on his side, his fingers lightly tracing circles around Rose's right breast. His hand stopped moving at the question.

"I mean, I think it's time we got on with it, or at least made a plan for when to start trying." She turned to look at him. "You still want kids, right?"

Peter sat up and leaned back against the wall. The window was open to the warm early September air and a breeze blew across his naked body.

"We can't have kids yet. I've got med school to finish and residency after that. Let's wait and talk about it then."

"But I want to get a sense of where we're going and when we'll get there. And I'm not happy taking the pill all the time. I don't think it's good for me."

His mouth twisted sceptically. "The pill's great. I don't think there's anything wrong with it and we never have to worry. And besides, I don't like wearing a condom. I hardly feel a thing with one on."

Rose slid her hand down his front and smiled. "I'll bet we can find ways to make it worth your while."

She kissed his belly and lay her cheek where her lips had been. Peter looked at the back of her head, at her straight blonde hair, tangled from their lovemaking and lying across his stomach, at her shoulder rising and falling with her breath, at the outline of her spine snaking down her back. The curtain swayed with a breath of breeze.

His hand reached to touch her, then hesitated, then rested on her arm. "I guess we can try condoms if you want. I think the concerns about the pill are overblown, but if you're really uncomfortable taking it…" Her hand squeezed above his knee and slid up the inside of his leg. "But we'll have to be careful once you go off it."

Rose turned over and looked at him. "Or we could just forget the condoms and go with whatever happens."

"Whoa, hold on. I just said we can't even think about having a kid now. It'd be crazy."

"No it wouldn't. My parents would help, so would yours." She sat up on the bed, her eyes excited. "Lots of people have kids while they're still in school."

Peter pulled his knees up to his chest and rubbed his fingers through his hair.

"Sweetheart, why can't we just keep things the way they are? We do our own things, we can go places, we have hardly any hassles. And besides, our parents already help us a lot." He looked away. "Too much, in fact. Makes me feel like I can hardly breathe sometimes."

"Well I like my parents, and yours too, and I don't see what's so wrong with letting them help us out. I know they'd all love for us to have a baby."

"Oh great. Let's have a kid to please our parents again."

Rose glared at him. "Again? You still hate the fact that we're married, don't you?"

Peter felt cold. He pulled the sheet over his legs and rubbed his arms.

"Rose, don't get me wrong. I really love you, but we could've avoided all the wedding stuff and just lived together. Everybody does that now, and that way we wouldn't be so…"

"So what?" Rose demanded. "So committed? So responsible?" She got off the bed and put on her dressing gown, tying it tight with its belt.

"I'll start dinner," she said. "Or is that too much togetherness for you?"

She left the bedroom. Peter stayed on the bed, feeling nailed to the wall by her words. He wanted to be with her on a faraway island. He wanted to be alone. He took his pipe from the bedside drawer, put a pinch of grass in it and smoked it by the window, blowing the smoke outside, then went to the kitchen to help with dinner.

SEVEN

Bob woke Peter at seven. "We're going in early," he said. "We'll get breakfast in the cookhouse."

Peter struggled awake and pushed himself off the couch, his head aching from a hangover.

"I'll get the truck started," Bob said as he stepped out the front door.

Peter lingered while lacing up his boots, hoping he would see Dianne to say goodbye, but the bedroom door was closed and he heard no movement behind it. Stepping out of the cabin into a brilliant morning, the air seemed to freeze the hairs in his nostrils and burn a cold, dry line to the back of his head. The sky was clear and pale, with a few stars and a faint moon visible in the early light. New snow squeaked under his boots as he walked down the path.

Bob had run an extension cord out to the truck to plug in the block heater, and he was shovelling snow from behind the vehicle. The road up to the highway had already been plowed out.

"We'll take the truck. I've gotta get groceries on the way home."

"How's Dianne this morning?" Peter asked.

"Fine," Bob's voice was short as he threw the shovel into the back of the pickup and climbed into the driver's seat.

They went slowly up to the road and turned towards town. Bob drove with one hand while he sipped coffee he had poured from a thermos. He offered the plastic cup to Peter.

"No thanks, I'll wait for the cookhouse swill."

The road was narrowed by fresh snowbanks on either side and they strayed into the opposite lane as they rounded a tight blind curve. A transport coming from Stikine, fully loaded with pallets of bagged asbestos, was entering the curve and suddenly was directly in front of the pickup. Bob cranked the wheel hard right and they skidded sideways. Black coffee flew from the cup he was holding onto Peter's hand, and the open thermos tipped onto his leg. Peter cried out in pain just as the transport's horn blared. They slid in a blizzard of kicked-up snow, then the pickup spun hard in the opposite direction as its back corner was nudged by the huge rear tires of the truck.

When they stopped moving the pickup was sitting crossways in the centre of the road. The transport was gone, vanished around the curve and on towards the Alaska Highway. Peter writhed in pain and lifted himself off the seat to escape the hot coffee that had pooled underneath him. he unzipped his jeans to pull them off his scalded thigh.

"Holy shit," Bob said, seeing the bright red patch of Peter's skin.

"Can you get some snow?" Peter said through his clenched teeth. "It'll take away the heat."

"I'd better get us out of the middle of the fucking road first." Bob drove ahead fifty yards. Something was banging on the back of the truck. "Sounds like the bumper got torn loose."

"Better it than our heads," Peter said, trying to laugh while grimacing with pain.

Bob got out of the truck and climbed over the snowbank to scoop up snow. He opened the passenger door and handed it to Peter.

"Will the snow be clean enough?"

"It'll be okay, the skin's not broken," Peter said, packing the snow and laying it on his thigh. "Jesus Christ that stings."

Bob dug around under the snow in the back of the pickup, found a rope and tied the loose bumper to the tailgate, then got back behind the wheel. "Let's get you to the Infirmary."

"Yeah, this could use some antibiotic cream. Pain killer wouldn't hurt, too."

Bob gunned the truck the rest of the way to Stikine. He slowed as they entered the town and glanced over at Peter.

"Sorry, Pete. That was all my fault."

"Don't worry," Peter replied. "The burn isn't bad. And like we know, shit happens."

"It shouldn't have." Bob was staring ahead intently. "I know that curve and I've seen accidents there before. I wasn't paying attention 'cause I was pissed off at you."

Peter felt his insides grip. He took the snow off his leg and rubbed some on his burned hand. "How come?" he asked.

"The talk last night brought back a lot of stuff for Dianne and I hate it when she's down."

"Shit, I'm sorry. I should've just kept my mouth shut about Rose."

Bob didn't respond. Peter looked at him again and saw the whiskers on the side of his face moving to the rhythm of clenched jaw muscles. The pain in his thigh returned and he rubbed a handful of the melting snow over the skin. They pulled up in front of the Infirmary.

Bob's hands stayed on the wheel. Peter carefully pulled up his jeans and put his hand on the door handle.

"I'm sorry," Bob said. "You didn't do anything wrong, Pete." He took a deep breath. "It's just that Dianne and I have had a really rough time since the second miscarriage. All kinds of tension between us and no sex for I don't know how long until the past few months when we're starting to get close again. And then last night I could feel that wall go up again and I'm lying there praying that we're not back in the fucking ice age."

Peter's leg throbbed and his head ached. He let go of the door handle and turned to Bob. "Maybe it's better if I stay out of your way from now on."

Bob shook his head. "No, man, it doesn't have to be like that. You and I go way back and I'm glad that you're here."

Peter's hand trembled as he grabbed the door handle again. "I better get this burn looked at." He hesitated a moment. "You two are great," he said quietly. "And I really appreciate you having me over." He opened the door and climbed out. "Say thanks to Dianne for me and give her my best," he said. "I'll see you around." He closed the door and went up the stairs into the Infirmary.

"How did it happen?" the doctor asked as he examined Peter's leg.

"Hot coffee."

"Clumsy." He opened a bottle of distilled water and poured some on the burn. "Seems to be a lot of particles on the skin."

"I used snow to cool the burn. It fell overnight so I thought it would be pretty clean."

The doctor looked closely at flecks on the skin. "As clean as snow ever gets around here. This is asbestos dust. Where'd you get the snow?"

Peter winced as his wound was cleaned. "Alongside the highway. Around where the Reserve is."

"The stuff can travel a long way." He wrapped the burn with a bandage and put the supplies back in a cupboard. He sat at his desk and wrote on a note pad. "I'll authorize you for light duty for four days. Come see me after that and I'll re-assess."

Peter took the note, but stayed sitting in the chair. The doctor wrote in a chart, then looked up.

"Anything else?"

"Well ... no, I guess not." Peter wanted to stay in the room with the doctor, smelling the familiar medicinal odours. He wanted to close his eyes and talk, but he stood up. "I'll come back in four days."

"That's what I said." The doctor tuned back to his notes.

EIGHT

Peter's shift went on graveyard. Midnight to eight. He showed the fore-man the doctor's note for light duty because of the burn on his leg.

"Light duty?" Clarkson laughed. "Everyone's on light duty in Rock Reject. If I were you I'd hang out in the lunch room and look like you're cleaning in there if De Vleit shows up. But there's a snowball's chance in hell of that happening on the graveyard."

Through the first few shifts he struggled to stay awake, reading in the lunchroom. Boredom forced him out to walk the freezing, dust-filled passageways, to look for recent spills of ore from the conveyors for something to do. During the dead hours he wasn't sure if he was awake or dreaming as he stood staring through the dusty haze, the crashing din of the crushing machines pounding into his body, fatigue letting the cold into his bones, the ache from the burn on his leg just a dull throb through his general numbness. Back in the lunchroom, his but-tocks numb from hours spent on the plywood bench, time passed so slowly he wondered if his watch had stopped. The end of the shift came at eight, and he trudged up the steel stairs beside the jaw crusher and out into the morning air, along the road to the Mine office to sit silently with twenty bleary-eyed miners waiting for the man-haul bus to take them down the mountain to the Mine Dry and to bed.

He slept in fits and starts, his body clock resisting being turned upside down. At five each afternoon he went to the cookhouse but his stomach turned at the sight of shepherd's pie and canned peas a half hour after getting out of bed. In his room each evening, he made himself sit at the desk with the letter to his father in front of him and try to write a sentence, hoping that a sentence might become a paragraph and then pages, saying something other than what the weather was like, something important that he needed his father to understand, something that he needed to understand himself. But all he could manage was a report on the depth of the snow, the length of the icicles and the late-night temperatures. Then his pen would stop and his mind would wander away, drifting into memories and light sleep, jerking awake only to float off again. At eleven each night he went to the cookhouse to drink coffee and make a lunch to eat at four in the morning. At midnight he boarded the man-haul bus and rode up the mountain, staring out the window into the dark, feeling lonelier than ever before in his life.

Temperatures slid steadily down as late November froze into December. A thermometer advertising Pepsi Cola had been nailed near the door at the top of Rock Reject and it read twenty-three below as Peter went out for a smoke break at four thirty in the morning. The moon had set, and in the frozen cold he watched the northern lights pulse and swirl across the dark sky, green sheets tinged with red, blue and violet flowing from the northern horizon and disappearing beyond the mountain peaks to the south.

At the edge of the slope he could see down the mountain to the lights of the town. Nearby, the door to the empty Mine office was half open. A radio was on inside and the voice reading the news carried clearly in the cold air. A plane had crashed in Washington D.C., killing ninety-two people. Suspects had been arrested for blowing up the pub in Birmingham. The cease-fire in Vietnam had been violated and more people were dead. He looked around at the dark masses of the mountains that surrounded him and at the scraped and blasted piece of earth that he stood on and felt he could cry.

The radio voice changed and someone in Whitehorse told him that the Red Wings had beaten the Leafs and the Canadiens the Bruins, that it was minus twenty-eight in Dawson City and minus twenty-four in Watson Lake. He threw his cigarette butt over the edge, walked across to the other side of the road and looked down into the pit.

At the bottom the mining proceeded under floodlights. Dump trucks lined up around a pool of light that surrounded the shovel, waiting their turn to be filled. He followed the headlights of a full truck as it climbed the slope from bench to bench to the top of the pit and along the road behind where he stood. The back-up horn blared repeatedly as the driver backed up to Rock Reject. The box of the truck tipped up and the load of ore thundered into the jaw crusher. A light was on inside the cab of the truck and he recognized Dave McGuinness, a thermos in his hand, pouring into a cup and drinking it down. The box lowered back onto the truck bed and as he pulled away his headlights fell on Peter and they waved to each other. The truck roared along the road and down into the pit. Peter turned to the sky to see the aurora swirling in a spiral overhead and watched the show of northern lights for another five minutes until the cold forced him back into Rock Reject and the heated lunchroom.

At six he took his shovel and went up the conveyor line to where he had seen an ore spill earlier in the shift, ten yards down from where the ore dropped out of the jaw crusher onto the moving belt. A load had been dumped into the crusher and the noise of the rock being ground by the massive steel plates was painful, even with hearing protection. He held his hands in their lined leather mitts over his ear muffs until all the ore had passed out of the machine, then resumed shovelling in the relative quiet, tossing spilt ore back onto the moving conveyor. A minute passed, then he was startled by the sight of a partially crushed red hard hat with a Union shop steward sticker on its side lying upright in the middle of the belt. Without thinking, he reached with his shovel and flicked it off the conveyor onto the floor, then turned in the direction it came from and froze.

Twenty feet away and coming towards him on the conveyor belt was a dark shape. A lumpy pile of rags. A parka, coveralls, boots. A pool of red. The back of the parka faced Peter as it went by him, hood up, hiding what was inside. He stared disbelieving, his insides shaking as the shape flowed past. A yell came from deep in his guts and he turned and sprinted down the corridor to the shut-off switch, cutting the power to the conveyor. The mangled shape, the crushed body, stopped five feet from the cone crusher that would have turned it to pulp.

Peter still carried his shovel. He swung it two-handed with all his strength against the plywood wall, then heaved it down the corridor where it spun off the conveyor and clattered to the dirt floor. He lifted his left leg up to climb onto the conveyor and gasped in pain as his pant leg tore open the burn blister on his thigh. He swore through his clenched teeth, then took a deep breath and vaulted up onto the steel frame of the conveyor. He stepped over the body to where he could reach into the parka and check for a pulse he knew wouldn't be there. The combined smells of blood and alcohol hit him as he looked for the place on the neck to put his fingers, but the landmarks were gone, the shoulders, collarbone, throat no longer recognizable parts of an anatomy. He glanced quickly at the face, wanting to know but not to see. Dave McGuinness was only just recognizable. Peter laid a hand on the shoulder of the parka, but withdrew it quickly from the feel of broken bone underneath the greasy, oil-stained material.

He began to lose sensation in his hands and cold sweat was forming on his forehead. He jumped off the conveyor, but his knees wouldn't support the landing and he fell against the wall. He struggled to his feet and stumbled along the corridor to the stairs up to the crusher operator's booth.

Paul Morino was asleep, slumped sideways in his chair against the filthy Plexiglas window of the booth, an electric heater by his feet going full blast. A paperback novel lay closed in his lap, his thumb marking his place. Peter shook him awake.

"Wake the fuck up," he shouted.

Morino startled awake. "What?"

"Goddamn it, Dave's dead."

"What the fuck are you talking about?"

Peter leaned towards Morino and screamed at him. "He's dead. Dave McGuinness. He went through the crusher."

"You're fucking nuts, man. I've been right here."

"You were asleep, for christsakes. You should've stopped the machine."

Morino pushed past Peter out of the booth onto the catwalk. Peter followed him and stood by the guardrail at the edge of the crusher pit. A dump truck sat with its engine idling on the other side of the pit, its box empty of ore. Another truck was on the roadway, waiting its turn to dump its load. The door to the outside at the end of the catwalk was half open, and ten feet inside the door the broken ends of the wooden guardrail dangled in space over the crusher.

"Holy shit," Morino said, taking his hands off the railing and stepping back. "He went right through." He turned to Peter. "Did you see the body?"

Peter glared at him. "Go to the Mine office and get on the radio," he ordered. "Get Clarkson, get De Vleit, get whoever you can."

Morino started along the catwalk then turned back. "Don't tell them I was asleep," he pleaded. "This wasn't my fault."

Peter looked at him and said nothing.

"They'll fire me."

It's what you deserve, Peter wanted to shout at him, but instead he turned and started down the stairs.

"Where're you going?" Morino yelled.

"Someone needs to be with Dave," Peter yelled without looking back. He hurried down to the conveyor where McGuinness's body lay and stood beside it to wait.

Ian Clarkson, the shift foreman, was there in three minutes. His face was white as he ran up to Peter. Fog from his breath hung thick.

"Did you see what happened?" he asked.

The image of McGuinness tossing back a drink in his truck flashed through his mind, but Peter shook his head. "Only his body on the conveyor," he said. "I shut off the power before it went into the cone crusher."

"That was quick thinking." Clarkson put a hand on the conveyor frame, ready to jump up.

"For sure it's McGuinness?" he asked. "You looked?"

Peter put a hand on Clarkson's shoulder to hold him back.

"Yes. I wouldn't advise you to, though."

"That bad?"

Peter nodded. Clarkson stepped back from the conveyor.

"I'd better put a barricade where the guardrail's broken." He looked at Peter. "You're okay until the doctor gets here?"

"Yeah, I'll be fine."

Clarkson looked at the body. "What a fucking waste." He turned and went back up the stairs.

Peter sat on the dirt floor and closed his eyes. His leg felt wet where the blister had broken and it throbbed with pain. Dust was thick in his nostrils and throat, and the smells of urine, feces, blood and booze that leaked out of Dave McGuinness's body spread through the cold air. He remembered the smell of Rose's blood in their bedroom, the heavy odour that filled the room and hit him when he stepped through the door. He remembered the weight of her soaked nightgown and his own voice asking, "What have I done? God help me, what have I done?" He felt his tears rolling down his face and dropping onto the folds of his parka. He looked down and saw how they mixed with dust on the nylon material and froze in tiny pools of mud.

Footsteps banged down the steel stairs. Simon De Vleit and the doctor were followed by Iggy Benedetti carrying an aluminum stretcher. Peter slowly got to his feet.

"Christ, what a mess," De Vleit said. "Did you touch anything?" he barked at Peter.

"Not really," Peter said. "I tried to check for a pulse at first, but there was no use."

"Well see that you don't." He turned to Iggy. "There'll be hell to pay because of that goddamn wooden guardrail. Why didn't you change the goddamn thing to steel?"

"It's been like that since the place was built," Iggy shouted. "The goddamn mine inspector's seen it a dozen times and never said a thing about it."

"I guarantee he'll give us grief about it now."

The doctor stepped around De Vleit and addressed Peter. "You had a look at the body?"

Peter nodded. "Massive trauma. Skull is crushed. I couldn't even locate a landmark for the carotid pulse. Death would have been very quick."

The doctor looked surprised at the answer, then nodded. "Very good. I'll confirm now." He climbed onto the conveyor and lifted open the hood of McGuiness' parka. He winced at what he saw, shook his head and climbed back down.

"I smell booze," De Vleit said. "Was he drinking?"

"It's possible," the doctor said. "I smell it too."

"He was drunk, then," De Vleit said. "That'll keep Compensation off our backs. Make sure you get a blood sample for evidence." He turned and walked towards the stairs. "I'm going to check his goddamn truck for a bottle."

De Vleit disappeared up the stairs. Peter and the doctor watched him leave. Iggy undid the straps on the stretcher.

"Bastard," Peter mumbled.

"He's famous for it," the doctor replied. "He came from the Company's South African operation with quite a reputation. Highest production rates. Highest fatality rates."

"Aren't we lucky to have him," Peter said with a sneer.

Iggy shot a look at Peter. "Go ahead and be smart, young fellow, but it doesn't absolve McGuinness from behaving irresponsibly. Drinking on the job. He's got only himself to blame, rest his soul, and your sarcasm won't change that."

Peter's cheeks flushed and he looked away down the corridor. Iggy's words repeated in his head, but the voice became his father's. An image of his scolding face flashed through his mind.

Iggy lifted the stretcher onto the frame of the conveyor. "Hold this steady, will you doc?" He climbed on the belt and positioned himself at McGuinness's head, then paused for a moment with his eyes closed and his breath rapid and shallow. "Sorry," he said to the doctor. "I hate this."

"I don't blame you. So do I."

Iggy motioned to Peter to climb up and take the feet. Peter grabbed the body by the boots and lifted, but there was no solidity to what he held and he let go involuntarily, fearing that he might pull away a part of McGuinness's leg.

"Better grab the clothing," Iggy said. "And roll it. He's too big to lift."

They turned the body and let it flop into the stretcher, the doctor groaning as he steadied it against the conveyor frame. An arm hung over the edge, bent the wrong way. One leg was twisted sideways over the other. Blood streamed out of McGuinness's clothing and splattered on the frozen floor. Peter and Iggy jumped down and took the ends of the stretcher, then laid it on the ground. The doctor arranged the limbs alongside the body and shook his head.

"Not a bone that isn't smashed. I've never seen anything so bad." He picked up the blanket and tucked it around the hood of the parka, then stretched it the length of the body before fastening the straps tight.

"It's going to take some muscle to get him up the stairs to the ambulance," Iggy said to Peter. "Go up top and see who you can find."

Peter looked at the stretcher, then into the grey faces of the doctor and Iggy. He wanted to stay, to put his hand on Dave's broken chest, but he turned and hurried down the corridor and up the stairs.

Clarkson was watching two men hammer a new railing in place at the edge of the silent crusher pit.

"Iggy asked me to get some men to carry the stretcher," Peter said.

"The truck drivers are all outside. They'll want to do that."

Peter followed the foreman out of Rock Reject. The sun had just risen over the peaks to the southeast and he squinted into the golden light. Six Haul Pac dump trucks were parked along the edge of the road and the drivers stood near McGuinness's truck, which was still at the edge of the crusher pit. De Vleit was climbing out of the cab, waving a thermos bottle.

"I've got it," he shouted. "Whiskey or something in here. Proof."

Clarkson ignored De Vleit as he went to speak to the truck drivers, who then followed him towards the door into Rock Reject. De Vleit called after them.

"Hey, hold up you. Who knew he drank on the job? Who saw him do it?"

They walked into the building without looking at De Vleit.

"Hey, I mean it. I want a report from all the drivers on this shift." He waved the thermos in the air. "It was deliberate negligence that got him killed."

A Chevy Suburban appeared from behind the parked trucks, the RCMP logo on the doors. It pulled up near De Vleit and an officer got out.

"Fatality?"

"That's right. Drunk on the job and here's the evidence." De Vleit proudly showed the thermos to the officer, then opened it for him to smell.

"You found this where?"

"Right in the cab of his truck." De Vleit pointed up at Dave's Haul Pac.

"You shouldn't have moved it," the officer said. De Vleit's mouth turned sour. "Show me what happened."

"He stumbled right through the railing into the jaw crusher," De Vleit said as he led the officer towards Rock Reject. "The crusher operator said he was in the shit house. This guy saw the body on the conveyor below the crusher." He pointed at Peter as he walked.

"I'll need to talk to both of you," the officer said, looking at Paul Morino and Peter before going into Rock Reject.

Morino came up to Peter. "They'll fire me for sure if you tell," he said in a whisper. "I need to keep this job."

Peter looked into his face. It was grimy with dust and looked small under his hard hat. His eyes were puffy and streaked with red

"What's done is done," Peter said. He turned from Morino to look at the sun, which seemed perched on a distant mountain top. "You probably couldn't have saved him. The crusher would've taken too long to stop."

"Thanks," Morino began, then the door to Rock Reject banged open and two truck drivers carrying the front of the stretcher squeezed through side by side. Morino ran to hold the door as the body, the stretcher bearers, the doctor, Iggy and Clarkson all filed into the cold morning light.

Peter watched the procession go by him, the bulk of McGuinness's body covered by the blanket, a thin stream of his blood falling from the underside of the stretcher and leaving a trail of red in the dirty snow. He closed his eyes and felt himself suddenly weak, his legs wobbly from fatigue and cold. Images flashed in his mind: Dave waving to him from his truck two hours earlier; Rose smiling; Rose lying pale in the hospital bed. He saw her funeral, saw her coffin sitting on the carriage in front of the altar. He heard her voice telling him something he couldn't make out. He strained to understand. Then other voices from above him and a sharp smell jolted his eyes open to the doctor kneeling beside him with Iggy and Clarkson looking on.

"You okay?" the doctor asked.

"I think so. Yeah." He pushed himself to sitting, felt woozy and lay back again. "I just need a minute to rest. I'm tired."

"In shock is more like it, seeing a body like that," the doctor said. "Just lie quiet for a while.

He lay on the cold ground, the spinning in his head slowly settling down. The RCMP officer stood nearby talking to Iggy, making notes.

"I should go with the body," Peter said. No-one looked his way. He wondered if he spoke the words or thought them. The officer crouched down beside him.

"I'll give you a ride down when I'm finished," he said. "If you're ready, you should probably get in the Mine office where it's warm."

Peter nodded and sat up. The ambulance pulled away with Iggy at the wheel and the doctor beside him. De Vleit got in his white pickup and drove off. The officer was talking with Paul Morino by the entrance to Rock Reject.

It was quiet. No vehicles or machinery were running. The sun was bright, but he felt no warmth from it as he slowly stood up and walked towards the Mine office. The trail of blood led in that direction, and Peter followed it to where it stopped, to where the ambulance had been parked and the stretcher loaded inside. He stared at the spot where the thin line of red ended and looked around to see if there was someone he could show it to, to point out where the trace of Dave McGuinness ended. His last imprint on this blasted wreck of a mountain. A pickup truck drove past and didn't stop. The Haul Pac drivers were nowhere to be seen. The officer left Morino and came up to Peter.

"I'm ready to go down now," he said.

Peter looked at the trail of blood. "But shouldn't we do something?" he asked.

"Yeah, get some sleep. Let's go."

His feet were numb from cold and his leg burned with pain as he eased himself into the police vehicle. He drifted in and out of consciousness as they drove down into Stikine and they spoke only as Peter got out of the Suburban in front of his bunkhouse.

"Come by the station later today after you're rested. I'll get a statement from you then."

"I'll do that. Thanks for the ride down."

"No problem. And if I were you, I'd take a day off. Get the doc to authorize it."

Peter nodded and went into the bunkhouse.

NINE

Peter sat on his bed, gathering the energy to undress. Every movement was heavy, every muscle ached. The fluid weeping from his burn had soaked through the bandage and he almost enjoyed the searing pain as he peeled it off, the sensation a jagged shock through his brain, jolting him awake. He stood for a long time under the shower, letting the heat penetrate his aching back and neck. He dried off and climbed into bed, but after two hours of light sleep he was wakened by pain and memories of Dave's broken body. He got up, sat at his desk and looked out the window at the slice of mountain that was visible to the north, the sun lighting the upper half of its slope. The lower half and the valley were in the shadow of the wall of mountains to the south. The sun hadn't shone on the town in two weeks.

On one side of his desk was a pile of pay stubs, books and magazines. The edge of the half-written letter to his father stuck out of the pile and he pulled it out, crumpled it and tossed it in the wastebasket. He took a new sheet of paper and began writing.

December 2, 1974.

Dad, What happens to you when you see death? How do you feel when you can't do anything? What did Granddad say to you about being a doctor? What did you ask him? Why were you always so hard on me?

His pen stopped and he stared at what he had written. The words broke apart into fragments and made no sense to his exhausted mind. He folded the page, put it in an envelope and addressed it, then pushed it to the back of the desk.

As if he would answer honestly.

He looked at his leg. Dots of fresh blood had emerged from the raw skin where the blisters had torn away, and the area surrounding the wound was swollen and red. He decided he would go to the Infirmary to have it dressed again.

The doctor's eyes were baggy and bloodshot as he ushered Peter into his office. A half-smoked cigarette burned on the edge of an overflowing ashtray on the desk. He stubbed it out as he sat in his creaky swivel chair. Peter stood on the opposite side of the desk.

"You look about as bad as I feel," the doctor said. "Have a seat."

"It's easier to stand," Peter replied. "The bandage you put on my thigh was a real mess, so there's nothing on it now."

"Right. The burned leg." He looked at Peter's file. "Scalded, wasn't it?"

"Yes. Second degree."

The doctor nodded and rose from his chair. "Let's have a look."

Peter gingerly pulled off his pants and eased himself onto the examination table. He wished he could close his eyes and fall asleep.

"It's a bit raw. Were you keeping it clean like I told you?"

"Sort of," Peter replied. "Last night it got torn open. Climbing up and down on the conveyor."

The doctor slowly shook his head. "A hell of a way to go, through that machine. I have to admit it shook me up." He went to a cabinet across the room, returning with a tube of ointment and bandages.

"Gentamicin?" Peter asked as the doctor spread the ointment on the wound.

"What'd you say?"

"The ointment. Is it gentamicin?"

"That's right. How do you know?"

"I got most of the way through medical school."

"And now you're a labourer in an asbestos mine."

Peter closed his eyes. "There's a reason," he said, his voice shaky.

"Everybody's got a reason for being here," the doctor said. He wrapped Peter's thigh with a clean bandage, then returned to his desk and lit another cigarette.

Peter slowly pulled on his trousers then sat in the chair by the desk. His eyes met the doctor's for a moment, then they lowered to the desk. He saw a framed photograph of two young children.

"Do you want some pain killers?" the doctor asked. "Tylenol 3s. Help you sleep."

He flipped a sample packet of the pills across the desk. Peter glanced at his left hand and saw no wedding band. He picked up the packet and turned it over in his hands. The doctor leaned back in his chair.

"Did you know Dave McGuinness?" he asked Peter.

"Just a bit. Not really," Peter said. "Did you know him?"

"Yeah. I spent some time with him. He was a decent guy and I think he really cared about this place and about being the president of the Union."

They sat in silence for several moments.

"My wife died this past spring," Peter said quietly.

The doctor's mouth opened in surprise. He looked intently at Peter then leaned forward and folded his hands on the desk.

"I'm sorry. It was sudden?"

Peter nodded. "Yes. It was…" He looked down at his hands in his lap, clasped together tightly, the knuckles white.

"Do you want to tell me anything more about it?" the doctor asked.

Peter felt paralyzed with fatigue, his mind a blank wall. "Not now," he said, his voice barely more than a whisper.

"That's okay, I understand." The doctor closed Peter's file. "Come see me again if you feel like talking."

Peter put the pills in his pocket and stood up. "Thanks. I might."

Outside the Infirmary he stood on the porch facing the mountains. They seemed to loom closer, steeper than before and he suddenly felt claustrophobic, breathless. He thought of walking to the Administration Building, quitting and getting on the ride to Watson Lake the next morning. Or going back to the bunkhouse, to bed and putting the past six hours behind him. Or to the Union office, fifty yards along the road. He remembered Dave asking him to help out, saying how they could use someone like him. He felt pulled towards the Union office but he held back, wondering if he would fit in, worried they would think he was nothing but a university city boy with no knowledge of the northern mining world. Someone with no substance.

A siren sounded through the town, the signal that a blast was about to happen in the Mine. He looked along the top of the wall of mountain to the jagged gap where the Mine was. Rock Reject looked like it was pasted to the side of the mountain, the Mine office a tiny dot on the crest of the peak with a serene blue sky as its background. In his weariness he had already forgotten that the siren had sounded and was startled when a cloud of rock and dust spewed up from the blast and seemed to hang motionless, as if it were a photograph. The noise of the blast hit him seconds later, as the cloud began to settle back, leaving a haze floating against the sky. He thought how this piece of the mountain would now be dug away and hauled to Rock Reject, crushed and milled to end up as brake linings in cars or fire-proof suits or whatever else they did with asbestos. He imagined countless trucks and boots travelling over the trail of Dave McGuinness's blood, wiping it away. He had had enough. He went down the steps of the Infirmary and turned towards the Administration Building to quit.

He was halfway there when two women came out of the front doors. Peter recognized Dave's girlfriend, Susan. The other woman had her arm around Susan's shoulders, steadying her as they walked down the stairs. Simon De Vleit came out a few moments later, calling after them from the top of the stairs. Peter couldn't hear what he said and the women didn't respond. They got into a pickup truck in the parking lot and drove past Peter. Seeing the shine of tears on Susan's face, he tried to imagine what she felt. He looked at De Vleit, walking to his truck while watching the women drive away. On an impulse, Peter abruptly turned and headed towards the Union office.

The office was a house trailer with a narrow porch. He stood at the door, hesitant, unsure, hearing voices inside, a chair scraping across the floor. A road grader drove by, pushing back the snowbanks and widening the road. Taking a deep breath, he opened the door and stepped into a room with a long table down the middle littered with styrofoam cups and papers and surrounded by stacking chairs. The room smelled of stale coffee and cigarette smoke. A velvet painting of a tiger hung on the dingy panelled wall behind the table, at the far end of which several men sat in silence. He recognized two of them from the head table at the monthly meeting: Alex Bruce, the vice president, and Chris Murton, the secretary. Peter stood by the door, waiting to be acknowledged, wondering if he should just leave when a toilet flushed behind a door at the back, and George MacDonald stepped out from the washroom.

"Pete, buddy, good to see you in here." George extended his hand to Peter.

"George, hi. I didn't know that you were involved here."

"Like I said before, it runs in the family. Must be in our blood or something. What're you here for?"

"I was wondering if there might be something I could do to help out. With the health issues, like Dave said when we were in the bar. But this is probably a bad time."

"You heard about Dave?"

Peter nodded. "Yeah. I was up there."

They looked at each other briefly, then nervously away to the floor. George put a hand on Peter's shoulder and steered him towards the back of the room.

"Let's see if Alex can give you something to do."

Alex Bruce sat at the end of the table, staring into an empty coffee mug. A dark shadow of heavy beard made his pale complexion look sickly.

"Alex, this is my buddy, Pete. He's studied medicine and wants to help out with the health stuff."

He looked up at Peter. His eyes were grey and dull. "Alex Bruce, Vice President of the Local." He offered his hand. It was cold and damp.

"Peter Stevens. I'm just a labourer up in Rock Reject, but I've got a bit of background in medical studies, and a while ago Dave…"

"Stevens," Alex straightened up and turned in his chair. His face opened to Peter. "Weren't you the guy who first saw him? You stopped the conveyor, right?"

"That's right," Peter said quietly.

"He wasn't…" He stopped to take a breath. "Was he still alive when you saw him?"

"No, for sure not. He died very quickly. Instantly."

Alex slumped back in his chair. "That's good to know. Christ, what a way to go." He ran his hands through his hair, pushing it back off his forehead. "What was it you wanted?"

"Just to know if there was some way I might help out here."

"Oh yeah, the health stuff. You can be on the safety and health committee. Go see Gord Evans, he's in the back office over there."

"Thanks. I don't know if I'll be of much use, but…" Peter's words trailed off as Alex seemed to fall back into the trance he was in a minute earlier. Peter moved away and knocked on the door of the back office.

There was no response from inside, but the door was ajar so he pushed it open. Gord Evans sat with his elbows on a battered desk, his head in his hands. Peter stood in the doorway for several moments, then sat in a chair beside the desk.

"Excuse me."

Gord lifted his head to look at Peter. His eyes were hidden by the deep sockets of his craggy face. "I let it happen," he said. "I'm to blame."

"I'm sorry?"

"That goddamn wooden railing. I looked at it on every safety tour with Iggy and I never wrote it in my report. I should have made them change it. Dave would still be alive."

"But Iggy saw it too," Peter said. "And so did the Department of Mines inspector. I heard Iggy say so."

"That Mines inspector is useless. They feed him a fancy dinner with all the booze he can drink, then he writes a glowing friggin' report about the operation. It was up to me to catch problems like that and I should've pushed for it. It was such a simple thing and I fucked up."

"It's not your fault that this happened. Don't blame yourself."

Gord's face tightened, as if holding back tears. Moments passed in silence then he looked again at Peter. "What is it you want?"

"I was thinking about being on your committee. I might be able to help out on the health problems."

"My committee," Gord sniffed with disgust. "What a joke. It's a committee of one and I'm fucking useless at it." He got up from the desk, took his coat from the back of the chair and went towards the door.

"So, is there something I can do? Anything I can look at until we have a meeting?"

Gord motioned to a file cabinet. "There's all the safety reports in there. You can read them if you want." His eyes were wet. Turning his back to Peter, he pulled a handkerchief from his back pocket and brought it to his face, then took a cowboy hat from a hook on the wall, pulled it down low and left the room. The front door closed a moment later.

Peter sat listening to the sounds of voices through the thin walls, then looked around the small room. It was gloomy despite the two long florescent tubes on the ceiling, the dark walls absorbing the light, making everything seem dirty. A small window looked like it had never been cleaned. The file cabinet stood in a corner with an almost empty beer bottle on top, two cigarette butts floating inside. A case of empties sat on the floor under the window.

Despite his fatigue, Peter's mind was clear and he felt a sense of purpose being in the room. From the file cabinet, he pulled out folders labelled "Reports" and "Correspondence," cleared the clutter from the desk, and sat in the battered chair Gord had vacated. He adjusted it to his own height and began to sift through the contents of the files.

An hour later he was startled out of light sleep by someone calling his name. Disoriented, he looked around, a letter with Department of Mines letterhead still in his hand. George stood on the other side of the desk.

"Pete. You okay?"

Peter shook his head awake and rubbed his eyes. "Yeah. Sorry, I didn't get much sleep."

"Can you talk to someone?"

"Who? What about?"

"It's Dave's girl. Susan Bradley. She wants to know if anyone saw what happened."

Peter looked past George and saw Susan standing outside the open door. George lowered his voice.

"I told her I wasn't sure, but that maybe you knew something. I can tell her I was wrong if you want."

His heart thudding, Peter closed his eyes and tried to breathe away the fear that rose inside him. "No, it's okay. I can talk to her." He stood up as George motioned to Susan. She came into the room. George stepped out and closed the door behind him. Peter thought about calling after him, to tell him to leave the door open, but it was too late. Susan looked at him across the desk.

"Did you see what happened?" she asked.

The look on her face tore Peter open. He had difficulty gathering the breath to speak.

"No. I don't think anyone did. I saw him after he fell, after he came out…" He stopped himself from going further.

"I heard how he died."

Peter nodded. They looked at each other for a moment. "Please, sit down," he said. "Can I get you something to drink? I think there's coffee or a glass of water."

"No, thank you." She remained standing and Peter didn't move. "Can you tell me what you saw?"

A wave of tiredness flowed over him and he longed to sit down.

"I was working by the conveyor below the jaw crusher. That's where the trucks dump the ore. A load had finished going through and maybe a minute or two passed and then I saw Dave's body on the conveyor. I stopped the belt before he got to the next crusher."

Susan stood with her eyes closed. "Do you know if he was already dead?"

"Yes, for sure. I checked for a pulse right away, and I couldn't find…" Peter stopped and swallowed hard. "I couldn't find one. There was no pulse. He died instantly."

She nodded, swaying slightly on her feet. "Do you know how it happened? Simon De Vleit said he had been drinking."

"I could smell alcohol from his body, but I don't know how much he would've had. It seems like he tripped or stumbled on his way to the latrine, and he fell against a guard rail and broke through it."

Susan shook her head slowly. "He tried so hard to stay off the hard stuff. I know he did." She looked at Peter. "I'm sorry you had to see it. It's been hard on you."

He thought for an instant to lie to her, but his head nodded the truth. He watched her face and felt the edges of his own grief.

"What will you do now?" he asked.

She shrugged. "They told me I can take time off. Maybe I'll go home for a while, stay over Christmas."

"Where's home?"

"Winnipeg. It's Dave's home, too." Her mouth tightened. "I'll have to visit his parents. This is going to just kill them. He's their only child." She reached into her pocket for tissue and wiped her eyes, then blew her nose. "I'm sorry. You don't need to hear all of this."

"No, it's fine, really. I… I think I know how you feel."

"I don't think you do," Susan said bitterly.

Peter looked down at the desk. "It's good to talk, anyway. That much I know."

Neither spoke for half a minute. The sound of voices from the main room filtered through the thin door. The hum of the florescent light seemed to gradually grow louder. Peter felt a pressure inside him and he was relieved when Susan took a deep breath and let it out. He did the same.

"Thank you for telling me what you saw. And for listening. I've got to go now." She turned and went to the door.

"If there's anything I can do…"

Susan didn't respond as she left the room and closed the door behind her. Peter stayed on his feet, struggling to avoid falling into the dark pit of his grief. The smell of her shampoo remained in the room, sweet and sharp in the stale air. He sat down and picked up a two-year-old safety report from the file and forced himself to read it.

He went to dinner early, wanting to get a few hours of sleep before the graveyard shift at midnight. He was pulling on his coat at the cookhouse door when Paul Morino came in, his eyes looking haunted and his face grey. Peter reached out and laid a hand on his shoulder, but his head was filled with the memory of shaking him awake in the crusher booth, of screaming at him to wake up. Without a word, he turned away and left the cookhouse. Goddamn liar. Coward. Selfish bastard.

Words chewed inside Peter's head as he walked through the cold to his bunkhouse.

He sat at his desk and picked up the letter he had written that morning, reading the single page that was inside. He then began to write more.

My life feels wasted, pointless. I need a father. I need you, father. Bless me father for I have sinned. I confess to you, father. I beg your forgiveness. Mea culpa, I am guilty. I am responsible for Rose's death. It's my fault. Punish me father. Forgive me father for I cannot forgive myself. I need you.

Laying down his pen he folded his hands, his interlaced fingers clenched and white, and let his head fall forward, pressing into his knuckles until the pain was too intense to bear. He lay his hands open on the desk. Callused and strong from swinging a pick and shovel, he clenched them into fists and watched his forearms grow, bigger than he had ever seen them before. He read the letter again, then took hold of the paper and tore it in half, then in half again and again, until his words became a pile of confetti that he swept into the wastebasket.

TEN

By the second week of December mid-day in the town seemed like dusk and up in the Mine there was only a glow on the southern horizon, a reminder that the sun and warmth still existed somewhere. The main room of the Union office was empty when Peter entered the trailer on a day off, and he headed towards the back room to see if Gord Evans was there.

"Stevens," someone called as he walked past the open door of the president's office. He stepped in to see Alex Bruce putting files in a briefcase.

"You're on the safety and health committee, right?"

"Yeah, I guess so. I was coming in to see about meeting with Gord and finding out what I could do."

"Gord's gone." He closed the briefcase and stood up from the desk. "And tomorrow's the monthly safety tour with Iggy, so you'll have to be the Union rep and go with him."

"But I can't do that. Can't the tour wait 'till Gord gets back?"

"I said he's gone. Quit and fucked off out of here yesterday. I guess he couldn't get over Dave's death. Blamed himself for some crazy reason." He picked up the briefcase and went to the door. "We're meeting with the Company in ten minutes about the contract. We're close to an agreement."

"But wait a minute. I don't know anything about safety. How the hell can I be the Union rep?"

"Don't sweat it. Just show up at Iggy's office in the Admin Building at nine tomorrow. He does all the work. You follow along and sign the report when he's done. It's no big deal, and you get your day's pay for doing it."

"Can't I talk to you some more about it before tomorrow?"

"No time. Gotta go." Alex was out the door. Peter heard his heavy footsteps descending the wooden stairs and watched through the window as Alex made his way to a pickup truck, walking with a limp that made his body shift from side to side. He climbed into the truck and drove the hundred yards to the Administration Building.

"Christ, how stupid is this?" Peter said to the empty room. He paced around the conference table, wishing he had quit the week before instead of walking into this ugly trailer. The thought of spending a day with Iggy Benedetti made his stomach clench. The velvet tiger on the wall stared at him, its eyes a garish yellow. They watched each other for a moment, then he shook his head in disgust and went to the counter to make a pot of coffee. In the back office he pulled out the safety tour files and spent the morning reading them.

Pellets of hard snow stung his face as he walked to the Administration Building the next morning at five to nine. Heavy clouds hung just above the tops of the mountains and the streetlights were on in the dark morning. He recognized the receptionist as he stood in front of her desk. She was the woman who helped Susan out of the building the morning Dave died.

"I'm here for the safety tour with Iggy."

"Mr. Benedetti," the woman corrected.

"Right. Sorry."

"I'll let him know you're here. Name?"

"Stevens."

She rang through on the intercom, then turned back to Peter. "He's with someone, but you can wait upstairs, down the hall to your right. There's a few chairs there."

"Thanks." Peter started to leave, then hesitated. "The other receptionist, Susan Bradley. Did she leave?"

"Yes. She went home to stay with her parents. Poor girl. Such a thing."

"It was a horrible accident."

"Accident my foot. That was sheer ignorance if you ask me."

Peter turned away without a word and climbed the stairs to the second floor. Doors led off both sides of the corridor, all closed except one. He glanced into that room and saw Iggy and a woman talking. He moved away from the door to look at the photographs hanging on the corridor walls. A tractor-trailer loaded with bags of Stikine asbestos, bulldozers pushing a road through in the early fifties, the Administration Building with management staff on the front steps, dated September 1963. He was looking at the faces of the people on the steps when the woman came out of the office and smiled at Peter.

"Good morning," he said.

"Good morning to you. I guess my husband's a busy man this morning."

"They gave me a number downstairs," Peter joked. "I hope I'm next."

She laughed, then broke into coughing. Peter waited until she recovered.

"Sorry." She dabbed at her mouth with a handkerchief. "A bad cough."

Peter thought he heard a rattle in her lungs. He watched as she walked to the stairs, then knocked on the open door of the office.

Iggy's face showed surprise when he looked up from his desk and recognized Peter.

"So you're Stevens. A Rock Reject labourer is the best that the Union can do to replace Gord?"

Peter looked down. "I guess so."

Iggy shook his head. "It's probably just as well that you've got no experience." He crossed the room and handed Peter a clipboard with blank paper. "Follow my lead, take notes if you like." He looked straight at Peter, his blue eyes stern. "And spend your time listening and learning. I don't appreciate trouble makers."

He gestured for Peter to go out, then closed and locked the door, trying it twice to make sure it was secure.

"Let's move it, Stevens. We're already behind schedule."

Peter hurried to keep up with Iggy through the building, across the parking lot and into his pickup. Iggy checked his watch as they pulled away.

"Normally I like to be inspecting the first worksite by nine. We're starting late, so we'll have to make up time."

"You were meeting with your wife this morning?" Peter asked, his voice as bright as he could make it.

"Yes. That was unexpected."

"She seems to have a chest condition."

"She has a cold," Iggy said curtly.

Peter shrugged, folded his arms and stared out the window.

Iggy parked in front of the Mill and got out without speaking. Peter sat in the truck, glaring at Iggy's back, then got out and followed him inside.

The Mill was another world, another version of industrial hell than the one Peter had been working in for the past six weeks. Unlike his frigid solitary days in Rock Reject, the Mill was hot and at a glance he saw six or eight workers, their faces blank under their hardhats and hearing protectors, moving almost mechanically at a pace that appeared dictated by the pervasive din and vibration of heavy machinery. Iggy was nowhere to be seen, but footprints in the dust on the floor led to a nearby open door. Peter felt like he was trailing after his father in the hospital and momentarily considered turning around and going back to his bunkhouse room. He tasted dust in his mouth, finer than the rock and ore dust in Rock Reject. Pure asbestos dust. Feeling suddenly hot and nauseous, he took off his parka, then followed Iggy's trail through the door that said, "Mill Supervisor."

"I just can't imagine how he could've fallen into the friggin' crusher." The supervisor sat behind his desk, leaning back in his chair. A nameplate on the cluttered desk said, "Carl Moffat." Breaking right through the damn guardrail." He shook his head sadly, his heavy jowls wagging over his open shirt collar.

"He was a big man," Iggy said. Peter thought he sounded defensive. "And don't forget, he was drunk as a skunk. The guard rail would've held up under any other circumstance." He looked at his clipboard and cleared his throat. "So, anything that should go into the report, Carl?"

"Naw. Things are pretty ship-shape." He broke into a cough, then took a handful of Kleenex from a box on the desk, horked from deep in his lungs and spat into the tissues. Sweat beaded on his forehead.

"Sheet metal guys are replacing a few guards around crusher motors. Some idiot got his sleeve caught in an exposed drive belt last week and it dislocated his shoulder. He was hung over, I'm sure of it."

"Was he off work long?"

"Nah, I told him to take a couple of days off, so it won't show up as a Compensation claim. Keep the slate clean. Anyway, the belt is covered now, so don't bother to put it in the report."

"No problem. I'm behind schedule, so I'll just take a fast run through the Mill." He turned and noticed Peter. "This is the new Union safety rep," he said, then started for the door.

Peter stood facing Carl for a moment, expecting him to say hello. Carl had turned his attention to papers on his desk, taking a handkerchief from his pocket to wipe his forehead. Peter shrugged, turned and followed Iggy. He was enveloped by the noise of the Mill, which was at once heavy, deep and piercingly sharp. A haze of dust gave everything the grainy appearance of an old photograph. He passed by three workers, each standing between two metal chutes about two feet square and hanging parallel to the floor at waist height. He watched the workers pull huge plastic bags over the chutes — like putting on condoms, he thought — and saw the bags fill with blocks of compressed asbestos that were pushed out of the chutes. The filled bags toppled upright onto a conveyor and past a man operating a machine that sewed closed the top of the bag, then on to a machine that stacked the bags onto pallets and strapped them together. A fork lift truck was moving a pallet through an opening in a wall, probably onto a tractor-trailer, he figured.

Two men and a woman stood at the bagging chutes, turning steadily from one chute to the other, never stopping. Sweat stained their t-shirts. As each filled bag dropped off, a cloud of dust followed from inside the chute and they had to lean into it as they pulled on the next bag. Peter watched the woman work, her movements like a dance, her thick black braid falling from side to side as she tended to each chute. She glanced at him and their eyes met for a moment as she paused to lift her hardhat and wipe her forehead with her sleeve, then reached for another bag to pull over the chute.

A finger tapped roughly on Peter's shoulder and he turned to see Iggy's scowling face.

"Dammit Stevens, we don't have all day. I've been standing at the man lift waiting for you."

"Sorry," Peter hurried after Iggy. "I've never been in here," he shouted at his back. "It's kind of… fascinating, I guess."

"Be fascinated on your own time. We've got work to do."

A moving conveyor belt went straight up through an opening in the fifteen-foot-high ceiling. Handles and small platforms were attached to the belt, and Iggy stepped onto one as it came up through the floor from a lower level of the Mill. "Get off at the sixth floor," he shouted before rising through the ceiling. As Iggy disappeared, a man descended from the floor above, riding down on the other side of the continuous belt.

Peter waited for the next handle to come into view from below, grabbed it and awkwardly stepped onto the platform. He rose through the Mill, looking around through the dusty haze at the heavy machinery on each floor. At the sixth he almost forgot to get off the belt and had to jump to the floor from several feet up. Iggy was watching.

"That was unsafe, Stevens," he shouted over the roar of the machines. "You weren't paying attention, and you could have injured yourself. That would have cost the Company in compensation. You need to be more responsible."

Go to hell, Peter thought.

"Listen up now and you'll learn something."

Peter turned an ear towards Iggy so he wouldn't have to look at him.

"The ore comes down the mountain from Rock Reject and a conveyor brings it up to this floor. It's crushed and screened, then drops down to the next floor for more processing. Each level down is finer screening. At the second floor the waste is taken by conveyor outside to the tailings pile. The pure fibre is light and a vacuum sucks it back up to this level where it's blown into storage bins. The bottoms of the bins are at the first floor and that's where the fibre is compacted into the blocks you saw coming out of the chutes." He paused and looked at Peter to see if he was following.

"I get it," Peter said. "So what do we do?"

"A quick look around to see if there's any obvious safety hazards. Missing guards on drive belts. Places where a man could trip and fall. Just follow me."

Iggy took off his safety glasses to clean them of dust. Peter did the same with his.

"The dust really cuts down your vision, doesn't it?"

"It's a dusty place," Iggy said, then set off at a fast pace through a maze of crushers and conveyors. The floor was slippery with dust, and vibrated from the heavy machinery. They came to a series of large hatches, one of which leaned open. Iggy looked around to see if any workers were nearby, while Peter peered down through the hatch.

"These are the storage bins I told you about," Iggy shouted above the roar of the machines. "Each bin is for a different grade of fibre, and by the look of it, this is high grade. Someone's left this hatch open. It could be a safety hazard." He wrote a note on his clipboard.

Peter watched as pure asbestos fibre was blown into the bin through an opening below where they stood. White, cloud-like, it looked like down, like it would make a perfect bed.

"That's white gold, Stevens." A note of pride was in Iggy's voice. "It's the best there is."

Peter watched a moment longer as the fibre floated downwards, innocent, white and soft, then Iggy dropped the hatch cover in place.

"Whoever left this open was negligent and they're lucky I didn't catch them. I would have charged them three demerit points." He turned and was off again on his inspection. Peter followed, but seeing his boot lace undone, he stopped to tie it, then hurried to catch up, forgetting his clipboard on the edge of a machine.

Iggy was waiting for Peter when he stepped off the man lift on the fifth floor.

"You're too slow, Stevens."

"Shit."

"What?"

"I forgot my clipboard where I tied my boot. I'm sorry. I'll just be a second." Peter went to the other side of the man lift to go back up.

"I'm not waiting for you. Look for me on the fourth floor."

Back on the sixth floor Peter tried to remember where he had tied his boots. He looked for footprints in the dust, but there were so many he couldn't be sure which were his. He hurried past conveyors and machines, anxious that Iggy was waiting for him again, until he saw the clipboard lying on the floor, having been shaken off the machine he had put it on. He picked it up and headed back to the man lift by a more direct route. He came around a wall and stopped in his tracks, quickly turning and going back the way he had come. He didn't want anyone knowing that he had seen his bunkhouse mate Claude opening the hatch of the fibre bin and pissing into the world's finest asbestos.

He got off the man lift on the fourth floor suppressing a smile. He carried the image of Claude in his mind as he trailed after Iggy, criss-crossing each floor back down to the first. They passed the workers at the bagging chutes, still moving steadily back and forth in the dust. Iggy leaned into Carl Moffat's office.

"We're off, Carl. No problems anywhere."

Carl waved from his chair. "Good. See you at curling Friday night." He broke into a cough, and grabbed Kleenex from the box.

They climbed into the pickup and Iggy made notes on his papers. "A good man, that Carl. Keeps things running smoothly in there. Nothing for the report." He made a check mark on a page marked "Mill." Peter looked at his blank page.

"But what about the dust in there? It's got to be worse than in Rock Reject, since it's all pure asbestos dust. It must be as much of a hazard as the things we were looking for. More, even, since everyone's breathing it in."

Iggy looked at Peter. "This asbestos isn't harmful. Didn't I tell you that when you were hired on?"

"Why would this asbestos be any different than the other types? Just listening to Carl coughing should tell you it's harmful."

"Carl's a smoker, and he should quit. And the dust likely doesn't help, but the scientists say that chrysotile fibre doesn't cause disease, and that's that." He put the truck into gear and accelerated suddenly, spinning the tires on the snow.

"The industry's scientists, no doubt."

"Scientists from McGill University, as a matter of fact," Iggy replied angrily. "And you listen young fella. Don't be causing trouble here. I'd just as soon be doing these tours on my own."

"But you can't. The collective agreement says there has to be a Union rep on the tours."

"And the Union shouldn't be sending a kid who knows nothing about mining."

They didn't speak for the rest of the morning as Peter followed Iggy through all the workplaces in the townsite: the power generating plant, spotlessly clean with its twelve huge diesel generators in a precise row; the laundry, steaming hot and smelling of bleach, where Chinese was the working language; the kitchen, where a rush was on to get lunch ready and Peter sensed that tempers were simmering just below the surface; the sheet metal shop; the carpentry shop; the garage. At each location Iggy talked with the supervisor, who assured him that everything was fine. No problems anywhere, they all said. Peter stood on the edge of the conversations, introduced to each supervisor by Iggy and then ignored. At first he tried to listen and take part in the discussion, but he soon gave up and mutely trailed behind as Iggy made a fast circuit of each workplace. He tried to understand what he was seeing, what was a hazard, what was unhealthy, but each department and the rest of the morning went by in a blur.

Iggy dropped Peter at the cookhouse at twelve thirty. "I'll pick you up here at one fifteen and we should be able to get the Mine done this afternoon. Providing we keep it moving like we did after the Mill."

"Providing we don't look at anything, you mean," Peter muttered.

"What was that?"

"I said one fifteen, I'll be here." Peter climbed out of the pickup and went inside for lunch. Iggy drove towards the streets of private homes.

George put his tray next to Peter's and sat down. "How's the safety tour going?"

"Don't ask," Peter said, his mouth full of tuna casserole.

George shrugged. "How bad can it be? A day away from Rock Reject. Checking out the whole operation. Sounds like a good thing to me."

"Then you should be doing it instead of me. Iggy treats me like I'm nothing. A complete nobody." He put down his fork and leaned his head into his hands. "He'd pay attention to you. You've got… I don't know what."

"A working-class background is what," George said. "Let's face it, Iggy's intimidated by you. You've got the upper-class upbringing, the education."

"As if that's of any use here."

"Bullshit. Iggy's no better than you are, Pete. But he's not going to give you a break, so you're going to have to demand it."

"George, why don't you be the safety rep?"

"No way. I've volunteered for the grievance committee and that's enough for me. Besides, you've got all the knowledge on the health issues."

"Nobody gives a shit about health in this place. All Iggy cares about is keeping to his schedule." Peter looked at his watch. "Christ, I'm supposed to be outside right now."

"So keep him waiting. Don't let him push you around. Remember, he needs you to sign the report, so you've got power because you can refuse. Make him play ball and treat you like an equal."

"That's easy for you to say," Peter said as he stood and picked up his tray. "I just feel like an idiot trailing behind him and being ignored."

"More bullshit."

"It's the truth."

"Sounds more like a cop-out," George said, stubbing a cigarette into a pool of gravy on his plate. He leaned back in his chair and raised his hands above his head. "I'm an idiot. I surrender," he said, then broke into a smile and threw a balled-up serviette at Peter. "Go do your fucking tour, man. Can't keep Mr. Iggy waiting."

"Goddamn weirdo," Peter said, and took his tray to the kitchen and hurried outside.

Iggy was sitting in his pickup, drumming his fingers against the wheel. Peter climbed in and stopped himself from apologizing for being late.

Iggy seemed startled by Peter's sudden presence, as if he forgot that he was waiting for him. He looked at his watch, put the truck in gear and started off. "Let's get this over with."

They drove up the road to the Mine. The clouds had thickened and lowered and as they neared the top Peter could no longer see the town in the valley below.

"It feels like it's going to snow," he said. Iggy didn't answer.

They drove past Rock Reject and made the turn down into the pit. Iggy drove cautiously down the slope and stopped at the first bench, giving way first to a Haul Pac loaded with ore and then to an empty one coming down from Rock Reject, which they followed to the bottom. They parked fifty feet behind the shovel.

Peter hadn't been close to the shovel before and was startled by its size. The operator's cab was more than twenty feet up and the boom that the shovel arm pivoted from rose on an angle to twice that height. Iggy's pickup would fit in the bucket, he thought. The machine scooped into the vertical face of blasted rock in front of it, then swung around and dropped the load into the waiting Haul Pac. The massive truck rocked side to side as the ore cascaded in and a cloud of dust rose into the frozen air. Iggy approached the back of the machine and tugged on a cord that hung from its corner, causing a horn to sound somewhere on the shovel, and it stopped digging.

He went to the side of the shovel and pulled on a rope that brought down a ladder. It looked new, in contrast to the rest of the battered machine. He climbed up the steel rungs to a platform ten feet above the ground. Peter followed, and when he stepped off the last rung the retractable ladder slowly rose to its original position. Two flights of steel stairs were attached to the outside of the machine and Iggy was already at the top and entering the operator's cab. Peter hurried after him.

The cab was small and Iggy stood beside the shovel operator in his high-backed chair. Peter recognized Bukowski, who'd lost the Union president election to Dave McGuinness, wearing a t-shirt in the over-heated cab. Peter closed the door and squeezed behind the chair. Foam padding poked out of rips in the vinyl fabric of the seat and duct tape held the corners together. Bukowski smelled of talcum powder.

"Everything fine down here in the pit, Joe?" Iggy asked. "No problems on the shovel?"

"Mostly good," Bukowski said, his Eastern European accent heavy. "My stupid oiler pulled down the ladder without sounding the horn two days ago. I kept digging and swung the shovel around with him hanging on the fucking ladder. It hit the tracks and bent in half."

"I thought you couldn't operate with the ladder down."

"Fucking lock-out mechanism must be broken. Idiot oiler's fault though. Didn't sound the horn."

Iggy made a note on his clipboard. "I'll get it seen to."

"Was he hurt?" Peter asked. "The oiler?"

"Not much. A few bruises, a scrape. He's now more useless than before." He took a cigarette from a package and lit it, holding it between his thumb and two fingers.

Peter looked out the window at the ore face in front of them. A few boulders tumbled down from above. Leaning forward and peering up through the falling snow, he couldn't see to the top of the face.

"It's a long way up to the next bench. Does the bucket reach that far?"

"No, it's ten or fifteen feet short," Bukowski replied.

Peter turned to Iggy. "I read in a report from the Department of Mines inspector that the shovel has to be able to reach within five feet of the top of the face. Otherwise there's the danger of large rocks coming down on their own."

"I know what the danger is," Iggy said. "And it's a big job to reduce the height of the benches. The whole pit has to be widened, and that's going to take a year or more."

"So is it unsafe to be working down here in the meantime?" Peter asked.

"It's safe enough. Especially with capable men like Joseph at the controls."

Bukowski looked at Iggy, smoke floating out of his nostrils. "No comment. And if you two gentlemen are through, then you can kindly get the fuck off my shovel and let us get back to mining."

"We're done," Iggy said, turning to the door.

Peter nodded to Bukowski, "Thanks," he said, and followed Iggy down to the ground.

"Those are just guidelines in the inspector's report, Stevens," Iggy said as they pulled away in the pickup. "They're not hard and fast rules."

"It didn't read like just a guideline to me. He referred to a regulation, and that would have the force of law behind it."

"You can't change these problems overnight. The inspector knows that."

"I think that report was dated over a year ago. Has the Company even started to widen the pit?"

"Not yet." Iggy's knuckles were white on the steering wheel. "But it's scheduled to begin soon."

"How soon?"

Iggy didn't respond for several seconds. "I'll send a memo to the General Manager asking when."

"So we'll wait until next month's tour and put his response to your memo in our report?"

"I'm not agreeing to that."

They drove up out of the pit and parked at the side of Rock Reject. Iggy led the way through the door and was headed across the catwalk towards the stairs to the lower levels. Peter stopped inside the door.

"Iggy," he shouted. "Hold on. Let's have a good look here."

"What for?" Iggy shouted back, irritated. "The guard rail's been replaced with a steel one."

"A man died here, for christsakes." Peter struggled against a rush of anger. He began inspecting the walkway around the area where McGuinness crashed through the old railing. He stepped on the edge of a section of the steel floor where it butted against the plywood wall and felt it shift down a few inches. The section popped up on the other side of the walkway at the edge of the crusher pit. He took his foot off and let it drop, then stepped again and watched it rise up.

"Come look at this."

Iggy watched as Peter rocked the section of floor up and down.

"A piece of the support must've broken away," Iggy said, making a note on his clipboard. "We'll get that fixed."

"But it's more than that," Peter said, his voice rising with excitement. "This is what happened to Dave McGuinness. He stepped on this spot and then his other foot caught on this piece that comes up. The lighting is bad here and he couldn't see. The floor tripped him up and he fell against the wooden railing, right where it was weakest."

Iggy tried stepping on several spots on the floor. "It only rises when you step in this one place and it's right up against the wall. Nobody walks on that spot."

"He had something to drink so he was unsteady. He could easily have put his foot there."

"This is nonsense. The reason he fell was because he was drunk. It was entirely his own fault."

"He was drinking, yes, but you don't know for sure how much. I think this might have been what caused his death. At the very least, it's a strong possibility."

Iggy stood with his hands on his hips, looking at the floor of the walkway, and at Peter, who returned his gaze without flinching. A Haul Pac backed up to the edge of Rock Reject and dumped its load of ore into the jaw crusher. Peter covered his ears against the noise as the rock was mashed until it fell through to the conveyor below.

"There was an investigation and the police were satisfied," Iggy said flatly when the crusher had emptied. "The accident report is filed. The man is dead and I don't see the point in dragging this business out any more."

"Sure he's dead. But what about his reputation? How will this make his parents feel? They've been told that their son was a drunk who got himself killed and maybe it's not as simple as that."

"This is nothing more than a wild theory, Stevens. There've never been any reports of people tripping on this section before."

"Because everyone walks down the middle. But if you stumble and your foot lands right next to the wall like this…" Peter stepped and made the grate rise up. "And then your back foot catches the edge like this…" He made himself trip and fall forward, then caught himself on the railing. He looked down into the jaw crusher for a moment, then turned to Iggy. "It's possible, whether you want to admit it or not."

"So it's possible. All kinds of things are possible, but it doesn't mean that's what happened." He turned towards the door to the outside. "I'm putting a traffic cone on that spot so nobody'll step there and I'll send a welder up here asap to fix the damn thing." He turned back to look at Peter. "But there's no way I'm going to change the report on McGuinness's accident. That business is finished, understand?"

Iggy went out the door to his pickup. "Do you get a bonus if the Company is liable for nothing?" Peter said to the twisted plywood door, then turned and looked across the crusher pit, thirty feet to the other side where the operator's booth sat. The Plexiglas window was filthy with dust, but he could just make out Paul Morino sitting inside, looking back at him. Morino gave a small wave. Peter nodded in return. We're all part of some lie or another, he thought. He looked down at his clipboard and made notes.

It was nearly six o'clock when they finished inspecting the Mine and began the drive down the mountain to town. Peter was chilled through from spending most of the afternoon outside in twenty below and his insides quivered trying to generate heat in his core. He huddled in his parka in the dark cab of the pickup and stared ahead at the snow-packed road lit by its bouncing headlights. Where the snowbanks weren't too high he caught glimpses of the lights of town below. He longed to be standing under a hot shower in the bunkhouse.

"I'll have the report done the day after tomorrow," Iggy said. "You can come to the Admin Building to read it over and sign it then. It'll be at the reception desk."

"That's what Gord did?" Peter's teeth were chattering. "Gave it the old rubber stamp?"

Iggy glanced over at Peter and turned the heater up full blast. He slowed down to take the hairpin turn at a switchback. "Gordon co-operated with me on the tour and we had no disagreements about what went in the report." Iggy's voice was weary. "And I hope you'll be reasonable and do the same."

"And if not?"

Iggy paused. "Then come to my office after you've read it and we'll talk." He turned on the radio. "Six o'clock news," he said.

Peter recognized the voice of the CBC announcer, the same voice he listened to in Toronto. It told them that four children died in a house fire on an Indian reserve in Ontario. Sextuplets were born to a California woman. The U.S. government proposed to pay the costs for sterilizing poor women but not for abortions.

"Multiple deaths, multiple births," Peter said. He looked out the side window at the dark moonless sky and the darker mass of the mountains on the other side of the valley.

"And the thousands not allowed to be born," Iggy said.

"People find themselves in difficult situations," Peter said, staring at the snowbanks blurring past them. He folded his arms tight across his chest and tried to stop himself from shivering.

ELEVEN

The receptionist handed Peter a brown envelope containing Iggy's report of the safety tour. A paper clip held a note to the top of the first page. "Come to my office when you've read this." He took the report to the Union office, poured a mug of coffee and sat in the back room to go over it.

He skimmed over a list of items under the heading "Housekeeping": cluttered passageways, slippery floors, uncollected garbage. Under "Maintenance" he saw the loose section of walkway by the jaw crusher, with a star next to it indicating it received immediate attention. The last section was headed "Ongoing." Iggy wrote that the bench faces in the Mine were still higher than regulations permitted, and that a program of widening the pit and lowering the bench heights was to begin in March of next year. A second item stated that half a million dollars was to be spent on improving the dust conditions in the Mill, following a study to be conducted the next summer.

With a loud, "Yes," Peter punched his fists into the air. He wanted to show the report to Alex Bruce, but he was alone in the building. He pulled on his parka and returned to the Administration Building.

Iggy was at his desk. "Come in, Stevens," he smiled.

Peter sat in the chair by the desk. He didn't wait for it to be offered.

"I put that note on the report 'cause I thought you'd want to ask about some of the items I've got in there." Iggy leaned back in his chair. "I met with the General Manager yesterday morning, and he filled me in on some plans the Company has. That's what you see in the Ongoing section of the report."

"It sounds really good, especially the dust control program. But that's just for the Mill. What about Rock Reject? It's just as bad in there."

"That's a very good point, and I think that once the study for the Mill is finished, there'll be one for Rock Reject too."

Peter couldn't help but smile. "This is great. It'll make it so much healthier here."

"That's right." Iggy slid the report across the desk to Peter, open to the back page. "So let's get your signature and then we're done."

Peter signed. Iggy put the report in a folder and pushed it to the side of his desk. They looked at each other for a moment.

"The walkway in Rock Reject got fixed that night. That was good, you finding that problem."

Peter's face flushed. "Thanks. I know you ruled it out the other day, but couldn't something be added to the accident report? That Dave might have tripped on it?"

Iggy shook his head. "It's too late now. But I was thinking about what you said about his parents. I'm going to write them a letter and let them know that he was a good man."

"Will you mention the accident or why it happened?"

"No. If they want to know the details they can ask for the report. This is just to help them feel a bit better. After all, there's no bringing back their son."

Peter looked out the window. A gust of wind blew snow horizontally. Spruce trees on the far side of the parking lot faded in the white blur.

"That's right. There's no bringing him back," he said, his voice distant. He turned back to Iggy. "So that's it until the next tour?"

"That's right." He checked a calendar on his desk. "The third Monday in January. I'll have a Xerox copy of this report sent over to the Union office."

He patted the file folder on the side of the desk, then turned in his swivel chair, opened a file cabinet and pulled out a binder full of papers. Peter stayed in his chair and watched him for a moment, his weathered neck, his fingers clumsy with paper. Iggy glanced at him.

"We're done. You can go."

"Oh. Sorry." Peter went to the door, then stopped and turned.

"It's a good idea."

Iggy looked up from his papers. "What?"

"The letter. To his parents."

Iggy nodded absently. "Close the door behind you."

Pulling the hood of his parka close around his face, Peter walked in the blowing snow to the Union office. Alex Bruce was looking through the mail as he entered the trailer and shook the snow off his coat.

"Stevens. Here's something from the regional office for you." He handed Peter an envelope addressed to the Safety and Health Co-Ordinator of their Union local.

"You had your tour with Iggy, didn't you? How'd that go?"

"Good. Really good, in fact. His report says that the Company is going to start widening the pit starting in March to make it safer and that they're going to do a study on the dust in the Mill, then put half a million dollars into reducing the dust levels. And they'll do the same in Rock Reject."

Alex put down the letter he was reading and looked at Peter. "I hate to rain on your parade, Stevens, but they've promised those things before and haven't done a goddamn thing."

"But it's in the report and Iggy signed it. And that goes to the Department of Mines."

Alex Bruce snorted a laugh. "Where nobody reads it and it's filed with ten thousand other reports. Welcome to the real world." He turned and limped into the president's office and closed the door.

Peter stood for a moment looking across the empty room, tapping the envelope against his leg. Naïve. Rookie. Pushover. Words bounced around inside his head. Hoping to shift his attention to something else, he tore open the envelope and read an announcement from the Union's regional office about a workshop on safety and health issues. January fifth and sixth in Whitehorse. Why not, he thought. Learn something. Get the hell out of here for a couple of days.

Alex was on the phone when Peter walked into his office without knocking. He gestured an apology and turned to leave, but Alex snapped his fingers at him.

"What?" His hand covered the phone's mouthpiece.

"They're offering a course in Whitehorse next month and I think it'd be good if I attended. It would help me with the safety tours and..."

"Yeah, no problem. You need my signature?" Peter handed him the paper and he signed without looking at it. "Take it to the Admin Building. Is that it?"

"Uh yes. I'm hoping that this course will help..."

"Sure. Close the door on your way out."

Peter went to the Administration Building and left the application form with the receptionist. As he was leaving he saw Iggy standing in an office doorway, laughing with whoever was inside. You won't be laughing at me next month, Peter thought as he pushed through the door and back out into the cold.

The wind had picked up and was driving snow down the valley. He bent forward into the storm and watched his legs trudge through the blur of white. A grader honked from behind, warning him out of the way. It roared past, throwing a foot of snow over his boots and making him tumble over the snowbank in front of the Post Office trailer. Pulling himself free from the snow, he stumbled up the steps and inside.

It was like an oven in the trailer. The heat hit his cold, wet face and he felt he was suffocating. His numb fingers fumbled with the zipper of his parka before finally freeing himself from it and wiping the melting snow from his face.

Hundreds of individual mailboxes covered two walls, each with a small, transparent window on its front. Inside his he saw a white envelope. My parents, he thought, and his heart rate increased as he imagined the reproaches it might contain. The heat and anxiety made him dizzy and he leaned against a wall for support.

The postmaster carried a parcel out of the back room and placed it on the counter. His t-shirt didn't cover the belly that hung below his belt. Sweat shone on his forehead and arms.

"A valve's bust on the steam system," he said as he rummaged through a drawer. "Can't shut the fucking thing off." He put an ink pad on the counter, worked a hand stamp into it then hit the parcel hard enough to buckle it. "Been sweating like a pig all day." He stared at the dent he had made, shrugged, then picked up the parcel and tossed it into a bin. "Hope it wasn't fragile."

Peter looked at the letter in his box and heard it speaking to him. *When are you coming home? Go back to school. After all we've done.* He felt suddenly cold.

"You okay?" The postmaster was looking at him. "You're white as a fucking sheet."

"It must be the heat."

Are you going to mass? Have you been to confession? How could you have left her?

The postmaster crossed to the door. "Let's get some air in here. Make you feel better." He opened the door to a blast of snow. Peter turned his face to the cold air and breathed deeply. The postmaster closed the door after ten seconds. "Fuck if I'm going to spend all day mopping the fucking floor." He scratched at his sweat stained armpit. "I called the Mechanical Department at eight fucking o'clock and no one's showed up yet."

Just shut up, Peter thought. He pushed himself away from the wall towards the mailbox and opened it with his key. The envelope was stiff. A card, Christ, a Christmas card. Stuffing it in his pocket, he went to the door.

The postmaster shouted to him as he stepped outside. "Hey, if you see anybody from Mechanical, tell them to get the fuck over here and pronto. Hope you're feeling better."

Peter stood on the steps of the trailer, his eyes closed to the snow on his face. He saw himself on the steps of the Medical Science Building, looking across the expanse of King's College Circle, the buildings of the University of Toronto fading in and out in a storm like this one. Walking through the drifting snow to Hart House, to the warmth of the second floor library, to sit with a dark-haired woman. Leaving with her an hour later by a side door to huddle behind the building by a loading dock where they shared a joint she took from a beaded bag. He shuddered at the memory and went to the bunkhouse.

George poked his head out of his door as Peter came down the corridor.

"Pete. I saw you coming. Care for a toke?"

Peter winced at the smell of marijuana seeping out of the room. "No, for christsakes."

"Hey, it's just an offer. You don't need to bite my head off."

"I'm sorry, George. I'm just not into it."

"Catch you tonight for a drink at Eric's then?" George called out.

"Yeah, sure."

Inside his room he sat on the bed holding the envelope addressed with his mother's practised handwriting. It hadn't occurred to him to send them a card—Rose had always taken care of that. He thought of dropping it in the trash, of explaining how unreliable the mail is in the North, then changed his mind and opened the envelope slowly.

O Holy Night, the front of the card proclaimed. Infants with wings hovered above the manger, blowing trumpets to the sky. Parents with halos gazed knowingly at the wise baby in the crib, whose own halo outshone theirs. He opened the card and two pieces of paper fell out. One a note.

Dear Peter, I'm so concerned that you are continuing on in that cold and dangerous place. Your father and I both want the best for you and we miss you terribly. We want you to come home for Christmas. If you like, you could give up this mining that you're doing and return to your studies in the new year. I know that you're not earning a great deal, so I've included a cheque to pay for airfare home. It will make us both very happy to have you back with us, to celebrate Our Lord's birth and a new, fresh start for you.

Thinking of you with love, Mum

p.s. Don't tell your father about this cheque. It'll be our secret.

The cheque was lying upside down on the bed. Turning it over he saw with a shock that it was for five hundred dollars. He covered it with the note, then looked again at the card. Inside, the flowing script wished him the holiest and happiest Christmas ever. His mother had added a line. *I pray, Peter, that one day you will experience the miracle of parenthood, in the spirit of the Holy Family.*

A change in wind direction drove snow against the window and he looked out into the feeble December light. The next bunkhouse was just

113

a vague shape in the gloom. He ached inside. He took the Christmas card in his shaking hands and imagined tearing it, ripping through the halos and the serene faces of Joseph and Mary, turning the manger scene into a hundred ragged pieces, but he opened his hands and let it fall on the floor. Picking up the cheque, he lay down and covered his head with his pillow. With deep breaths he tried to fill the emptiness in his chest, but it made him ache all the more. He felt the paper between his fingers, the impressions made by his mother's pen. He tore the cheque in half, and in half again.

"I'm sorry, Mum," he said into the pillow. "I just can't come home."

He lay still for ten minutes, dimly aware of his clenched jaw and fists. He pushed himself suddenly to sitting, grabbed the fragments of the cheque and flung them across the room.

"Goddamn it," he shouted. "How the hell could I go home?" He slammed his hand against the bed.

Someone pounded on the wall next to his. "Keep it down, for christ-sakes, I'm trying to sleep."

"Go screw yourself," Peter said. He fell back onto the bed and let his eyes drift closed.

He laid a twenty dollar bill on the coffee table. She went into the bed-room and came back a moment later with a bag of grass.

"Mexican, my dear. Your favourite." An ornate urn sat on a bookshelf and she put his money in it, then raised it above her head as if it were a chalice. "Thou art Peter," she said. Her silk top showed the outline of her breasts. "And upon your stone I will build my church."

"You mean rock."

"Stone, my dear." She put the urn back on the shelf and sat in her fan wicker chair, her dark eyes steady into his. "I'm afraid you're a rock in name only." She took a joint from an inlaid box on the coffee table and lit it.

"And your name says it all," Peter replied. "Luce." He let his tongue linger over the word. "Lucifer."

Smoke snaked through her parted lips. Her thin arm extended to him, offering the joint. As he reached for it she crossed one leg over the other, opening the long slit up the side of her Chinese skirt. Peter looked at her thigh as he took a toke.

She rested her arms on the wide sides of the chair and stared at Peter. A black cat stirred and stretched in a corner behind her. Shifting uncomfortably on the couch, his eyes broke free from hers and roamed the room, settling on a Jimi Hendrix poster, tracking the psychedelic curves and swirls that surrounded his image. He took a deep breath.

"Rose is pregnant." The words rushed out of him with his exhale. He glanced at Luce to see her face freeze for a moment, then her mouth curl into a half smile. The cat leapt into her lap and turned to stare at him.

"Well, well. And how does young Peter feel about this turn of events?"

He sighed and looked down at his hands, seeing that he still held the joint. He held it out to her but she shook her head. He stubbed it into an ashtray, sat back and closed his eyes.

"I…I don't know. I love Rose. For sure. But a baby…" He shook his head slowly. "I don't know."

"You don't know love. It's an idea for you."

"That's not true."

"It is true." Luce's voice was hard, sharp. "You're a boy, Peter. And a jerk. Your notion of love is bullshit. You come here month after month to score weed and to score me. Why?"

Peter's hands went to his face, his fingertips digging into his eyes. "Because you're different. Because Rose doesn't understand things like you do."

"More bullshit. You're afraid. Scared shitless of being real with Rose. You come here to relieve the pressure of your lie. You smoke weed to buy time away from the truth."

He stared down at the threadbare oriental carpet. "Fuck off, Luce," he said quietly.

"You are a boy. And I fear that something's going to have to bite you hard to make you grow up."

A feeling of dread crept into his body and he looked at her sitting regally in her chair, watching him. A lamp on the floor covered with an orange shawl made shadows on her collarbone and high cheekbones. Through the window behind her, weak winter light filtered through a half dozen hanging plants. He heard the rumble of a streetcar outside on Bathurst Street. He looked at his watch.

"Thinking about where she is?"

"She started teaching this week at St. Raymond's. She loves their music program."

Luce didn't respond. Her eyes held Peter's. He wanted to run, he wanted to stay. He felt an electricity in his groin. Her eyes shifted to the bedroom door, then back to his. A half minute passed.

Peter's jaw clenched. He put his hand on his bookbag and shifted to the edge of the couch.

"I'd better go."

Luce slowly nodded. One hand went to stroke the cat in her lap. "Don't come back, Peter."

TWELVE

A northwest wind out of Alaska drove snow relentlessly through Stikine. The powerful lights up in the Mine were invisible from the town. Heavy, low clouds walled the two worlds off from each other. Peter pushed his way through the weather along the road from the cookhouse, the hood of his parka open so he could feel the sting on his face and head. He stopped in front of the bar, where an arrangement of Christmas lights hung unevenly from the eaves, swaying back and forth in the wind.

He pictured the precise lines of lights that outlined his parents' home in Toronto. The rhododendron and cedars in the front yard multi-coloured and snow-covered. The front door ringed with light and welcoming. A decorated ten-foot fir in the living room, perfectly symmetrical and centred in the picture window, on display to the families driving by to look at the lights.

What are they doing this year, he wondered. Are they keeping up appearances, or mourning? A gust of wind drove a hanging strand of lights against the log building, breaking a bulb. He shook snow off his shoulders and went into the bar.

It was packed inside, hot and moist. Miniature lights were strung haphazardly along the walls, their light blurry through the haze of cigarette smoke. Beer bottles filled every table. Voices were already loud at seven thirty, drowning out Elvis singing "Blue Christmas" on the juke box. The place felt pressurized.

Peter threaded his way through the crowd towards the back room where he knew he'd find George. Men were weaving back and forth to the bar, clutching beer in both hands. Someone bumped into him, spilled beer on his leg and stumbled away. A fiddler started playing and a cheer went up. He pushed towards the music and saw Bob and Dianne waving him over to a chair next to them. Close to the fiddler stood George, his head tilted back, emptying a beer into his open mouth. Bob handed Peter a beer as he sat down and Dianne leaned over to squeeze his arm and smile, her loose hair falling over her collarbone. Her low-cut blouse was revealing and Peter made himself turn back to Bob.

"What's happening in here?" he shouted so he could be heard over the din. "Seems like everyone's gone wild."

"'Tis the season," Bob shouted back. "No sunlight. Christmas is near. Guys are lonely and get all fucked up." He drained a beer and grabbed another from the supply in the middle of the table. His shirt front was open down his broad chest showing thick curly hair. "It happens every year."

The fiddler began a Maritime tune. George whooped and came to the table to grab another beer. He bumped hard against Peter's shoulder.

"Pete, buddy," he slurred. He clapped a hand on Peter's shoulder. "Sorry about that, man."

"It's okay." Peter pushed him back towards the music.

"He's been hitting it hard for a couple of hours already," Bob said. "Must've had eight or so by now."

"What are you doing for Christmas?" Dianne asked. "Are you going to go visit your parents?"

"Go to Toronto on three days off?" Peter shook his head. "No way. I'll just take it easy here." Dianne raised an eyebrow to Bob, who nodded.

"Would you like to come out to the Creek and have Christmas with us?" she asked. "It'd be a lot nicer than turkey in the cookhouse."

Peter hesitated. "Can I let you know in a day or two? I imagined being alone on Christmas. It's the first one since…"

"I know, man," Bob interrupted. "No need to go into it."

"But maybe I'll change my mind."

"No problem. Just let us know and I'll come and pick you up."

Peter cradled his beer bottle, absently picking at the label with his thumbnail. A new fiddle tune began and George shouted approval.

"Peter, will you dance with me?" Dianne looked at him hopefully. He looked at Bob.

"No problem with me, man. I'm no dancer."

"He never will, the big lout." Dianne punched him playfully in the arm. "But I love to dance."

Peter watched her sway in her chair for a moment, then he stood up. "Let's give it a try."

They moved onto the tiny open space in front of where the fiddler sat. Peter took her hands in his and they began a jive to find the rhythm. Her hands felt soft and warm.

George was stomping his feet to the beat. "Hey Pete," he shouted. "Is that how you Toronto pussies dance?" He did an effeminate imitation, then laughed loudly.

Peter put a hand on Dianne's waist and turned her away from George, dipping and twirling her in the process. She smiled at him. "You're a terrific dancer."

He smiled back.

Dianne matched his steps perfectly. He remembered dancing with Rose at parties, how their bodies moved together, pressed together. And alone in their living room, slow dancing to Nashville Skyline or Maria Muldaur and ending up in bed. Dianne's body was fuller than hers, softer. Her breasts brushed against his arm as she turned and he forced himself to focus on the music.

He spun Dianne as he was turning himself. George lost his balance and stumbled against Peter, knocking him into her. Peter pushed him away with his shoulder, not looking at him. He rolled his eyes at Dianne.

"Just ignore him," she said.

"If that's possible," he said, smiling.

He put an arm on her shoulder and they began a polka step in the confined space. Dianne laughed and the fiddler caught on to their movements, playing to their dance. Peter felt light as they moved back and forth, his smile lifting his face and his feet. He thought again of Rose, her skirt and hair spinning outwards as she twirled, her eyes shining. He felt his eyes start to well up.

George stuck his hand on Peter's shoulder. His eyes looked wild and a fierce grin made the gaps from his missing teeth look huge.

"You Toronto people don't know any fucking thing about dancing. I'll show you how to dance, Cape Breton style."

Peter shrugged away the hand. "For christsakes, George. Get lost."

"No, Pete, I'm cutting in."

Peter was barely aware of his arm swinging and his hand making contact with George's head. He seemed to fall in slow motion and Peter wanted to catch him before he hit the floor but he couldn't make himself move fast enough. George lay motionless, his eyes closed. Peter bent over him.

"Are you okay? George."

George half opened his eyes. They were bleary and red.

"I'm sorry. But you were being a jerk."

George's fist came up and caught the side of Peter's face. Hands grabbed him from behind and pulled him away.

"That's it, bud." The waiter pinned his arm behind his back. "Get your coat and get out."

"I was trying to help him up, for christsakes." Peter tried to get free of the hold but the waiter tightened it.

"After decking him? Sure you were."

"Take it easy, Shaun," Dianne shouted to the waiter. "He didn't mean it."

"I don't fucking care. You fight outside, not in here."

"Alright, I'm going," Peter said. "Let go of my goddamn arm."

The waiter released him and watched while he grabbed his coat. "Thanks for the dance," he said to Dianne.

"Let us know about Christmas," she said.

Someone pulled George off the floor and sat him in a chair. He waved at Peter, who pushed through the crowd to the door. "Pete. Old buddy. You Toronto piece of shit. Get back here and I'll show you how to fucking dance."

The cold air felt good after the smoky, stale heat of the bar, and Peter stood in the road for a minute without his parka on, listening to the noises from inside. "Jingle Bell Rock" on the jukebox, a dull roar of voices, then some shouting. The door opened and two men were pushed out and immediately began swinging at each other. Peter turned and began the walk back to the bunkhouse.

His wrist ached as he pulled on his parka. Must've bent it back, he thought. He remembered hurting it falling on the steps to the Mine Dry his first day at work. He remembered hurting it in the apartment, one night the winter before. He held the wrist in his other hand as he walked through the snow.

Rose was standing in the living room when he came home. A Thursday evening in late February. His stomach tightened when he saw the look on her face.

"Are you okay?" His voice was unsteady.

"Who is she?" Her arms were folded across her chest. Her jaw muscles clenched.

Peter felt unable to breathe. "Who?"

"You goddamn know who. I'm on the Bathurst streetcar taking a pupil to Toronto Western to get a sprained ankle looked at and I see you and her get out of a cab and go into a goddamn rooming house or something."

"She's just the person I get grass from." Peter's voice was raised, strained. "That's all."

"Then what are these?" Rose held out her hand. Three condoms lay in her palm.

"Where did…"

"Your other coat. I found them last week but I didn't put two and two together until today. I suppose you were too damn stoned to hide the evidence."

Peter's legs felt weak. He sat down in the chair by the telephone table.

"Well?"

He shrugged with his hands. "I don't know… She and I used to…"

"Used to? You expect me to believe that?"

"No I don't, but it's true." Peter looked up at her, seized with fear, pleading with his eyes. "I just bought grass today. That's all." He paused, flooded with feelings he struggled to suppress. "Other times," he said slowly, "yes." He rubbed the back of his neck. "Sometimes it's so long that you and I don't have sex."

"What's that supposed to mean? That it's all my fault? I'm not putting out enough for you so it's okay for you to screw your dope dealer?"

"No, I don't think that. It is my fault. It's just that…" He shrugged and shook his head. "I don't know."

"What *do* you know? I'm pregnant and you can't make up your mind about being a father. Or a husband, it seems. And I'm supposed to be having sex with you all the time?" Rose paced to the window. "Goddamn it Peter. What do you want? Tell me the truth."

He sat looking at the floor, unable to move. He wanted to speak, but couldn't.

"At least look at me," she shouted.

He raised his head to look at Rose. She was still slim. He couldn't tell she was pregnant.

"I'm sorry." The words sounded hollow in his ears. He wanted them to come from his heart but he couldn't feel anything below his throat. He wanted more words to pour out of him but no more came. He wanted her to believe he was sorry but he wasn't sure he believed himself.

Rose stood waiting for more. "That's it?" she said after a minute passed. "What does that mean? What good is that to me?"

She took two steps to the coffee table and picked up the ashtray, full of Peter's cigarette butts and ash from his joints. Two more steps and she flung the contents into his face. She dropped the empty ashtray into his lap, then threw the condoms against his chest. She went into the bedroom and slammed the door.

"I can't have a child with you," she shouted through the wall.

Peter sat for a minute, the taste of ash in his mouth, a black coldness seeping through his chest, then stood up, scattering the ashes and butts and condoms onto the floor, and threw the heavy glass ashtray at the couch. It bounced off, flew across the room and hit the wall underneath a Group of Seven print. Leaving a gouge in the plaster, the ashtray broke and fell to the floor. He wheeled around, saw the coat-stand by the door, holding his old winter jacket where Rose found the condoms, strode to it and swung, sending it crashing to the floor. His arm carried through and his hand hit the wall, bending it back at the wrist. The pain made him want to scream, but he clamped his mouth shut. Instead he kicked at the coats lying on the floor, then leaned his back against the wall and slid down, his wrist and hand throbbing. Rose cried in the bedroom. He pushed himself to standing, welcoming the searing pain from the effort, took the broom from the closet and swept up the mess he had made.

THIRTEEN

At the two pay phones in the Recreation Centre a half dozen men waited for their turn to make calls on Christmas morning. Peter stood behind two tall men who spoke together in their own language. Serbian, he guessed. The smell of alcohol wafted from their breath. On one phone someone was speaking Greek, on the other, Spanish. Peter's pockets were full of quarters and he let them slip through his fingers while he waited.

His mother answered the phone.

"Merry Christmas, Mum."

"The same to you, dear. Have you been to mass yet?"

"No, Mum. It's just nine here. Noon your time. Did you and Dad just get back?"

"Yes. It was lovely." There was a long pause with muffled voices and whispers. "We both miss you terribly today."

"I just got your card the day before yesterday," Peter lied. "The mail here has been really slow. That was a great idea, me coming home, but I got it so late and we've only got a few days off, so…"

"That's all right, Peter. I'm sure you're very busy."

"I have been. And that's why I didn't get anything in the mail for you two. I'm really sorry."

"Don't worry about us. Here's your father. He wants to say hello."

Peter held the receiver so tightly his hand shook.

"Hello, Son."

"Dad. Merry Christmas."

"And the same to you. Your mother and I have been wondering what your plans are. How long you'll be continuing in the Mine."

"I... I'm not really sure. I like it quite a lot here. I'm involved in safety and health issues and I've got a position with the Union..."

"That's all well and good," his father interrupted. "But we'd like to see you back here in civilization. I won't hide my disappointment that you're not putting the past behind you and returning to your studies for the winter term."

Peter took a deep breath to try to calm himself. "Maybe one day I'll feel ready to go back to school, but right now I can't."

"What's done is done, Peter. You need to move forward."

Peter shut his eyes and leaned his head against the wall beside the phone. "Damn it, Dad, I'm haunted every day. How can I pretend it never happened? You're a doctor. Why don't you understand that?"

His father didn't respond. Peter heard his slow breathing, as if he were inches away. Pressing the phone closer to his ear, he imagined for a moment that he was pressed against his father, held by him. From behind he heard impatient murmurings from the men waiting for the phone.

"Dad. I can't stay on the line. There's a bunch of people wanting the phone."

"Of course. You need to go."

Peter felt he could cry. "I hope you and Mum have a good day."

"Yes, thank you."

"Well, bye for now." Peter waited a moment.

"Son..." His father's voice sounded small. "Merry Christmas."

"Thanks Dad," he replied in barely more than a whisper.

The inside of Bob and Dianne's cabin was like a Christmas card. Warmth, a tree in the corner, the smell of turkey roasting. Fresh snow reflected light through every window.

"How was the walk out from town?" Dianne asked as she took Peter's coat.

"It's beautiful out. There's no wind." He took two bottles of wine from his backpack and handed them to her.

"I can't thank you enough for having me today. It's really good to be here again."

"We're glad you decided to come." Bob went to the fridge. "Care for a beer?"

"Sure. I guess the wine can wait 'till dinner." Bob handed him a Molson's and they clinked their bottles together.

"We'll eat around four," Dianne said. "And there'll be two more joining us."

"Yeah," Bob said, wiping beer foam from his moustache. "I ran into George and Claude in the liquor store yesterday and we got to talking so I invited them." He looked at Peter. "I hope you're cool with that."

"Uh, sure. I guess so. I actually haven't talked much with George since that night in the bar. Does he know I'll be here?"

"Shit yeah. Don't worry. I'm sure that was no big deal to him."

"I hit him. I've never hit anyone before."

"He had it coming. Besides, you didn't hit him hard."

"Hard enough to knock him over."

Bob laughed. "My grandmother could've knocked him over that night. Go sit down and relax."

Peter sat on the couch by the tree and looked at the opened presents that lay under it. Books. Record albums. A bottle of Crown Royal. A wrapped gift lay off to one side. He hoped it wasn't meant for him. He realized that he should have brought gifts for them.

"Looks like you two did alright this Christmas," Peter called out to the kitchen. "Where did you get it all?"

"Mail order," Dianne said. "It was easy. Other years we've gone to Toronto for Christmas, but it's nice to be here for a change."

"Your folks must miss you, Bob."

Dianne looked at Bob, who busied himself at the sink peeling potatoes. "Bob's parents split up a couple of months ago. He hasn't wanted to talk about it."

"Jesus, that's awful," Peter said. "I remember your parents being, I don't know, just normal. People who'd stay together."

"Not fucking normal enough," Bob said.

Dianne put her arm around him. "I know it's hard for you, sweetheart, but I really think it's for the best. I saw them getting frustrated, especially since your brother Jimmy left home. I think they had to move on. It's what people our age do all the time."

"It's weird when it's your parents, though," Peter said. "You want to know that they're still around, still together. I know for me it's in the back of my mind that they're at home and that won't change. Everything else changes, but not that."

"Well I can tell you that's bullshit," Bob said. He took his beer into the living room. "My old man had a fling with some young chick. The old lady finds out and tells him to pack his bags. No talking it through. No working it out." He paused and took a drink. "Seems it wasn't the first time he'd been screwing around but he swore to her it'd be the last. That didn't cut any ice with her though. She says they're through. Hit the road. Thirty years together and bang." He turned his head and looked out the window.

"I'm sorry," Peter said. "I liked your parents. It must be a real drag for you."

Bob shrugged. "I'm pissed off about it, but that sure as hell won't change anything. So our merry Christmas is right here in the Creek."

The cabin was silent except for the turkey sizzling in the oven.

Peter turned to Dianne. "What about your parents?"

"Both gone," she said. "Mum from cancer four years ago. Breast cancer. Dad…" She stopped what she was doing and took a breath. "Dad killed himself a year later. It's funny, but it's still hard to say it. I guess he just couldn't go on after she died." She raised an arm and dabbed at her eyes with the sleeve of her shirt.

"I'm sorry to bring it up. I didn't think…"

"It's fine, Peter. Really. It's years ago now." She reached for a glass on the counter and took a drink. It looked like sherry, the way it coated the sides of the glass.

"Your dad must have loved your mum so much. It's like he lived for her and then… and then he died for her." Peter stared at the Christmas tree. "In a way it seems really unselfish."

"I don't agree." Dianne's voice was sharp. "It doesn't even the score, it's just the easy way out. My father lost the love of his life. Granted. But there were other reasons for him to keep on living. Like his children and seeing his grandchildren grow up. But my brothers and I didn't matter enough to him, so he just left us. Took himself into the woods and hung himself."

Peter looked at her, then down at the floor. "You're right. I'm just wrapped up in my own shit, I guess."

Dianne leaned her head back and let out a deep breath. "Don't mind me, Peter. I can still get riled up about what happened even though I went through years of therapy after losing Mum and Dad. It's not even a year since you lost Rose."

"Rose would be having Christmas dinner with her family today if it wasn't for me."

"Pete, don't say that, man," Bob said. "You were good for each other."

"He's right, Peter," Dianne said. "Don't be so hard on yourself. You just need to keep going."

"I've been so goddamn selfish."

"Bullshit, man," Bob said. "You're no different from the rest of us. Maybe you did some bad shit when you were with Rose, but who hasn't? I've screwed up plenty before, you know that. But you and me, we're still figuring shit out. Someone like my old man should know better. And maybe my mum should know enough to not be such a hardass about it. But the point is that we've gotta accept responsibility for what's gone down, learn from it and move on."

"And suicide's just escaping responsibility," Dianne said. "My dad could have done something to help himself deal with his loss, but he refused."

"You mean counselling?" Peter asked.

"Exactly. It helped me a lot."

Peter stared at the half-empty bottle in his hands. "The idea of opening up to a stranger scares the shit out of me."

"Maybe at first," she said. "But then you build trust. After a while I realized I could say anything without being judged and that really felt freeing."

"Maybe. I don't know." Peter looked at Bob. "Have you done it?"

Bob shrugged. "Yeah. A bit. After we lost the baby I talked to the doctor in town. I guess it helped."

"You guess?" Dianne laughed. "You couldn't stop talking about how great it was. You macho guys and your pride."

Bob reddened. "Okay okay. I confess. I got a lot out of it." He looked at Peter. "Just don't go telling the world or I'll break your arm."

Peter raised his right hand. "Scout's honour." He paused for a moment. "He's a good guy?"

"Who, Bob?" Dianne screwed up her face. "I guess he'll do."

"No." Peter smiled. "I meant the doctor."

Bob checked his beer for a few last drops. "Yeah, he was pretty easy to talk to. You should give it a try. What've you got to lose?"

Peter looked out the window. What little daylight there had been was almost gone at three in the afternoon. A breeze blew snow off a nearby spruce. He shrugged. "I don't know. Nothing? Everything?" He took a deep breath and blew it out. "Man, what is it about this place? The conversations get so heavy."

"It must be you," Dianne laughed. "This never happens with other visitors. At least not with any of Bob's friends."

"Oh great. I'm a freak." Peter made a grotesque face.

"Merely exceptional, my friend," Bob said. "Just don't let it go to your head."

Looking around the room, Peter noticed a sculpture on a small table by the window.

"Is that the eagle you were working on? It's finished?"

"Yes," Dianne said proudly. "Finally. It's my Christmas present to myself." She rose, went to the sculpture and picked it up, caressed it and traced its lines with her fingers. She placed it in the middle of the coffee table. "We can see it better here."

The emerald green of the jade shone in the light from the kitchen. Veins of darker green snaked across the bird's chest and through to the feathered tips of the outstretched wings. Its legs were rooted in the base she had left rough, but claws emerged in front, powerfully gripping the stone from which it was made.

Peter looked at Dianne. "You're really talented."

Dianne beamed.

"She's not bad in the sack, either," Bob said.

Dianne swung a pillow at his head. "Moron. Get your ass into the kitchen and get your potatoes boiling. Our other guests will be here soon."

"So authoritative. So sexy." Bob pushed himself out of the chair and blew her a kiss through his bushy beard. "I'll get my French maid's outfit on."

Peter laughed as Bob turned and wiggled his large backside in his baggy jeans. He noticed a guitar leaning against the wall by the table.

"Is the guitar new?"

"Dianne got it for me. Said I needed something to keep my hands busy."

"And off of me," she laughed.

"Hey, you play, don't you?" Bob asked.

"Yeah," Peter replied. "Not in a while, but…"

"You should play for us after dinner," Dianne said. "If you want to."

Peter nodded. "Maybe I could."

The sound of car doors closing came from outside.

"Must be the rest of the country," Bob went to the door. "Quebec and the Maritimes."

Dianne went to join Bob at the door. Peter moved to the Christmas tree, to sneak a look at the card on the unopened gift. He wanted to be prepared in case it was for him. Bending quickly, he turned over the tag. "To Laura. With love from Mum and Dad."

The kitchen erupted with noise and commotion as George and Claude came inside.

Claude gave two bottles wrapped in coloured tissue paper to Dianne, a ribbon tied around the neck of each. "Merry Christmas," he said smiling. "For sure you'll never guess what they are."

"Thank you, Claude." Dianne kissed him on the cheek. "That's so thoughtful of you."

George handed two cases of beer to Bob, gave Dianne a kiss and came towards Peter. He brought up his fists and crouched in a boxer's pose, throwing a few jabs towards him. Peter smiled uneasily.

"Pete," he grinned. "My old bar fight buddy. How's she goin'? Haven't seen you in a bit."

Peter responded awkwardly to George's play punches. He tried to fend them off with open hands.

"You're a lover, not a fighter," George laughed. "You better stick to Toronto, Pete. Cape Breton'd be too rough for you." He put an arm around him and dug a fist playfully into his ribs. "Merry Christmas," he whooped. "What're you drinking? Claude, let's get this party going. Where'd that beer get to, Bob? Jeez it smells good in here."

Bob handed beer to everyone. They stood in a circle in the kitchen and clinked their bottles.

"Merry Christmas and Happy New Year," Dianne said.

"To a new year not breathing in all that goddamned dust," Claude said, wiping his handlebar moustache with his sleeve. "My aim is to get out of the Mill and up into the Mine."

"Out of the dust, into the cold," Bob said. "Good luck."

"Thanks. I'm gonna get my air brake ticket for the trucks and drive a Haul Pac. That's my plan. I'm studying for the test."

"How's that going?" Peter asked.

"It's all in English, so it's pretty hard."

"Your English seems pretty good to me," Bob said.

Claude shrugged. "Reading and writing not so good. I got two cousins who drive trucks at the asbestos mines in Quebec. Thetford Mines. They told me a year ago I should get my air brake licence. I wish I took their advice and done it there, back home in French."

"You can't make them give you a test in French?" Dianne asked. "What about official bilingualism? Services in both languages and all that?"

Claude shook his head. "That's only for federal services. Getting the licence is a provincial thing so I'll just have to manage it in English."

"If you want any help," Peter said, "let me know."

"For sure. Thanks."

"You can all get out of the kitchen and go sit at the table," Dianne said. She handed two bottles of wine to Claude. "Mr. O'Neil and I have things under control. As long as he stays sober, that is."

"Sober on Christmas," Bob said. "What a concept. My old man used to be shit-faced by two every Christmas afternoon. He'd start as soon as we got home from mass. It was some kind of weird Irish ritual for him.

Then he'd pass out 'till dinner at five. Like clockwork, every year."

"At least he passed out," George said as he sat at the table. "My dad was a friggin' nutcase most Christmases. I remember once he takes the friggin' tree, lights and all, and tosses it out the door. There she lay, on top of the snowbank on the side of the friggin' road. Stayed there till after New Year's. He wouldn't let my mum touch it. She said at least drag the thing around back so the neighbours don't have to stare at it all winter." He shook his head. "Goddamn psycho," he muttered.

George seemed to fall inward. He picked up his fork and examined it, turning it over in his large hands. Peter wondered if he was thinking of his son, missing him at Christmas, and he wished he could ask how he felt.

Bob came to the table with a bowl of mashed potatoes. "What's Christmas like at your place, Claude?" he asked as he sat down.

"Pretty boring, compared to you guys. Lots of family. Lots of food and wine. Guitars, accordions, singing. Pretty happy time."

"No trees tossed out the door," Bob said.

"Nope. No drama like that." Claude reached for a bottle of wine and a corkscrew.

"You Frenchies just don't know how to live," George said. "Too god-damn much happiness, that's your trouble."

"No better than us Toronto types, eh George?" Peter said.

"Jesus, now that you mention it. It's probably a fucking love-in scene there, just like at Claude's."

"It'd make your hair stand on end," Peter said. "The carolling, the caviar and champagne, father carving the perfect turkey and mother smiling at their perfect son. Oh, it's all just like on tv there in Toronto."

George laughed. "Goes without saying, Pete. Toronto. Streets paved with gold. Everyone's happy as pigs in shit."

Peter laughed and held out his wine glass for Claude to fill. Bob and Dianne brought the turkey and vegetables to the table. They toasted the food and fell to eating.

Little was said for three-quarters of an hour. Plates and glasses were filled and re-filled. They sat back in their chairs, eyes glassy with the food and the wine.

"Best I've ever had," George said. "No question."

"A fantastic meal," Peter added. "It's so good to be here and not in the cookhouse."

"We're glad we could rescue you from the steam table," Dianne said.

"Hey," Claude said. "We should make a toast to the new contract. Our Christmas present from the Company."

"A damn good settlement," Bob said. "Almost makes me wish I was still in the Union."

"It's great on the money side," George said. "But Alex said he had to let go of the health demands that Dave had on the table. I'm thinking about standing for vice president, now that Alex has taken over as president."

"That's a good idea," Bob said. "You should do it for sure."

"I think Chris Murton is going to offer. He's been secretary for quite a while so he'd have a lot of support."

"Don't let that stop you, George," Dianne said. "I'm sure you'd be great in the position."

"I would try to get more happening around health. Where I come from you can't count the number of old miners with black lung. A couple of my uncles died of it." He shook his head and drained the last of his wine. "But I hear from Alex that you've been doing a good job of twisting Iggy's arm, Pete. The Company's made some promises about dust control."

Peter grimaced. "Sure. Rub my nose in it now that we're too full to fight. It's more like Iggy's got me twisted around his little finger."

"Don't get me wrong," George said. "I think it's great what you've got out of him. Alex told me about what was in the safety report. It's all right on."

"Didn't he also tell you that all that's been promised before and nothing's happened? It's all bullshit and I'm their new patsy."

"Don't be so negative," Claude said.

"That's right," George said. "The Company's supposed to hand you a blank cheque because you complained to Iggy about the dust? Jesus, you gotta fight for shit. That's what my old man taught me. He's a prick sometimes, but he's a hundred percent union and they've had to fight for everything in those Cape Breton coal mines."

Bob turned in his chair and leaned towards Peter. "I hope you don't mind me saying this, Pete, but this sounds like classic you. Either you get what you want totally, right away, or you're ready to throw in the towel. Like how you didn't stay on the basketball team in high school because the coach didn't make you a starter. Shit, you could've kept working at it and been a starter the next season. Or a really good sub. You would've been a big asset to the team if you stayed."

"Bob," Dianne said.

"No, it's okay," Peter said. "Bob's right, I can give up too easily and look for an excuse to walk away." He stopped for a moment, the wine buzzing his head. "But in fact I'm going to take a workshop in Whitehorse next month on safety and health stuff. Maybe that'll give me more confidence."

"Right on." George put his arm around Peter's shoulders and gave him a shake. "Stay in there, buddy. Give the Company shit."

"You're right. Give them shit," Peter said, unsure of his conviction.

"Enough work talk," Dianne said as she stacked up their dirty plates. "Peter, how about playing something for us? Give Bob some inspiration to learn."

"Well..."

"Go on, Pete," George urged. "Give us a tune."

Peter pushed back his chair and picked up the guitar. It was badly out of tune, and he took a minute to set it right. He began to pick away at melodies, searching for a song, and found a James Taylor intro. He stopped for a moment, unsure if he wanted to go there, then closed his eyes and carried on into "Fire and Rain." He felt himself fill with emotion as he sang, "they let me know you were gone," felt his playing come from his heart, felt himself open with each repetition of "I always thought that I'd see you again."

When he was done, the room fell quiet. He opened his eyes after a moment to see everyone lost in their own memories. Bob slowly shook his head. "That was beautiful, man. I had no idea you could play like that."

"Yeah, that was great," George said. "Play another."

"Okay, but we need a change of pace." Peter started strumming hard, and worked his way into "Blue Suede Shoes," standing up and giving an Elvis imitation. The table was cleared and the dishes done to his beat, with everyone singing along loudly.

Peter got into the back seat of Claude's car, an old Pinto with Ontario plates.

"When did you get this?" he asked.

"Day before yesterday." He turned the key and bobbed his head back and forth in time to the starter, as if sending more energy under the hood. "Come on. Tabernac son of a whore." His breath formed a fog that hung in the frozen air. The car didn't start and he let go of the key. "From a guy in the Mill. French guy from northern Ontario. He drove all the way here in this shit box and quit after like two weeks or something. Told me he just wanted to make enough money to fly home. Never been in an airplane, he says."

He turned the key and put his whole body into motion, urging on the engine. George joined in, banging the dashboard with the flat of his hand.

"You can do it, baby."

The engine caught, sputtered, then revved up. A loud roar came from under Peter's seat.

"Muffler's shot," Claude said. "But for two hundred bucks you don't get a Caddy."

They backed out of the parking spot and turned around. Peter looked back at the cabin, its lights a warm yellow against the snow and trees. He caught a glimpse of Dianne through a window as the car started up the road, and then the cabin was gone.

A headlight beam bounced high in the trees on the left side of the road. On the right the beam lit up the ditch.

"Something's weird with your lights," George said.

"First time I've driven it in the dark. The guy said something about it being hit in a parking lot in Edmonton. I guess the focus is screwed up." At the top of the road up from Crystal Creek he turned towards town. "Like I said, two hundred bucks. But the heater works good."

The car roared like a tank as it picked up speed. Peter sat back and looked across the valley. A three-quarter moon shone through a window in the clouds, lighting the spruce forest with silver. A pocket of mist rested above the frozen river. He looked between George and Claude at the road ahead. The moonlight was enough that it didn't matter the headlights shone off to the sides. It felt like they were driving into a dream and he let himself drift on a cushion of food and wine. His mind roamed through the day, through the emotions he'd felt— the phone call to his parents, the hour-long walk in the sun to Crystal Creek, the exquisite sadness as he sang "Fire and Rain," the delicate outstretched wings of Dianne's jade eagle. The unopened present under the tree. He wondered how they chose the gift, how they would feel when Christmas ended and they put it away.

As they neared the tight turn in the road, lights appeared from the other side of the rock outcropping, and Claude slowed and hugged the shoulder to make room for the vehicle coming from town. A car emerged and Claude's left headlight shone up into the face of the driver. Her hand came off the steering wheel to shield her eyes from the glare, and the car didn't make the turn. The car hit the guardrail and spun around. After two revolutions on the snow-packed surface it came to rest. Claude stopped and Peter followed George, who ran along the road and opened the driver's door. He leaned into the car, turned the key and killed the engine.

"Jesus, Anna Mae," George said. "You okay?"

She shifted in the seat. "I don't know," she said slowly.

"You know her?" Peter asked.

"Of course. We're on the same shift in the Mill." George put a hand under her arm. "Let me help you out."

"No," Peter said, his voice authoritative. He put his hand on George's shoulder to move him away. "Stay still," he said to Anna Mae. "You might have injuries."

George stepped back. "Okay, Pete. You're the boss."

Peter leaned into the car to get a good look at her and saw blood flowing over her temple from a cut. "Are you hurt?"

"I don't think so. My head hurts. I'm not sure."

"Can you move your feet?"

She flexed both feet. "Yes."

"What's your name?"

"Anna Mae Johnson."

"Do you know what day it is?"

"It's Christmas. Why are you asking?"

"I just want to see if you remember. Does your neck hurt?"

"No. I don't think so." She slowly turned her head from side to side. "It's a bit stiff, that's all."

"Does it hurt if you take a deep breath?"

Anna Mae inhaled. Peter watched her chest expand.

"No, that's fine."

"Good." Peter straightened up. "Can I take a look at your cut?"

She looked at Peter. "I recognize you. You're the Union safety guy. I saw you in the Mill. So are you a doctor too?"

"Pretty close. Do you have a first aid kit?"

"Yeah. Under the seat." She began to bend forward. Peter put a hand on her shoulder to stop her.

"Hold on. I'll find it." He reached under the seat and pulled out a plastic box. "Just the thing," he said, looking inside.

"Mum's a nurse at the Infirmary in town." She winced as Peter gently wiped blood from the side of her face with an alcohol swab. "She always dreamed about being a doctor."

"Maybe she still could," Peter said as he applied a gauze pad to the cut. "The cut's not big. It probably feels worse because of all the blood, but that's what happens with wounds around the scalp."

"It feels like it's pouring out."

"It's really vascular in this area," he said, wrapping the bandage in place. He worked quickly, deftly unrolling gauze through his fingers, neatly circling her head several times, then tucking the end securely.

"That's some slick, Pete," George said, watching from behind. "Looks like you've done that a lot."

Peter finished the bandage. "Now we need to get you to the Infirmary to get checked over."

"No way," Anna Mae said. "Mum's waiting for me at home. She'll have a look at me, and besides, I'm sure I'm fine."

"Are you sure?" Peter asked. "Nothing else hurts? Chest, back, hips, legs?"

She shook her head. "I need to get home." She reached forward and started the car. "Thanks for your help."

"Hold on," Peter said. "You shouldn't drive, let me. Is it far?"

"No." Her eyes closed as she held tight to the steering wheel. "In the Reserve. Second street. Left. Fourth house."

Peter repeated the directions to Claude, who stood beside George. "You go first. I'll follow," he directed, then turned back to Anna Mae. "Can you get around to the passenger side?"

She nodded, and slowly got out of the car. Peter saw that she was pale.

"I feel really weak." She gripped the door for support.

"You need to lie down." Peter opened the back door and helped her in, then turned her and lifted her legs so her feet rested up high on the far door.

"This'll get the blood to your head," he said. "You're in shock." He covered her with his parka, then closed the rear door.

"Let's get going," he shouted to Claude. "But take it easy, it's gotta be a smooth ride."

Claude led the way to the road into the Reserve, then down into the village alongside the river, stopping in front of a one-storey house neatly outlined with Christmas lights.

"Is this your house?" Peter asked.

Anna Mae propped herself up in the back seat. Curtains opened in the front window of the house.

"That's it. There's Mum. I hope she doesn't freak out."

Peter helped her out of the back seat as the front door of the house opened and a woman hurried down the porch steps and along the shov-elled path.

"Anna Mae. What's happened? Are you hurt?"

"I'm okay, Mum. I'm just a bit groggy."

"You look worse than groggy. Let's get you inside." She looked at Peter as she put her arm around her daughter's shoulders. "How do you fit into this?"

"We were heading back to town and Anna Mae was blinded by our headlights as she came around that sharp turn in the road. She spun out and hit her head on the window."

"He really helped, Mum. He's the Union safety rep."

"Are you? Well, come in with your friends for a minute while we see to my daughter."

George rolled down the window as Peter approached the car. "Come on inside. We're invited."

George turned to Claude, then back to Peter. "We'll wait for you here. You won't be long, eh?"

"I guess not. Just don't leave without me." He followed the women into the house. A Christmas tree stood in the far corner of the front room, opened presents scattered around. "O Come All Ye Faithful" came from a record player in a corner. Family photographs were arranged on the walls. Open doorways led to a kitchen and a bedroom. The floor was painted plywood.

"Don't bother with your boots. I'll mop up later." Anna Mae's mother called to Peter. She had her daughter on the couch and was inspecting her head. "Louis," she called. A young boy appeared from another room. "Get a plastic bag from under the sink, go outside and fill it with snow. Your sister needs cold on this head of hers." She turned to Peter. "Did you do the bandage?"

He nodded.

"Well done. My name's Theresa. What's yours?"

"Peter. Peter Stevens." He glanced out the window at Claude's car. "If everything's okay with Anna Mae, I should probably get going."

"You've done this before," she said.

"Bandaging? Yes, I have."

The boy ran into the room with a clear plastic bag full of snow. A burly man in an open ski jacket followed him into the room. A white Vancouver Canucks t-shirt stretched across his wide chest. Peter recognized him from the Union meeting the month before.

"What's happened, Terry?" he asked.

Theresa took the bag of snow from the boy and laid it on the side of Anna Mae's head, then wrapped a towel around it to hold it in place.

"Anna Mae's been in an accident up on the highway but she seems all right. This is Peter Stevens. He bandaged her and brought her home."

A hand that seemed twice the size of his own was extended over the coffee table to Peter. "I'm Dan Grandison, Theresa's brother. Thanks for your help."

"It was no trouble."

"He's the Union safety and health rep," Theresa said to Dan. They exchanged a look.

"Is that so? Safety and health. Then you took over from Gord Evans."

"That's right. So I'm pretty new to the position." He half turned to the door. "I've got friends waiting in the car. I really ought to get going."

"Have a look at this," Theresa said, taking the bag of snow from Anna Mae's head and holding it out towards Peter. "You see what's in there?"

He leaned forward to look closely at the bag. The snow inside was flecked with green.

"You know what that is?"

Peter nodded.

She carefully laid the bag back on Anna Mae's wound. "Winter and summer, my kids are outside playing in that asbestos dust. And it's all through our houses. We've been after the Company for years to control it but all we get is the runaround. They tell us that the dust isn't harmful, but I've done enough reading to know different."

"And we've been after the politicians up here," Dan said, "but the Company has them in their back pocket. They couldn't care less about us."

Theresa's face hardened. "My husband can't walk half a mile without having to sit down and catch his breath and there are many more here on the Reserve that are just as bad. The dust is making us sick."

Peter's mouth went dry. He was hot in his parka, but didn't want to take it off. "Have you talked to anyone in the Union before?"

"Oh yeah," Dan said. "I had a long talk with Dave McGuinness last summer and he sounded real sympathetic. He promised he'd fight to get all this dust pollution cleaned up and I believed him. But now he's dead and Alex Bruce couldn't give a goddamn about us here."

"I'll say this for sure," Theresa said while adjusting the bag of snow for Anna Mae. "This is the first time a Union rep has set foot in the Reserve." She turned back to Peter, her eyes grabbing his. "So. What have you got to say about our situation?"

Peter looked at Anna Mae on the couch. He was tired. His eyes were heavy and they drifted closed for a second. Anna Mae became Rose, pale, lips cracked, afraid. The image startled him and his head jolted back, his heart suddenly pounding. Theresa watched him, waiting.

"It's not good." He turned and looked around the room. A sampler hung on the wall beside the tree. Bless This House, it said. A child's crayon drawing of a house was taped underneath. "The dust gets everywhere."

"Tell us something we don't already know," Dan said.

"I can talk to Iggy about it on the next safety tour."

"I just told you we've been given the runaround by him," Theresa said. "We need something done."

"What can I do that you haven't already tried?"

"Put pressure on them. You're the Union health man. We're choking in this stuff out here."

Peter nodded agreement. "Okay. I'll see what I can do, but like I said, I'm just new to the job." He made a move toward the door. "I really have to get going."

Theresa followed him to the front door. "I'm sorry for throwing all this at you. You helped out my daughter, and I thank you again for that."

"It's okay. I can understand how angry you must be," Peter said, stepping onto the porch. "And I just helped Anna Mae like anyone would have."

"No. You came down here. That's more than most white people would do."

Peter looked down for a moment, embarrassed, then back at Theresa. "Merry Christmas."

Theresa smiled. "The same to you. Come again. Come for supper sometime." She turned to a small table by the door and wrote on a piece of notepaper. "Here's our phone number. Give a call and we'll make arrangements."

Peter took the note and put it in his wallet. "Thank you. I'll do that."

Claude's car struggled back up the road from the river. The hole in the muffler made a deafening roar and the vibrations rattled Peter, sitting in the back seat.

"So what happened in there?" George shouted back to Peter over the noise, a quizzical look on his face. "What was it like?"

"It was nice." Peter shouted back. "They're a nice family."

George gave Peter a dubious look, then turned in his seat to face forward.

"There's asbestos dust everywhere in the Reserve," Peter said.

"That doesn't surprise me," George said. "It blows off the tailings pile, down the valley."

"Yeah," Claude said. "They're not supposed to use the stack piler on the tailings when it's windy, but they always do."

"Goddamn it," Peter said. "Why the hell do they do that?"

"I complained to the Mill foreman about it once," George said. "He said the stack piler's way more efficient. He said don't worry about it, it's only Indians live down the valley."

"And the hippies in Crystal Creek," Claude laughed.

"Those people are living in that dust," Peter said, anger rising in his voice. "We can fuck off out of here anytime we want, but that's their home."

"You're right," George said. "But it wouldn't be easy to convince the membership to fight that battle. It's one thing to demand that the Company clean up the dust in Rock Reject and the Mill, but to go after the tailings pile to benefit the Indians, I'm not sure about that."

"That's racist bullshit, George. Unions are supposed to be about justice, not just fat paycheques."

"You're a rich doctor's son," George snapped back. "What the fuck do you know about unions?"

Peter was silent for a moment. He felt his face flush. "You're right," he said at last. "Nothing."

The car reached the main road and turned towards town, the roar of the engine quieter on level ground. Clouds had covered the moon and outside the car it was black. Peter settled back in the seat and closed his eyes. The challenges from Bob, George and Theresa played in his mind. *You give up too easily. We need your help.* His hands were cold. He put them in his pants pockets where his fingers toyed with coins and with his wedding ring, which was always there. He turned his head to look out the side window and saw his face reflected in the glass, his beard hiding his mouth, his eyes shadowed in the dim light from the instrument panel. He looked for evidence of his father, of his determination and certainty, but only saw his own weakness. He closed his eyes and again felt the ring, its engraved pattern, and remembered how it felt when Rose first slipped it on his finger and how he thought in that moment that he would change, that he would have clarity and purpose in his life. He realized how quickly that belief had vanished, how he had never changed, never made a true commitment to Rose, to his life, to anything. That was the truth. He had never made a commitment. He turned again to his reflection in the window and looked into his shadowed eyes. In the roar and vibrations and darkness of the back seat of the Pinto he nodded yes to himself.

FOURTEEN

January fourth was barely light at nine in the morning. A low pressure front from the Pacific had brought warmer temperatures and eight inches of snow to Stikine. The thermometer mounted beside the doors to the Administration Building stood at minus ten.

"It's all relative," Peter said to Brad Johnson, a truck driver from his shift. They stood at the top of the stairs waiting for Reinhard's station wagon to take them to the airport at Watson Lake. Two other men sat on the stairs, their belongings around them packed into duffel bags and back packs.

"Come again?"

"Ten below it says." Peter nodded at the thermometer. "It feels fine compared to a couple of days ago. What was it, thirty five below? It's all relative."

Johnson stared blankly at Peter. "Whatever. Just get me the fuck out of here." He lit a cigarette and offered one to Peter.

"You're going on leave?" Peter sucked in the warmth of the smoke.

"Goddamn right. De-bushing leave, and not a fucking minute too soon."

"I'm heading to Whitehorse," Peter said. Johnson stared across the road, his cigarette hanging from his mouth. "Going to a union work-shop," he added.

Johnson shook himself and turned to Peter. "What? Did you say something?"

"Never mind."

The Company station wagon slid to a stop in front of the building.

Reinhard got out and looked at the two men waiting with their bags. "Didn't I just bring you pussies in here a week ago?" he said to them as he opened the back of the Suburban.

"Three weeks," one of them replied, tossing a bag inside.

"Had enough of the Mill," the other said. "Too much dust."

Reinhard snorted. "Wimps. I've been here fifteen years. Do I look sick to you? This dust stuff is all bullshit."

"Fifteen years in this place?" the first man said. "If you're not sick, you're crazy."

They followed a snowplow out of town. Heavy, dark clouds hid the top half of the mountains along the valley. Passing the road down into the Reserve, Peter caught a brief glimpse of Theresa's house. He thought of her living room, the photographs of family, the dust in the snow, and then the view of the village was gone, blocked by the forest, thick and plastered with snow.

Johnson stretched up his arms and pounded on the ceiling of the station wagon. "Mexico, man," he shouted. "Weed, tequila, women and sun. Fucking paradise."

"Save your enthusiasm, Johnson," Reinhard said. "I can't drive with a lunatic next to me."

"It's time you went on de-bushing leave, Reinhard," Johnson laughed. "When were you last out of here? Nineteen fucking sixty-two?"

"Fuck off. Some people prefer not to throw their money away on expensive vacations. Some people have financial obligations."

"Screw obligations. I'm out of here." He turned to Peter. "You said you're off to Whitehorse, Pete? The bar and hooker capital of the North."

"I don't know about that, but I'll be three nights at the Yukon Inn for this workshop."

"What's it about?"

"It's training in health and safety issues. Put on by the Union's regional office."

"Health," snorted the man next to Peter. "That's nothing but a joke at Stikine with all that goddamn asbestos dust."

"No shit," said the man next to him. "I heard that stuff'll kill you. That's why I'm out of there."

"Bullshit," Johnson said. "But even if it does knock a few years off of being old, who cares. I'm making good money and I'm off to Mexico."

"The dust is bad and the Company has made some promises to do something about it," Peter said. "And it's not just us in town that are exposed to the dust. There's all the other people living in the valley."

Reinhard looked at Peter in the rear view mirror. "Just don't go stirring up a lot of shit over this. I don't want any clean-up coming out of my pay packet, especially if it's for the hippies or the Indians, if that's who you mean."

"That is who I mean," Peter said. He stared back at Reinhard in the mirror until he turned back to the road ahead. Peter sank back in the seat and was silent for the rest of the trip to Watson Lake.

Riding in a cab from the airport into Whitehorse, Peter found himself staring at the lit-up shops and restaurants. In the hotel lobby he was disoriented by the lights, carpets and upholstered chairs, and put off by the snooty attitude of the desk clerk. In his room he stripped off his clothes and went into the bathroom, looking at himself in the large mirror, almost not recognizing the person he saw. The eyes and mouth, yes, his, but the full face under his beard, the muscled chest, biceps and forearms didn't seem like they could belong to him. He showered then went down to the restaurant and was served food without standing in line. He listened to live music in the bar. He wondered if he had ever been so free in all his life.

The workshop wrapped up late in the afternoon on day two and the ten participants poured out of the conference room and across the lobby to the bar. Peter was in the midst of the group when he caught sight of the profile of a woman standing at the front of the lobby, looking out the plate glass window. He stepped aside as his companions filed into the smoky bar.

The woman's back was to him, her long blonde braid catching the light from a table lamp in the corner. Peter moved towards her and waited for for her to turn around.

"Susan?" She looked at him, but showed no sign of recognition.

"It's Peter. Stevens. From Stikine, the Union office. We talked there the morning after…"

Her face opened. "Right. Sorry, I should have remembered."

"That's okay. It was a while ago."

She seemed to fall back into memory. "It was kind of you that day. You were really helpful." Her hand reached over her shoulder and pulled her braid in front of her chest. They stood awkwardly for several moments.

"Why are you here?" they said in unison, then laughed, breaking the tension. Each waited for the other to begin.

"You first," Susan said.

"A union thing. A training workshop in safety and health."

Susan nodded. "Dave used to come up here for those. Was it good?"

Peter shrugged. "Not as good as I had hoped. What about you? You're not heading back to the salt mines, are you?"

She turned to the window. Her face looked thin. "Yes, I'm going back," she said without conviction. "I had to come to Whitehorse to get my truck. I parked it here when I left Stikine."

"So since you're this far, you might as well go back and make some money?"

She turned back to Peter and shrugged. "Why not? I couldn't think of anything else to do right now. Better the devil you know and all that," she said with a small smile.

"It's a rough time for you no matter what."

Susan nodded and turned away again, looking towards the front doors of the hotel.

"Are you waiting for someone?" Peter asked.

"Oh. No, not really. I'm just, I don't know. Scattered, I guess."

The door to the bar opened and loud voices spilled out. Two of the men from the workshop crossed the lobby. They saw Peter and waved.

"Pete, buddy," one shouted. "You'll be joinin' us, right?"

"Not too sure of that, Joey," the other said. "Pete looks pretty occupied to me."

They disappeared into the men's room. Their voices could be heard through the closed door.

"Newfoundlanders," Peter said. "There were some great guys at the workshop."

"So are you going to go on in and join the fun?"

"I could, I guess. Although I haven't been outside at all since I arrived. I don't suppose you'd like to go for a walk? Get some air."

Her mouth twisted sceptically. "I don't know, I think I'm okay." She looked out the window at the banks of snow on the sidewalk. A car passed on Main Street, its exhaust hanging in the air. "Besides, it looks as cold as Winnipeg out there."

"Well then, I should leave you." Peter took a step back. "I was pretty sure it was you, even from across the room. Your braid's pretty distinctive." His hands fumbled together. "Anyway, I just wanted to say hi."

He waited. She kept looking out the window, her jaw muscles working.

"I went to see Dave's parents," she suddenly said, her voice flat, colourless. "They were devastated." She shook her head. "I'm sure they feel I'm partly to blame for not keeping him off the bottle." Her hands fidgeted with her braid. "I guess that's how I feel, too."

Peter waited, unsure if he should speak. Moments passed, and she seemed to break free from a trance.

"Anyway, maybe I would like to go for a walk. Do me good, as my dad would say."

She started towards the elevators. "I'll get my coat and meet you here in five minutes."

The street outside the hotel was busy with people shopping, heading home from work, going out to eat. As they walked, Peter kept turning and looking into the shop windows.

"After three months in Stikine, this feels like New York. Sidewalks. Stores. Civilization."

"I guess I got my fill of it in Winnipeg. It seems pretty dreary to me."

"So you're here because of your truck?"

"Yeah. The Company said I could take a leave of absence to go home but I couldn't stomach the thought of riding in Reinhard's station wagon. So I took the pickup and parked it at the airport. Cost me ninety-two-fifty to leave the parking lot today."

"How come you didn't just go to Watson Lake and fly from there?"

"I don't know. I got to the junction of the Alaska Highway and wanted to keep driving. Edmonton seemed too far, so I turned west and drove here, stayed the night and flew to Winnipeg the next day. It was all a blur. My parents picked me up and took me home. I went to bed in my old room and hardly came out for a week."

They came to Second Avenue and turned right. Across the road and the railroad tracks was the frozen Yukon River, white in the light of the moon.

"It feels really weird to be back here in the North. It's like I was in a time warp in Winnipeg. There was Christmas and New Year's, but I can't say I remember any of it. Then I started to get really antsy. Agitated all the time. I had to get out of there and I didn't know where else to go." Her arms were swinging in front of her, her hands fists in her gloves. "Do you think I'm nuts for going back to Stikine? Is it a really stupid idea?"

"Maybe. I don't know. I guess you're doing what you need to do and you'll know if it's right when you're back there. All I know is that it's hard when you lose someone and there's no recipe for dealing with life afterwards."

Susan didn't respond. They continued along Second Avenue, drawn to the bridge over the river. They stopped halfway across and leaned against the railing, looking south.

"I was reading a brochure in the hotel room that said there are only four bridges over the Yukon River. Two thousand three hundred miles from northern B.C., across the Yukon and Alaska to the Bering Sea, and only four bridges."

"I like that," Susan said. "The thought of so little human interference in so huge an area. It seems hopeful, somehow. What else did it say?"

"They didn't think that this was a part of the Yukon River. On the early maps it was listed as the Lewes River, named after some Hudson's Bay Company bigshot. Then geographers discovered that it really was part of the Yukon and they changed the name in 1949. Lewes's name was erased from the map." He fumbled in his pocket for his cigarettes and lighter and lit one. "I like that," he continued. "Re-write the books. Wipe out the mistakes like they never happened."

A truck rumbled over the bridge, its engine vibrating the heavy, cold air. Peter turned and looked north. The northern lights were dancing above the horizon, their colours weakened by the light of the moon. He watched them for a minute then glanced at Susan, who was staring into the distance. Tears rolled from her eyes, freezing on her cheeks.

"I'm getting cold," he said. He flicked his cigarette off the bridge and watched the small sparks fly off the tip. "I saw a Chinese restaurant down the street from the hotel. How would you like to get something to eat?"

"I suppose." She wiped her eyes with the back of her gloved hands. "Please don't mind me, I'm just a bit of a mess."

"That's okay." He felt his own tears close to the surface. "I understand."

Hurt, wary, her eyes met his for a moment. "Do you?"

A wind from the north numbed Peter's face as they walked back to Main Street. He covered his cheeks and nose with his hands in their leather mitts. "I feel like my face will freeze off," he said. Susan wore only earmuffs. "The cold doesn't bother you?"

"I'm from Winnipeg," she said.

"Right."

Steam covered the restaurant windows. Peter held the door open for Susan, who hesitated on the snow-packed sidewalk.

"After you."

She shook her head.

"Are you okay?"

"Dave and I ate in there last summer. We took this great road trip..." her voice trailed off. She turned and looked down the street, towards the hotel. "I think I'll head back to my room. I don't really feel like eating."

"You're sure? Or maybe another place?"

"No, thanks." She gave Peter a quick smile. "And thanks for the walk, I enjoyed talking with you."

She climbed over a mound of snow on the edge of the sidewalk and crossed the street. Peter watched until she was through the doors of the hotel. Then his friends from the workshop filed out, led by the two

Newfoundlanders. They trooped off down the street and he thought of catching up with them but couldn't make himself move. A group of people came towards him and he stepped into the doorway of the restaurant to make room for them to pass. The door opened as three diners left, the last one holding the door for him. Disoriented and light-headed, he stepped through the open door into the heat and aroma and clatter of the small restaurant. A waiter in slippers edged by him with plates of food. A small child wandered among the tables. A posterboard menu hand-written in Chinese hung on a wall alongside a framed photo of a Mountie on horseback. A young woman cleared a nearby table of dirty dishes and, catching Peter's eye, she gestured to the empty chair. He sat and watched the child, now drawing shapes in the moisture on the window. A boy, he thought, but wasn't sure.

A menu in English and a pot of jasmine tea were placed in front of him, steam curling delicately from the spout. He watched as the vapour floated and vanished before filling the round handle-less cup left by the waiter.

He cradled the cup in his cold hands and inhaled the aroma. Closing his eyes, he saw Rose sitting across from him in a Chinese restaurant on Spadina Avenue, her smile wavering in the heat from the cup of jasmine tea that he held close to his lips. Laughing as she struggled with her chopsticks, she was young and shining, full of the love of being six months married. His hand reached across the table to touch hers.

"You ready to order now?"

His eyes snapped open. His arm was suspended over the table, reaching for the empty seat opposite, and he quickly drew it back.

"Uh. A dinner for one, I guess. And a couple of Molson's."

The waiter left and the child appeared by the table, peering up with open, unquestioning eyes. Aware that his own had filled with tears, Peter held his gaze, a thread of connection through the clatter of dishes and noise of voices swirling around the room until the waiter came and shooed the child away.

He drank another beer after his meal and was unsteady on his feet entering the hotel lobby. The desk clerk calling 'Sir' didn't register for him until the third time when Peter looked over and saw him waving an envelope. "This is for you," he said. "It's from the lady."

Peter tore it open, then glanced up to see the clerk watching him. He turned away from the desk, his nervous hands unfolding the note. It was written in a neat, printed hand on hotel stationary. *Just a thought, Peter. You could ride with me in the truck back to Stikine tomorrow. Sharing the driving would be a help to me. I'm crashing early tonight, so if you want to come, meet me for breakfast at six. Susan.*

He looked at his watch. Only eight thirty. The doors to the bar opened and the band started up a song he liked. He re-read the note, tucked it into his coat pocket, and followed the music into the bar.

It was packed with a Friday night crowd. Peter sat at the bar with a whiskey and watched the band play to the crowded dance floor. They started a Doobie Brothers song and he got up and moved closer to the band, feeling the rhythm in his legs and hips. He thought of calling up to Susan's room to see if she'd like to come and dance with him, but decided not to bother her. A woman sat alone at a table on the other side of the floor, smoking, watching the band, one leg over the other and bobbing to the beat. Why the hell not, he said to himself and made his way around to her.

"Would you like to dance?"

She looked startled. Her hair fell across her face and she quickly tucked it behind her ear.

"Would you like to dance?" he repeated, thinking she hadn't heard him.

She shook her head. He smiled.

"Are you sure? Just one?"

She turned her head away as a hand landed on Peter's shoulder and turned him around. He looked up into a heavily bearded face.

"Get lost."

Peter stepped back from the huge chest that pushed into his face. "I just wanted to dance. No harm in that, is there?"

The beard leaned towards him. "Find your own fucking woman. This one's mine." A thick finger thudded into Peter's chest, pushing him back. The man banged his beers on the table and sat down, glaring at

Peter as he tipped a bottle to his mouth. Peter imagined punching him in the face, then turned and slowly made his way around the edge of the room, trying to listen to the band but hearing only blood pounding in his ears. He picked up his coat and went to his room.

FIFTEEN

They pulled out of the hotel parking lot at quarter to seven, the headlights of Susan's Ford pickup cutting through darkness and ice fog as they drove along Fourth Avenue, up Two Mile Hill and onto the Alaska Highway. As they passed the airport Peter realized that he hadn't cancelled his reservation for the flight back to Watson Lake. Reinhart and the company station wagon would meet that flight to drive him to the Mine. He felt a twinge of anxiety and wondered if he should have Susan pull into the terminal so that he could do what was expected of him. The landing lights of a jet were visible in the sky ahead, another was taxiing to the runway, the emblem of Canadian Pacific on its tail. He closed his eyes for a minute, and when he opened them they had left the airport and the city behind.

He leaned forward and looked at the sky through the windshield.

"There's no moon and the stars are incredible."

"It was right above us on the bridge last night," Susan replied. "It probably won't rise until this afternoon."

He leaned back in the seat and shifted his feet to catch the warm air from the heater.

"I love driving in the dark," he said. "When I was little, my family used to go south in the winter. Dad liked driving at night. Less traffic, I guess. Mum used to make me a bed in the back seat and I could look out at the stars through the windows. It was so cozy in the dark with the humming of the road and the lights of other cars coming and going." He stared out at the white Alaska Highway flowing past them under the truck's headlights. "Like right now," he continued. "I can imagine myself being little again, curled up and looking at the stars."

"You must have had a happy childhood."

Peter shrugged. "I don't know. It doesn't seem like it was, but maybe... Anyway, the idea of being a kid again, starting everything over..."

"You don't like who you are?"

"No." He cringed inside as the word came out. He took a cigarette from a pack and lit his lighter.

"Don't smoke in the truck," Susan said.

His hand and the lighter stopped an inch from the cigarette. "Sorry," he said, and put it away.

"So what's so wrong with your life?"

Peter shifted in his seat, uncomfortable. He felt like he was sliding into a familiar pit, and fought to climb out of it. He looked out at the wall of spruce forest flanking the highway, dense in the pre-dawn grey. The edge of their headlight beam shone on the mounds of snow that had been thrown into the ditch by the highway plows. He focused on the line of light and dark, letting the snow become a blur that blended with the drone of the truck.

"Maybe we should change the topic. You probably don't want to hear me going on about my life."

"I can be the judge of that. Besides, what else are we going to talk about for the next eight hours?"

Peter didn't respond. A transport truck passed them going the other way. The pickup rocked in its wake and Susan wrestled with the wheel to stay in control.

"There's no way I'd want to be young again," she said, once they were cruising smoothly. "And to have to go through the pain of learning what I know now." She shook her head. "Since Dave died, every day it comes over me in waves. Sometimes I can hardly breathe, but I know that this is what life is about, and that I'll get through it. I've just got to carry on living and not forget him."

Peter felt himself sliding backwards, downwards. "Sometimes I'm not sure if I deserve to."

"To?" Susan asked.

Peter sighed. "To carry on living. I know that sounds stupid, but... Shit, I'm sorry. I'm kind of spinning my wheels here. Maybe I shouldn't have come with you today."

"For godsakes, Peter, I didn't put a gun to your head. But you go and make these heavy comments and then you run away from them. What the hell am I supposed to do?"

"I don't know. I wanted to come with you so that we could get to know each other and have some fun. I wasn't thinking that the conversation would go to these places, I thought we could just..."

"Pretend?"

"If that's how you want to put it, fine. I thought we could do without our baggage for a while."

"Peter, that's bullshit. You think I can get to know you without you telling the truth about yourself, or that I can carry on as if Dave didn't die six weeks ago? Give me a break."

Peter lifted his hands in surrender. "Okay, I'm sorry. I know how you feel, so maybe we can start this conversation over."

He looked over at Susan. Her jaw muscles were clenched, her eyes strained. She took her foot off the gas and geared the truck down. A highway maintenance yard was off the road to the right and she pulled in and parked.

"Everything okay?"

Susan got out without answering and slammed the door. Two men working on a snowplow looked over at them. She went behind the pickup then appeared a few seconds later on Peter's side, ten feet from his face in the window, with a snowball in her hand and an angry glare in her eyes. They looked at one another for a moment, then she wound up and fired the snowball at his head. He flinched as it crashed against the glass, and watched stunned as the snow melted on the warm window and slid away, blurring her image through the window. Peter opened the door and jumped out.

"What the hell is that about?"

"You do not fucking well know how I feel," she shouted. "You told me that the day Dave died and now you've got the nerve to say it again."

"I'm just trying to be nice to you, goddamn it." Peter felt heat building in his face and throat.

"I don't give a shit about nice. It's phony."

"Piss off. Who are you to accuse me of being phony? You don't know anything about me."

"How the hell could I? All you do is make these cryptic comments that go nowhere. You haven't told me a goddamn thing."

Peter turned away. The mechanics had put down their tools to watch the scene. "What are you staring at?" he shouted at them. They looked at each other and grinned, then went back to working on the plow's engine. He turned to Susan. Her face was still hard.

"Well I'm telling you right now that I'm not a fucking phony, that I'm for real and I've been through shit too."

"But you don't know anything about how I feel." She stabbed the air between them with her finger. "You don't know anything about losing the one you love."

"I do so, goddamn it." He swung his fist through the air, hitting nothing. "My wife died last spring. She died because I screwed up royally and now half the time I wish that I was dead." His insides shook. He spun away and looked across the maintenance yard, past the piles of sand and derelict dump trucks to hills in the distance that had become barely visible in the sunless morning light. "Does that explain enough?"

He heard Susan's boot kicking the ground and saw a clump of ice fly off towards the edge of the yard.

"Yes," she shouted. "It explains a lot. Why didn't you tell me that before?"

"Because..." He took a deep breath and sighed it out. "Because I'm ashamed. I want to get past this place and..." he paused again and shrugged, "and just live. I don't want to always be dragging my shit along everywhere I go."

"But all that is important. It's who we are."

"Like I said, I'm ashamed of it."

"But if it's the truth..." She kicked at another clump of frozen snow. "Jesus, I hate it when people hold out on me."

Peter looked at her. Her face had softened. "I'm sorry," he said.

Susan nodded. "I knew last night there was something that you weren't telling me, but I had no idea that it could be this. I'm sorry, too, Peter."

He shrugged. "Now you know." He walked away from her, breathing deeply to calm his insides. He watched one of the mechanics start up the plow, while the other stood on a platform, adjusting the engine.

"We'd better get moving," Susan said after a minute had passed. "We've got a long way to go today."

"You've got a hell of an arm," Peter said as he opened the passenger door.

She looked at him across the box of her truck. "I play third base. We won the provincials two years ago."

They pulled out of the yard back onto the highway. Susan accelerated to seventy and settled back in the seat. The land gradually became more visible as it rolled by, and the knot in Peter's stomach slowly relaxed. Susan switched off the pickup's headlights as the dawn turned to morning.

"I like this soft light to drive in," she said. "Easy on the eyes."

"You like driving?"

"Love it. My dad taught me when I was fourteen. We'd go to the back roads north of Winnipeg and he'd let me drive the car for hours. Seemed like hours, anyway. I bought a car as soon as I got my licence. What about you?"

"I had lessons through school and my mum let me practise on her car until I got my licence. Dad wouldn't let me touch his. Rose and I had an apartment near the university, so we didn't need a car. If we wanted to get out of the city, her mother let us borrow hers, on the condition that Rose did all the driving."

"Rose. Your wife?"

Peter nodded. "Yes."

"What a beautiful name. What happened? How did she die?"

The forest opened on the right and Peter looked across a frozen lake to the horizon, to someplace where the sun that he hadn't seen in four weeks was up and shining. The heater blew warm on his legs and for a moment he imagined them driving on to the end of the Alaska Highway and then on and on to the south, not stopping, not talking, just moving together towards the sun. Her voice brought him back.

"If you don't want to talk about it, I can understand that. Sort of. I mean, we've both been through the same mill and ..."

"No, no," Peter interrupted. "I was just ... It's hard to go back there."

"It is. I know."

"It was last March. I was writing exams and when I came home she had already gone to the hospital. It was sudden." His voice trailed off. A westbound transport truck approach them, kicking up a cloud of snow in its wake, and for a few seconds they drove blind.

"She had a miscarriage," he said while they were enveloped in the whiteout. "And she hemorrhaged afterwards. She couldn't recover."

"Peter, that's so tragic. I'm so sorry."

Peter nodded. He felt numb.

"But ... What did you mean about screwing up? Like it was your fault or something?"

"I wasn't there for her." He felt he had no breath for his voice. "I left her when I should have stayed. I knew what to watch out for but I didn't pay attention. I didn't listen to her."

Susan watched the road ahead, her jaw muscles knotting under the skin. "That's hard, feeling you could have done something and didn't. I feel that about Dave, that I could have done more to keep him sober."

"You didn't get to say goodbye to him."

She shook her head. "And that kills me. It had been tough for awhile between us and I can't remember the last time either of us said I love you." Her face was heavy with sadness. "Did you get that chance?"

"Not in a way that mattered. I saw her in the hospital ... And then she was gone."

They fell into silence for half an hour, the drone of the truck's engine filling the space between them. Susan geared down as they approached a service station overlooking Teslin Lake.

"We'll get gas and I'm desperate for a coffee. How about you drive for a while?"

"Uh, okay, but, like I said, I haven't driven much."

Susan laughed. "It's not like there's a lot of traffic to deal with."

They climbed out of the truck and stretched. Across the frozen sweep of the lake three mountain peaks stood out against the sky.

"That's Lone Sheep Mountain," Susan said. "And its peaks are called the Three Aces. Dave and I stopped here on our trip last summer and got the low-down from the people in the café."

"Three Aces. I guess they're supposed to bring you luck?"

Susan stood with her hands in her back pockets, staring at the distant mountains. "They sure as hell didn't give any luck to Dave." She started towards the café, with Peter a step behind. "My dad said you make your own luck," she said. "That's what I intend to do."

Peter turned slowly out of the service station lot onto the highway and ground the gears of the manual transmission up into third. He drove across the half-mile-long Nisutlin Bridge at forty.

"Jesus, Peter," Susan laughed, "the truck has another gear. We want to get there today."

"I've never driven a truck before." Glancing in the rear view mirror, he saw five vehicles lined up behind him. He put in the clutch and lurched into fourth, sending the speedometer up to fifty.

Susan bunched up her coat in the corner and leaned against it. "I'm going to nap, let me know when you want to switch."

A transport truck passed them going west and Peter slowed to forty in its wake. He hugged the edge of the road as several cars and trucks accelerated past them, then eased the pickup up to sixty. The highway wound through the Cassiar Mountains and dipped south into British Columbia to the Swift River. His attention wandered to the scenery when there was no oncoming traffic, then he white-knuckled the wheel when a vehicle appeared. The vastness of the landscape tugged at him, drawing him to the hills and rivers, empty of evidence of humans. He was relieved when Susan stretched and rubbed her eyes.

"How are you doing?"

"Coping. It's tough when a semi goes by the other way. I feel like we're going to get blown off the road."

"It's a light truck, an F-One Hundred. For sure next time I'll get a One-Fifty." She opened the glove box and pulled out a map. "Have we gone through Rancheria yet?"

"I don't think so. There was a sign a while back saying ten miles to Swift River."

"Oh. I was hoping I'd sleep through that goddamn place."

"I guess I'm kind of slow." He glanced at Susan. "Did something happen there?"

"Yeah. We stayed at the motel there on our trip. Had a nice dinner with a couple of beers. I was really tired and went to the room and Dave stayed to talk to some guys. A couple of hours later I hear all this shouting in the parking lot and he's out there in a fight. I go out and get him into the room and he's so drunk he can hardly stand up. They were drinking shooters." She started playing with the glove box knob, opening and closing it. "He shoved me against the wall. The next day he had no memory of doing it." She slammed shut the compartment door. "Pull over. I'll drive now."

They switched places and Susan tore off, quickly hitting seventy. They sped through Swift River and wound into the mountains, twenty minutes later crossing the Rancheria River. Peter looked at the map. "We just crossed the Continental Divide."

"Really? Where?"

"About five miles back. We've been travelling upstream all day until now. Everything until Swift River flows northwest to the Yukon and out into the Bering Sea. But now we're going with the flow. The Rancheria here flows east into the Liard, then to the Mackenzie and out the Beaufort Sea. The Arctic Ocean." He looked over at Susan. "I think that's amazing. You cross a line and the flow of nature changes."

She sniffed a bitter laugh. "So what is it with human nature? Why is it so goddamn hard to change?"

At two-thirty they neared the junction with Highway 37. The light was almost gone and snow blew across the roadway as they made the turn off the Alaska Highway onto the road south to Stikine. A familiar vehicle passed them going the other way.

"There's Reinhard in the Company wagon," Peter said. "I suppose he's going to Watson Lake for a fresh batch of new hires. He would have picked me up, too, except I'm right here."

"And how do you feel about that?"

"About having come with you?"

"Yeah. Do you regret it, like you said earlier?"

"Not at all. In fact, until I just saw Reinhard, I had forgotten where we were going."

"Dave was always excited to get back to Stikine. He always had something he wanted to get done. He lived and breathed for the Union."

"He also had you. That made a difference in his life."

Susan made a sceptical face. "Obviously not one that mattered enough. So what'll be exciting for you back in Stikine?"

"Doing something about the dust. One of the presenters at the workshop said that the asbestos industry might be hiding evidence about the long-term health hazards of being exposed to the dust."

"That's what Dave thought," Susan said. "He was really worried about the Mill workers getting sick later in life. He called it a ticking time bomb in their lungs."

"And not just the Mill workers. The dust is everywhere."

"Does it worry you?" Susan asked.

Peter thought for a moment. "I guess I don't know if the Company will really do anything about it, or if Alex Bruce will agree to making it a top priority."

"That's not what I meant," Susan said. "Are you worried about your own health, spending all that time in Rock Reject, breathing in the dust."

Peter shrugged. "Oh, I don't know. I suppose not, but maybe I should be." He stared out the windshield at the white road and the endless forest. "What about you?" he asked.

"It's clean in the Administration Building. They make sure of that."

Peter laughed. "As clean as it can be. There's probably lots of the stuff floating around in there." He sank back in the seat and hugged his arms across his chest. "So what will be the attraction for you in Stikine?"

"A paycheque, I guess. I like my bunkhouse room. It's quiet. And it's not Winnipeg."

"I guess that's how I feel about Rock Reject," Peter said. "It's not Toronto."

SIXTEEN

It was minus five and it smelled like snow as Peter walked from the cookhouse to the Union office after dinner—January ninth and he wore just a jacket and no toque.

The door to the president's office was open, Chris Murton and Alex Bruce huddled in conversation inside. They didn't acknowledge Peter, so he poured a coffee and went into the back office to read over the materials from the Whitehorse workshop. At eight thirty he heard someone leave the trailer and a few moments later his door opened and Alex limped in, took a chair from alongside the wall and sat heavily across the desk.

"Chris is the new vice-president?" Peter asked.

"That's right. It was a close vote between him and George. Chris'll be good." He grimaced as he shifted in his chair. "Goddamn leg aches like hell when the weather's like this."

"What's the problem with it?"

"I was smashed up pretty good on my bike when I was a kid and it never healed right. Leg's a lot shorter than the other one now."

"Didn't you get proper treatment for it? Kids' bones heal pretty well."

"Proper treatment? I was a foster kid, Stevens. I was limping around doing grunt work on construction sites in Edmonton since I was four-teen." He grimaced as he shifted in his chair. "Ancient history crap. How was Whitehorse? And was that you driving into town with Susie what's-her-name? McGuinness's girlfriend."

Peter looked down at the desk and re-arranged some papers. "That's right. I ran into her at the hotel. She came back from her leave in Winnipeg. Anyway, she was driving back here the same day, so I thought I'd catch a ride with her. See the country."

"Nice."

"It's not what you think."

Alex said nothing.

"What the hell." Peter sat back in his chair. "Think whatever you want. What difference does it make?"

"I think a few things about that girl. But Dave had her figured out. He knew what she was up to."

"What do you mean?"

"I mean getting him tied down to the kids, house and picket fence scene. I mean clipping his wings. But maybe you don't want to be hearing these things, since you've been riding around the country with her."

"I don't know, it sounds to me like she was pretty good for him."

"That's a good one," he laughed and coughed. "She had her fucking head in the clouds about Dave. Thought she was some kind of saint that could save him from himself. A big mistake, thinking you can change someone."

Peter lit a cigarette. They stared at each other.

"The course in Whitehorse," Peter said. "There was a lot about legislation and safety regulations and the power of union reps on safety committees. But they didn't have much to say about environmental problems, like what to do about dust. So I want to sit down with you and maybe the rest of the executive to talk about a strategy for getting the Company to clean up this place."

Alex leaned forward in his chair. "Listen, Stevens. Getting this place all cleaned up like your mother's kitchen is a fucking pie in the sky fantasy. There's dick-all the Company's gonna do about it because it's so fucking expensive and most of the membership don't give a shit."

"That's not true. People care a lot about their health. Guys are quitting because of the dust, and Dave told me that he wanted to make it a priority."

"Dave's dead. Look, we won a new contract with a twelve and a half percent increase retroactive to November plus pension improvements plus stronger grievance procedures. That's what the Union's for and we've done a goddamn good job negotiating this deal. Mining is dirty work and we're getting paid for it and that's what people care about. If you think different, run against me next election."

Peter shook his head. "Alex, you're the president now, and I don't want your job. But how are you going to feel when people here start getting asbestos diseases? Think about that, because it's going to happen."

Alex studied Peter. "And what makes you so sure of that?"

"Jesus, look around here. You can't see a hundred feet in Rock Reject, the Mill's dusty as hell, it's all over the town and the valley. Of course people will get sick."

"But the scientists say it's not harmful."

"Why would you believe what the asbestos industry scientists say? Just think about it."

Alex's eyes lowered and his mouth tightened. Moments passed, then he pushed himself to standing. "As far as I can tell the stuff's not poison and nobody's dropping dead around here. So just do your thing with Iggy and make sure nobody gets their fucking arm ripped off in a conveyor or falls through another goddamn guard rail. We've got to keep people from getting killed here." He hobbled to the door where he turned to look at Peter. "You'd be the picket fence type," he said, then left the room.

Peter sat, angry, listening to the shuffling sounds of Alex moving in his office and back into the main room. The trailer shook as the front door slammed shut. A truck door opened and closed, an engine started and the sound faded away down the road. He shuffled together his notes and materials and put them on the corner of the desk, then put a clean sheet of paper in front of him and began to write.

Dear Dad,

Can you help me? People here keep insisting that there is no link between the chrysotile asbestos they mine and asbestos-related diseases or cancer. Could you possibly find any studies that establish a clear link? I could take that information to the Company and get them to take the problem seriously.

He looked at what he had written, then added:

I worry that people's health and lives are at risk here. I know you're busy, but if you can send me information it could help me get the ball rolling.

I'll be grateful for your help.

Peter

SEVENTEEN

"Who is it?"

He leaned against the crumbling brick by the front door, his mouth close to the intercom. "It's Peter."

"Stone. Well, well. What do you want?"

"I'm not sure. Just to see you, I guess."

He waited. A warm spring wind blew dirt and litter down Bathurst Street. Cars and a streetcar rumbled by behind him and he turned his face to the door, hiding. It opened as wide as her thin body.

"I'm surprised to see you," Luce said.

He shrugged and pushed his unwashed hair back off his forehead. "Can I come in? I feel kind of exposed standing here."

"Wouldn't want any of your parents' friends to see you slumming it, would we."

He shrugged again. She opened the door wider and he stepped in.

He didn't take his usual place on the couch, choosing instead a high-backed chair. She sat in her wicker chair and watched him stare at a vase of dried flowers on the coffee table.

"Are you wanting to buy?"

He shook his head. "Do you have anything to drink?"

"Wine?"

"Yes. Please."

Luce pulled the cork from a half-empty bottle and poured him a glass. He drank it down as she watched.

"You're needy."

"And you wouldn't be?"

She nodded slowly. "I'm sure I would. This is your test of fire. How will you get through it?"

"I don't know if I can."

"And your option would be…?"

"Some days I want to kill myself. Most days."

She looked at him. Into him, he felt, and she shook her head. She opened an inlaid box on the coffee table and took out a joint, lit it and took a toke. She waved it in his direction. He shook his head.

"Rose's parents hate me. I'm too ashamed to see my own." He watched smoke curl upwards from the burning joint. "I can't go on like before, that's all over."

"I always said you needed to split from all that family bullshit. Devout Mummy and Daddy and their dutiful doctor-to-be and the Sunday dinners in Forest Hill. I'm sorry it took this to make you see the light."

"Rose is the sorry one. I hear her voice all the time, like she's whispering in my ear."

"What's she saying to you?"

His jaw quivered and he wiped at his red eyes. "That she's afraid. That I left her." He struggled to push down the feelings rising up inside him. "That I cheated on her." The words were bitter in his mouth.

"All true. All bad." She leaned forward to stub out the joint. Her loose top sagged open and for a moment he saw her breasts. He closed his eyes and turned away. "So now what? How do you make amends?"

He opened his eyes to the psychedelic posters on the wall, their dizzying patterns disorienting, nauseating.

"I leave."

"Town, or the planet?"

"Whatever I've got the guts for."

"Go to be with Rose? Dust to dust?" She shook her head, her eyes softer. "I don't think so, Peter. It's not in you."

He ran a bath in the apartment, stepped in and lay back. The back of the tub was square, not sloped like the old claw-foot one in his parents' home, but his head rested comfortably on the blow-up pillow that Rose used.

It was deep and almost too hot to bear. Steam curled up from the surface, drops falling from the faucet made a small noise. He slid down so his ears were under water, where the sound of the drops was clearer. He heard water running in the pipes of another apartment, and then the sound of his heartbeat, which he tried to ignore but gradually it filled the tub, his ears, his whole body, until he sat up to escape.

His arms and hands were pink from the heat, the tips of his fingers wrinkled. On the edge of the tub lay his Swiss Army knife, open to the blade. A Christmas gift from whom? When? He had been smoking pot before arriving for gift opening the past several years and couldn't remember who gave what. Rose saw to those details. The blade was clean, almost never used, intended for camping trips they talked about but never made. He lay it flat against his forehead and felt its coolness against his flushed skin. Then on his cheek, the tip just under his eye, rotating it to feel its sharpness.

He raised an arm out of the water. Thin, long, the artery pulsing in the wrist, beads of water hanging from the hairs.

Is it in you?

He put the flat of the blade against the wrist to see how it looked, then searched in the steel for the reflection of his face. He could see pieces of himself: one eye, mouth, part of his nose. He twisted the knife, pretending to try and find other body parts, pretending not to feel the edge pressing into his skin. A thin line of blood appeared beneath the blade.

Did it hurt? I never asked. Were you afraid? I wasn't there.

He watched his blood creep down his arm to the elbow, then drop off the bone into the water, staining it pink to the edges of the tub. The hand holding the knife shook.

"Is it in you?" he screamed, his voice ringing off the tile walls. Pounding through the wall from next door was the response.

He threw the knife away. It stuck for a moment in the wooden bathroom door, then fell clattering on the tile floor. He covered his face with his hands and moaned.

Jolted out of sleep, heart pounding, breath coming in short gasps, he got out of bed to go to the bathroom but there was a wall where the door should be. He pulled open the curtains and saw snow up to the windowsill, not parked cars on St. George Street. He stood for a moment in the centre of his room pressing his palms into his eyes, vaguely aware that his pyjamas were sweat-soaked and cold. A door banged open and closed, footsteps thudded down the hallway. The clock said seven-thirty. Men were coming home after dinner. He started graveyard shift at midnight. He stood shivering until his head cleared of his dream. He dressed and went out.

He walked fast along the service road behind the bunkhouses, trying to throw off the shakiness he felt. People were filing into the Rec Centre to see a movie, and from fifty yards away he could see Susan in the line with Simon De Vleit beside her. He watched them standing together for a moment, then turned away and kept walking. Beyond the Rec Centre and the bar were the streets of private homes. Neat log bungalows with pickups in the driveways. He walked up one street and down the next, glancing through front windows into the lives of the permanent employees. Finishing their dinners, helping their kids with their homework.

He came to a t-junction at the top of the last street. To the left a road went past a yard with derelict trucks and heavy equipment, then on into the darkness of the forest. He turned right and the road curved past the Catholic Church, where a sign by the walkway said, "Saint Jude's, Always Open, Always Welcome." Tall and narrow, sided with wood, the building contrasted completely with the imposing stone greyness of Peter's parish church in Toronto. A faint light came through the window above the door. He walked up the steps and inside, sitting in the far corner of the last pew. A single lightbulb burned high in the ceiling, and in the murky light it seemed the crucifix was floating above the altar and the tabernacle. The shadowy image of the suffering Christ made him feel uncomfortable, and he closed his eyes to the statue, letting his head bow forward, hands folded in his lap, breathing in the familiar thick smell of incense still lingering from Sunday's mass. He felt himself drifting in the silence.

A sound startled him awake. Something loose in the wind or a tree branch scraping against the wall. He looked at Christ hanging on the cross, sorrowful eyes half open, half dead, looking down at him reproachfully.

He stood and walked up the side aisle to the metal stand that held the votive candles. Above it hung the first of the Stations of the Cross, a plaster relief depicting Jesus being condemned to death. He took a quarter from his pocket and dropped it in the offering slot, the sound of metal hitting metal sounding unnaturally loud in the empty wooden church. He struck a match and lit a candle in a red glass, then stepped back and watched the flickering light play on the scene of Christ's trial, animating the characters.

Jesus stood with his head bent, surrendering to his fate, his garments and the frond of palm in his hands seeming to move in the light as if a hot breeze had sprung up. Pontius Pilot's outstretched arm wavered up and down as he dismissed the defendant, telling him to go home and to stop causing trouble. The scribe and soldier shifting in the background, wishing for the morning to pass quickly so they could be sitting at their mid-day meal.

The scratching noise came again. Peter felt the hair on the back of his neck rise, and he turned to look at the closed door, the empty pews. He moved to the next station, which showed Jesus carrying his cross, bent by its weight, jeered by onlookers. In the third scene he is on the ground, fallen, being whipped.

Peter turned to the altar and the crucified Christ hanging above. The red light from the tiny candle played on the icon, highlighting the blood dripping from the crown of thorns and the nails in the hands and feet. "Jesus suffered for your sins." He heard his teachers in Catholic school, the parish priest on Sunday, his mother.

"I'll suffer for my own sins," he said, the words echoing off the high walls and ceiling.

EIGHTEEN

Peter came into the Rock Reject lunchroom and put his shovel and pick by the door. Michael Koopman sat with his feet up on a bench and his back against the wall. He looked up from his book.

"Since when did you start wearing a mask?"

Peter pulled the industrial dust mask off his face, the imprint of its edges remaining on his cheeks and forehead. Moisture from the condensation of his breath dripped off the end of his nose, and he wiped his face dry with the sleeve of his dusty overalls.

"Day before yesterday," he said as he sat on the bench opposite Koopman. He knocked the dust off the outside of his lunch bag and took out a sandwich. "I asked for one two weeks ago and it took that long to get it."

"You think it does much good?"

"I'm not blowing my nose and coughing up green for an hour after shift is over."

"I should probably get one to wear on my drill. It's fucking dusty as hell."

Peter poured coffee from his thermos. "How come you're in Rock Reject? Drill down again?"

"Third time this month." Koopman put his book in his knapsack and took out a package of cigarettes. "The production schedule is going all to shit. I heard there's a big shake-up in the works." He lit a cigarette and offered one to Peter who shook his head.

"I can't smoke in here. With the dust it makes my lungs burn. I should probably quit for good."

Koopman blew smoke rings into the air. "I'm afraid I like these too much to give up. If my life is short, what the fuck."

"If it's going to be short, you shouldn't be spending it in here."

Koopman looked at him sideways but didn't respond.

"What's this shake-up about?" Peter asked. "I haven't heard anything."

"I don't know details, but apparently the head office people aren't happy with the levels of production, especially since the new contract was signed. I guess they're not seeing twelve percent more revenue to match the twelve percent wage increase we got."

"Head office is where?"

"New York. Pan-American Asbestos is the parent company and it's been pretty profitable for a long time, but the markets are getting soft and expenses are rising with the high inflation. They were pretty pissed off with the big contract Miller signed here."

"How do you know all this?"

Koopman grinned. "I'm a shareholder. Just small-time of course, but I get quarterly reports on what the Company's doing." He flicked his cigarette ash onto the floor. "And it doesn't hurt that I work in the fucking ore pit."

"So are you going to be buying more stock?"

Koopman shook his head. "Sell, man. Christ, the way this place is run. For years they've been digging the pit down, going after the ore that's easiest to get at, and now it's too deep and narrow and they've got to spend a bundle to widen it from the top down. And I figure that sooner or later the shit's gonna hit the fan about asbestos disease, then the world market will really go south."

"They're talking about spending millions on dust control," Peter said. "They must think there's enough ore still here to justify that."

"If you ask me, that's just PR bullshit. It's one thing to build a new Mine and Mill and have dust control from day one, but to retrofit a place like this? Too expensive. Won't happen." Koopman stood up and stretched. "The future of this place is for shit, but for now the money's too good to leave."

He opened the door and stepped out. A load of ore was dumped into the jaw crusher fifty feet away, sending dust and deafening noise down the passageway. "I'm going for a walk," he shouted. "If the fore-man comes by, tell him I'm in the can."

The door banged shut, shaking the plywood room. A clump of dust dropped down from the ceiling and landed in Peter's coffee. He looked at the green flakes floating in his cup, then picked it up and flung the liquid against the wall. He removed the felt filters from the sides of his dust mask and knocked them against the edge of the table. A stream of dust fell from them to the floor. He snapped them back into place on the sides of the mask, then pulled it snug over his face. Taking his pick and shovel to a remote corner of Rock Reject, he continued digging away at twenty years of dust and conveyor spills.

NINETEEN

Peter sat outside Iggy's closed office door, holding a clipboard and a large envelope full of papers with his father's handwriting on the front, rehearsing in his mind how he wanted to begin the safety tour. "Before we start, Mr. Benedetti...Before we get going, Iggy...I want you to see these studies I've received." From the envelope he took out the single sheet of his father's letterhead paper that came with the reports and read it again.

Peter,

These are the most recent studies that I have been able to locate. As you will see, while chrysotile fibre is not as problematic as crocidolite or amosite fibres, nonetheless clear links have been proven between exposure to chrysotile and asbestosis and mesothelioma, as well as a variety of cancers.

I urge you to take seriously the long-term risk you are putting yourself under by working in that place. If you must continue, please try to limit your exposure to dust. And if you are still smoking, quitting would be wise. Cigarettes appear to increase one's susceptibility to the diseases by as much as five times.

I know you are struggling. I can imagine that you are having difficulty finding meaning for your life. Working for the health of others may provide you that meaning, but at the same time you must protect your own health. For your own sake, for the sake of those you may help in your lifetime, and for the sake of your mother and I who love you despite all that has happened.

Sincerely, Father

Peter read the words and heard his father's authoritative voice speaking them. He saw him at his desk in his study at home, his large hands folded on the leather desk blotter.

He looked up as Iggy came down the corridor, sorting through his keys as he walked. He looked tired and anxious. "Sorry to be late, Stevens. Couldn't be helped." He found the key to his office and opened the door. "We'll get going in a minute."

Peter glanced at his watch as he followed him into the office. Twenty after nine.

"I know it's late, sir, but before we start the tour I'd like you to have a quick look at these reports I received in the mail. I think they're pretty important"

"We're behind already. Why not leave them on my desk and I'll have a look at them later?"

"It's about asbestos and lung disease. Chrysotile asbestos. New reports released in the States."

Iggy gathered his clipboard and papers.

"Mr. Benedetti. Iggy. The asbestos dust here can cause cancer. Asbestosis, mesothelioma. It's been proven."

Iggy looked at Peter. "Where did you get these reports?"

"From my father. He's a specialist in lung disorders. Something has to be done here."

"I told you last month that the Company plans to spend a lot of money on dust control."

"And the Union president told me that it's been promised before and that nothing happens. People's health is at risk."

Iggy looked at Peter. His eyes were different, Peter didn't feel pushed away by them. Then he looked at his watch. "I'll read your reports, Stevens, but we have to get this tour done. We can talk about what's in them some other time." He turned back to his desk and his papers.

"Some time that'll never come?"

Iggy snapped the clipboard closed on his papers and looked out the window. "I said I'd read them, and I will."

"We'll start with the powerhouse today," Iggy said as they drove off in his pickup.

"No dust problem in there." Peter tried to make his voice light to soften the sarcasm.

Iggy didn't respond. His fingers drummed nervously on the steering wheel as he made the thirty second drive to the powerhouse. He parked in front of the entrance but didn't open his door.

"What do you know about asbestosis?" he asked.

Peter turned in surprise. Iggy was staring ahead at the blank wall of the powerhouse.

"It creates scarring in the lung tissue that can't be treated. Lung function is reduced and that causes chronic shortness of breath. The risk of getting it is related to how long your exposure has been, but it seems that even a minimal exposure can cause it."

Iggy nodded. "Is there a cure? Or is it..."

"There's really no cure, but it isn't always fatal. They can treat the symptoms."

Peter waited while Iggy sat motionless, his hands clenching the wheel.

"It's mesothelioma that has no cure," Peter added.

"Right." Iggy opened his door. "Let's get going."

They quickly toured the spotless powerhouse, then drove to the carpentry and sheet metal shops. At quarter to eleven they were on their way to inspect the laundry when they were waved down by a Mine foreman driving past them in his pickup.

"They've been calling for you on the radio, Iggy. There's been an accident behind the Mill."

"My radio's down. Any idea what's happened?"

"No, but it doesn't sound good."

"I'm on my way." Iggy turned around in the middle of the road and accelerated towards the Mill.

"That's crazy you not having a radio," Peter said.

"You're goddamn right it is. I've been waiting two weeks for a new one." He turned hard into the Mill parking lot. "Goddamn Company cost-cutting and the safety supervisor doesn't have a goddamn radio in his truck."

They drove around to the back side of the Mill. The ambulance, the RCMP cruiser and a group of men were bunched together. Iggy jumped out and ran up to the Mill supervisor.

177

"Carl, what's happened?"

"Two men were up on the swing stage fixing some loose siding. One of the cables gave way." His face was pale and his voice weak as he spoke. He coughed deeply and spat.

Two stretchers lay on the snow behind the ambulance, the doctor bent over one, a blanket covered a body lying in the other. Peter stepped forward to get a look over the doctor's shoulder. He saw Claude, his head moving side to side. The doctor finished giving him an injection and looked up to see Peter watching.

"A sedative. He was delirious."

"Is he badly injured?" Peter asked.

"I don't know for sure. It seems he was hanging by his safety harness for a while up there."

Peter looked half way up the side of the six-storey Mill. A swing stage dangled vertically, hanging at one end by a cable running up to the roof. Another cable hung limply from the roof at an angle. It went through a mechanism on the bottom end of the stage. An open safety harness hung from a ring on the stage's railing.

Four men were lifting the second stretcher into the back of the ambulance. Its weight shifted and the blanket fell away, revealing the face of George MacDonald. His neck was bent at an impossible angle and blood covered the side of his face and matted his hair. Peter breathed deeply to hold back his tears. Claude was lifted on his stretcher and slid in alongside George. The doors were closed. Someone got behind the wheel and the ambulance was gone.

Peter stared at the low, grey sky, his grief turning to anger then back again. Images of senseless death paraded through his mind; young car accident victims during his emergency room rotation, Dave McGuinness lying on the conveyor belt, Rose. He shook his head to clear away the memories, and went to join Iggy, Carl Moffat and the RCMP officer, who was writing in a notebook.

"Did the survivor say anything about what happened?" the officer asked.

"He was mostly going on in French," Carl Moffat said, "but it seems that the hoist got jammed on the left side, and MacDonald tried to free it up. He unhooked his safety harness to lean over the end when the hoist let go of the cable. He dropped straight to the ground."

"He unhooked his harness," Iggy said.

"That's right," Moffat replied. "And I told them both to be sure and keep them on."

The officer looked up at the stage, swaying in the wind, banging against the metal siding of the Mill. "It seems pretty straightforward. I don't see that I need to be involved in this. The Workmen's Compensation people will likely want to have a look at the hoist and the cable, so make sure it's stored the way it is and that nobody works on it. Otherwise, that's it for me."

"Thanks, John." Iggy said.

"Yeah, thanks," Moffat said, sounding relieved.

The officer put his notebook in his belt, walked to his cruiser and drove off.

"I guess I'll get some guys from Mechanical to take down the goddamn stage," Moffat said. He looked up at the wall. "Jesus, hardly any of the repair got done. The fucking siding's still all loose."

The three men looked up at the side of the Mill.

"So does that mean the mechanism got jammed right away after they went up?" Peter asked.

Moffat shrugged. "Maybe. Or maybe those guys were just doing fuck all the whole time they were up there."

"What time did they go up?"

Moffat looked sideways at Peter. "Who are you?"

"I'm Stevens. The Union safety rep." Peter looked at Iggy. "In fact, we're on the safety tour right now."

"That's so?" Moffat asked Iggy.

Iggy nodded.

"So what time did they go up on the stage?" Peter asked again.

"I guess about eight fifteen, eight twenty."

"We heard about the accident at about ten forty-five?" Peter asked Iggy.

"Yeah, roughly."

"So when was it discovered? Ten thirty?"

"What're you driving at, Stevens?" Iggy said.

"I'm saying that those guys were stranded up there on a stage that was jammed for what, two hours before anyone checked on them. And when did the thing let go? How long was Claude hanging up there looking down at his dead friend?"

"What difference does it make how long?"

"A man died here, for christsakes. What's wrong with you? Where was the supervision? Those guys were labourers, sent up on a piece of shit equipment with no-one around to keep an eye on them."

"I've got a whole fucking Mill to run. I can't be out here holding the hand of some idiot who doesn't have the sense to keep his safety belt on."

"Well someone should've checked on them, and you should've seen to it. They were your responsibility, goddamn it."

Moffat pointed a finger at Peter. "I'm not on trial here and I don't have to put up with this shit from a fucking rookie. The man was working unsafely and there's nobody to blame but him." He coughed and cleared his throat and spat into the snow, then turned and went into the Mill.

"I can't believe that guy. All he cares about is whether the goddamn siding got repaired," Peter said.

"It's called a dead man," Iggy said, looking up at the swing stage.

"What are you talking about?"

"That's what they call a swing stage. A dead man."

By the wall of the Mill underneath the hanging stage lay a red labourer's hardhat. Iggy picked it up and looked for a moment at a patch of blood-stained snow, then with his arm he swept clean snow to cover what George MacDonald had left behind.

"I never know if the families might want these or not," he said, holding the hardhat. His fingers slid over the cracked dent in its side. "I've had people write and ask for something they can have for their memories. Others are so angry they want to tear my head off."

"You've been through this often?"

Iggy nodded. "You get used to it. That's the goddamn problem."

They watched the stage sway in the wind, then Peter turned to look at the tailings pile at the far end of the Mill, twice the height of the building itself. A steady stream of crushed waste rock and fine dust dropped onto the top of the pile from the end of a conveyor belt. Wind from the west gusted, catching the falling waste and sending a plume of dust eastwards down the valley.

"Take a look at that," he said, pointing to the blowing dust and watching for Iggy's reaction.

"That's not supposed to happen."

"You know where that's blowing?" Peter asked.

"Of course I know."

They walked back to Iggy's truck. George's hardhat sat on the seat between them.

"What happens now?"

"I have to contact Workmen's Compensation, his next of kin, write a report." Iggy's voice was weary.

"What about blame?"

Iggy looked at Peter. "This was a tragic accident, Stevens. There's no point in us pointing fingers. We'll let Workmen's Comp take it from here."

"But will they come and investigate, or just go by what's in your report?"

"They may do either."

"So will you mention about them being unsupervised? Being left stranded up there with the hoist broken for all that time? There needs to be some blame here. Don't you think something should happen to Moffat, like being fired or demoted?" Peter's voice was shaking and he struggled not to shout in the cab of the truck.

"Carl's a good man, and I know he's torn up over this."

"He sure as hell didn't seem torn up to me. All he cared about was if the cop was going to ask tough questions."

Iggy's jaw muscles clenched under his lean cheeks. He took a deep breath and blew it out. "I'll talk with Carl and with Miller, the General Manager. Carl should've known better, but he's management so that makes it strictly Company business and the Union's not involved in what happens to him."

"I just hope you make sure that it's not swept under the carpet like the dust and health problems have been."

Iggy didn't respond. He started the truck and drove slowly back to the Administration Building. In the parking lot Iggy kept the motor running and the heater on full, his hands resting on the steering wheel. Peter stared out at the blowing snow.

"When does spring arrive up here?"

Iggy shook his head. "A long while yet. Late April, May. Do you think you'll still be here to see it?"

Peter shrugged. "I haven't thought much about it. What makes you ask?"

"Most men like you, single men, they leave when winter's over." He turned the key and killed the engine. The noise of the motor and the heater was replaced by the sound of wind whistling around the truck. Peter's hand was on the door handle, but Iggy made no move to leave.

"Do you fish, Stevens?"

"Fish? No, I never have. I'm a city boy. Toronto."

"That's what spring is for me. Fishing the lakes and rivers up here when the days get so long. My wife and I have a cabin on a lake." Iggy seemed far away. "It's beautiful there. So peaceful."

"Does Carl fish with you?"

Iggy shook his head. "No, it's just Lynn and I that fish together. Carl likes it here in town. Told me he can't stand the bugs."

A gust of wind rocked the truck. Peter looked at his watch.

"Your father. You said he's an expert? A specialist?"

"That's right, in lung diseases. Is there something specific you wanted to find out?"

Iggy shook his head. "No. Not now. I've got work to do for this accident report." He opened his door and got out, and Peter pushed his open against the wind.

"What about the rest of the safety tour?"

Iggy looked confused for a moment, then nodded. "Right. I'll be tied up with this for the rest of the day." He paused and his fingers went to his forehead, trying to recall something. "And tomorrow won't work. I'm busy. Just take this afternoon off and meet me here the day after tomorrow."

Iggy entered the Administration Building and Peter walked away into the snow. He stopped in front of his bunkhouse but couldn't bear the thought of the walls of his room, so he carried on, past the Union office, where he slowed and saw through the window people gathered, discussing the news of George's death.

He kept on going, past the cookhouse with men filing in for early lunch, past the bar, past the church and the family houses and the maintenance yard and into the forest and a half mile farther to where the road crossed a timber bridge to the other side of the river. He stopped halfway across and looked up the valley into the mountains, up the river of ice that curved out of sight into the forest a hundred yards away. Crows called in the silence, and from trees to Peter's right a pair appeared and flew up the valley, gradually disappearing into the haze of falling snow.

Under the bridge, the wind had swept the ice clean. He tried to see through it to the bottom, to see if anything moved, if water flowed, but the ice was fractured and cloudy, revealing nothing. He put a cigarette between his lips, but the sharp smell of tobacco hit him in the back of his throat and turned his stomach. He took it from his mouth and stared at it for a moment before crushing it in his gloved hand, then took the rest of the smokes from the package and tore them apart, letting the shreds of tobacco and paper be caught by the wind and carried out of sight beneath the bridge.

He waited outside the door to the dining hall until Susan came out from lunch, talking with one of the secretaries from the Administration Building.

"Hi."

"Peter."

"Do you want to go for a walk?" he asked.

"It's not my day off. I have to get back to work.."

"How about tonight then?"

Susan looked at him for a moment. "I guess so. Sure."

The door opened and Simon De Vleit came out. Susan gave him a thin smile.

"Are you free tonight, Susan? There's a cocktail party at the manager's house and I hoped you might accompany me."

"A cocktail party? Goddamn it, a worker was killed this morning at the Mill and management's having a party tonight? That makes me sick."

"Nobody's talking to you, Stevens. Back off." He smiled at Susan. "Well?"

"I'm sorry, Simon. If I had known earlier, but I can't make it now. Another time maybe." She looked at her watch. "I've got to get back to work."

The two men watched her walk away.

"I can get your ass fired out of here in no time, Stevens."

"Not without cause, you can't. You forget this isn't South Africa." Peter turned away and walked to the bunkhouse.

He slammed shut the door to his room and leaned against it, trembling with rage. His arms and shoulders grew tense, and he felt he could tear the sink from the wall and hurl it through the window. Pushing away from the door, he paced to the window and back, retracing the four steps again and again until he grabbed the pillow from his bed and threw it across the room with all his strength, then leaned against his desk, gasping for breath, trying to slow his racing heart.

He stood under the shower for a long time, letting the heat soak into the tension in his back and neck, letting his insides relax, letting soundless tears flow out of him and be washed away. He looked at himself in the steam-covered mirror: his face hidden beneath his beard, his eyes dark and red-streaked. From the bottom of his toiletries bag, he found the straight razor Rose had bought for him the summer they were married. The bone handle felt cool, the blade sharp, hardly ever used. He lathered his face and began the slow work of shaving off his beard.

At eight o'clock he knocked on Susan's door. She opened it and looked at him quizzically.

"You shaved."

"It's been a hell of a day. It seemed like a good time for a change."

"You seemed pretty changed today, the way you went at Simon. I didn't exactly appreciate being in the middle of that."

"I was angry. George was my friend and he was killed in an accident because of an idiot manager and then De Vleit with that cocktail party thing really pissed me off." They stood silently regarding each other. "So, are you going to invite me in, or should we go for a walk, or should I just bugger off?"

"You're not the only one who's upset, Peter," she said, giving him a look that made him pull back. She stepped aside and gestured him into her room with a sideways nod of her head. "Take off your coat. I just made tea."

Peter dropped his parka on the bed and looked around. "It's huge in here."

"Oh please, it's twelve by sixteen."

"Compared to what I'm living in, it's a goddamn palace." There was a hard edge to his voice.

Susan poured tea into pottery mugs. "This bunkhouse was originally put up for visiting management guys."

"Typical. Management gets everything laid out for them."

Susan put down the teapot and glared at him. "Jesus, Peter, if you're just going to stand there and be pissed off, then I'd rather you didn't stay. Go find a punching bag in the Rec Centre."

"Well I am pissed off," he said. "Everything about this fucking place. George dying today. Dave. It's all so stupid, and all over what. Goddamn asbestos." He grimaced, holding back grief as he shook his head, then he took in a deep breath and let it fall out.

Susan watched him, a hand around her tea mug. "Dave got so angry sometimes. It scared me, he'd be so worked up."

"I'm sorry," Peter said. "I hope I don't scare you."

Susan smiled. "You're not exactly his size, and I can't say you're the frightening type."

"I guess not," he shrugged. "You could likely take me out."

She pushed the empty chair towards him with her foot. "Come sit down before your tea gets cold."

Peter sat and brought the mug to his lips, inhaling the aroma of bergamot. "Earl Grey. Nice." He sipped the tea and looked at the posters and hangings on the walls. Over the bed was a wilderness image of rock and water.

"That's a Macdonald, isn't it?" he said, gesturing with the mug.

"Who?"

"J.E.H. Macdonald. One of the Group of Seven. I've seen the original in Toronto."

"Dave bought it for me when he was down in Vancouver."

Peter nodded, looking at the print.

Susan placed her mug carefully on the table. "George's death hit me really hard," she said. "It took me right back to the day Dave died." She shook her head and turned to Peter. "You knew George pretty well, didn't you?"

Peter nodded. "And Claude too," he said. "I hope he'll be alright."

They looked at each other across the small table. A nervousness grew inside Peter and his heart began to beat harder. His eyes slid away from hers and returned to the print on the wall.

"Rose and I had a Macdonald in the living room of our apartment. *The Wild River.*"

"An original?"

"God no. A print, like yours. A wedding present." He closed his eyes and saw Rose hanging it on the wall, the day after they moved into their first place. "It's been almost a year now since she died. Three more weeks."

"I can't believe how the time goes," she said. "Sometimes it seems like the day before yesterday that Dave was killed. Other times it's like years ago."

He put down his tea and looked across the room. An open closet was to one side of the door and he could see the edge of the skirt she was wearing when he saw her with De Vleit. The silence in the room weighed on him.

"What was the movie you saw on your date?"

Her hand paused bringing her tea to her lips, then she took a sip. "James Bond. *Live and Let Die.* Why do you ask?"

Peter shrugged. "Did you enjoy it?"

Susan put her mug on the table and folded her arms. "It was nothing special."

Peter's mouth went dry. "Why do you go out with him?" As soon as the words left him he wished he hadn't spoken them.

"Why do you think it's any business of yours?"

"What about Dave and what he stood for?"

"You didn't know Dave."

"I knew him enough to know that he couldn't stand De Vleit."

"Damn it, why are we having this conversation? Simon's a gentleman and he treats me with respect. I loved Dave, but there were some things he wasn't, and one of those was a gentleman."

"But De Vleit's a complete asshole. You should see him in action in the Mine. You should've seen his attitude with Dave's body lying on the conveyor. I can't stand the thought of him touching you."

"Touching me?" she said angrily. "What the hell makes you think I let him touch me?"

"Because you both get dressed up to go out. He probably takes you to his nice house. Why wouldn't he be after you?"

"He lives in a goddamn bunkhouse, for christsakes. He sends his money to his children in South Africa. His wife divorced him for someone else. And no, I haven't slept with him and I think you should probably go before I really get angry at you."

Peter stood up and strode to the bed where his parka lay, but spun around before reaching it. Susan was two steps behind him.

"I think of him touching you because it's what I want to do." The words came in a rush, before he could stop himself from saying them. Embarrassed, he couldn't look at her, and his eyes settled on an arrangement of dried flowers on top of her bookcase. For a moment they were the dried flowers Rose had arranged in their living room. In his head he heard the words I'm sorry, I shouldn't have said what I said, I won't bother you any more, but he knew his lips hadn't moved. He knew he hadn't taken a breath. Only his heart seemed able to move, beating hard in his chest.

Susan turned her back to him and went to the wall beside the door. Feeling he could breathe and move again, he picked up his parka from the bed.

"I should go now. Thanks for the tea." He waited for a reply while she stood, hugging herself tightly, looking down at the floor. People came down the bunkhouse corridor, their shrill laughter grating in the room's stillness. The front door banged shut, leaving only the sound of the hissing radiator.

Susan's arms slowly fell to her sides. "So do I," she said, her voice hesitant.

"Sorry?"

She turned to him and took in a breath as if gathering strength. "Want to." She looked at him, her eyes serious.

Peter dropped his coat and stepped towards her, reaching for her arm, his fingers shaking as they touched the skin of her wrist. He felt breathless again.

Her hands floated up to his face and her fingertips traced the line of his jaw. He shook as she caressed his new-shaved skin and undid the buttons on his shirt, resting her hands on his chest. The warmth made him afraid he would cry, and he took her hands in his and kissed them.

"They're beautiful, your hands," she said. She felt the calluses on the palms then turned them over and traced the tendons of the fingers up into his wrists. "They're strong and have character." She looked into his face, his eyes. "I think you do, too."

Her words sliced into him. He felt like a fraud. "That's not what I think."

"It's what I see."

With an effort he stopped himself from denying her words. He put his arms around her and hugged her close to the ache in his chest. They swayed slowly in the silence. She kissed the hollow in the front of his neck then leaned her head back to look at him.

"Have you been with anyone since Rose?"

"No. I just feel too much…"

"I know. Me too."

He looked at her lips, the bones of her cheeks, the line of her hair pulled back across her forehead. She stepped away and turned off the light. Streetlight filtered into the room through the thin curtain.

He watched her take off her sweater and pull her t-shirt over her head. Her shoulders were wide and square, so different from Rose's.

Her hands came around her back to unfasten her bra. Her braid dangled down her spine, then fell to the side as she bent over to step out of her jeans. He turned his back to her, his nervous hands fumbling with the buttons of his pants. He heard the bed creak as she got in, the sheets rustle as she arranged the pillows and blankets. He kept his underwear on and slid in beside her, then pulled them off and tossed them on top of his pile of clothes.

Their hands found each other, and their fingers laced together.

"You're sure?" he asked.

"Yes." She shifted onto her side. He turned to face her, tried to see into her eyes but they were hidden in shadow.

"Is it safe?" he said. His voice sounded too loud. "Sorry," he whispered. "I mean..."

"Shh. Yes, it is." She moved closer, putting an arm around his shoulder. Peter felt her breasts against his chest, her thighs against his. She put her lips to his neck, his collarbone. He smelled her shampoo. He thought it was the one that Rose used.

He ran his hand down her spine and over her hip. She did the same.

"Lie on top of me," she said.

They rolled together. She lifted her lips to his and he lowered his head to kiss her. Her arms went around him and held him hard, shifting her legs open for him. He squeezed shut his eyes and pressed against her, imagined being in her, but knew he couldn't.

"I'm sorry," he said.

Her arms let loose around him. Her head turned away and she bit her lip. Peter saw tears in the corner of her eye. "Don't worry about it."

"It's me," Peter said, shifting his weight off her. "I just can't... Maybe it's too soon for me. And George dying today."

"That's kind of you, but Dave couldn't either, unless he got stoned. He had lots of reasons why, too, but I'm the common denominator here." She rolled away from him.

"No, you're wrong. It's just that..."

"It's okay, Peter. I've heard it before."

"No you haven't, damn it." He sat up and leaned his back against the wall. "You don't know what's inside me."

"I'm sorry. I'm not Rose. Right?"

Peter pulled his knees up to his chest and leaned his forehead on them, hugging his arms around his legs. "No, you're not." He spoke into the dark cocoon of his chest, thighs and arms. "Rose didn't die from a miscarriage," he said.

Susan turned to face him.

"She died because of an abortion. Because I was afraid to become a father. Because I was afraid to confront our parents. Because I made her do it my way." He lifted his head and looked at her. "She bled to death because I was too afraid to get her to the hospital in time." He leaned his head back against the wall and closed his eyes. "That's why I can't make love with you."

Susan reached over and laid her hand on the top of his foot. He flinched at her touch.

"She died and it was my fault." His arms fell limply onto the bed. "Christ, there are moments even now when I'm certain that it's all been a dream and I'll wake up and be in Toronto with her." Looking at the MacDonald print above the bed, he saw himself in the scene, alone, arms outstretched, offering himself to the wilderness. A shudder ran through him and he felt suddenly agitated. "I should go."

"It's not late, if you want to stay and talk more."

"I don't want to bother you any more tonight." He slid across the bed and sat on the edge.

"If you were bothering me, Peter, I'd tell you to go."

He stared down at his naked thighs. "I feel a million miles away. Like I'm on the moon." He pushed himself up and got dressed. Susan came to the door in her bathrobe.

"Listen," he said, "I just want you to know that… if things were different…" Tears gathered in his eyes and he wiped them with his sleeve. "God, I wish they were different."

He leaned forward and kissed her, then left.

In the dark of his bunkhouse room he lay in bed, listening to the wind driving snow against his window. He wondered what the weather was like in Toronto, if it was like last March, cold and miserable and dirty from the winter, like the day of the funeral. Or was there an early spring and the snow all gone.

He closed his eyes and saw the dangling swing stage banging against the Mill wall. George's bloody face. Rose in the hospital. His heart pounded and he opened his eyes again. By the light coming under his door from the hall he counted the holes in the ceiling tiles. After four hundred he drifted away onto a river and was standing in a canoe as it slid through a rocky Group of Seven landscape, his arms stretched wide and warm rain in his face. Susan sat in the front saying something to him. He heard her voice but couldn't make out the words.

TWENTY

Peter stood in the hallway, in front of the door to their apartment. Inside his coat pocket, his hand held the key but he was unable to make his arm move to bring it out. He knew Rose was inside since the newspaper wasn't by the door. He pictured her at the table in the kitchen reading the note he left for her that morning. The door to the apartment next to his opened, and he forced a smile at his neighbour, who stepped out to pick up her paper.

"Mrs. Jenkins, hello."

She shook her newspaper at him. "I don't appreciate the racket you two were making last night. Yelling, throwing things. I've a mind to report you to the superintendent."

"I'm sorry." Peter looked down at the worn carpet. "We'll try to be more quiet from now on."

She glared at him. Peter got his key into the lock and went inside.

He was shaking as he took off his coat and hung it on the stand. "I'm home," he called weakly.

"I'm in here." Rose's voice came from the kitchen. He couldn't tell her mood from its tone.

He stood in the archway that connected the living room to the small kitchen. Rose sat at the dinette table facing him, her hands on the Formica surface, on top of his note. The dozen yellow roses he bought after she left that morning sat in a vase in the centre.

"The flowers are nice," she said.

"They're drooping a bit."

"Did you crush the bottom of the stems?"

"No, I didn't think to do that. They haven't opened up yet. The guy in the shop said they'd last longer since they were still closed."

Rose leaned forward and smelled the buds. "Not much fragrance yet. Maybe in a few days."

She smoothed her hands over the note. Peter felt weak and he wanted to sit, but he wasn't sure if he should. The refrigerator clicked on and rattled through the first five seconds of its cycle, then settled into a loud hum.

"What am I supposed to make of this?" she said finally, picking up the note. "Why should I believe you?"

"I…" Peter gestured with his hands. He felt like he was standing on a ledge, trying to find something to cling to. "I don't know why you should, but I hope you can. I've really screwed up, I admit it." He felt himself tipping over the edge. "I hate myself because of it. I mean it that I'll stop smoking dope and that I won't see her again. I just want us to be happy like we used to be. Believe me. Please." He was sweating. "Do you mind if I sit down? I feel kind of weak."

Rose pulled out a chair, ran him a glass of water and sat back down. "You're pale."

"I'm scared."

"What about?"

"That you won't say yes. That I've ruined everything."

"But what am I saying yes to? Peter, I'm pregnant. Remember?"

"Of course I know that. But…but not now. I can't be a father right now, I'm not ready." He looked into Rose's eyes, and he saw fear. "Later, I promise you, but first I want us to do things together. Just you and me. Travel, move away, be different than we are here in Toronto."

"Back to that again."

"Well why not?" The words burst out of him and Rose flinched. He took a deep breath to calm himself. "I'm sorry. I didn't mean to shout but I'm just so anxious."

"I don't care if you shout. At least you're being real with me. But I can't cope with hearing about how you want to run away to Mexico or wherever while I'm in the condition I'm in." She looked down at her hands. "Truthfully I'd want to have the baby. And even more truthfully I wonder if you'll ever feel ready to have a family." She picked up his note again and held its edges with the tips of her long fingers. "But I'm not having a kid on my own, and…" She looked at his face for a moment and her eyes softened. "And as much of an asshole as you are I don't want it to be over for us, and if that means we have to do something about the pregnancy, then I guess it's what we have to do."

Their eyes locked on each other's. Rose's image became blurry and he blinked to make it clear.

"I've never seen your tears before."

He wiped his eyes with the back of his hand. "I can't remember the last time I had any."

She put a hand on his forearm. "I don't like this, Peter. And my father won't like it at all."

"Your father? God, you can't tell him."

She pulled her hand away. "What are you talking about? He's got admitting privileges at Toronto General. He'll make the arrangements. Don't you know how hard it is to get an abortion?"

"He'll freak out, that's what he'll do. Your mum will know, my parents will find out. Christ, my folks are so devout the bishop and the Pope will know. They won't let us get away with it, guaranteed."

"I've always confided in him."

"That's been easy because you've always done what they wanted." He slumped back in his chair. "Except for marrying me."

She rolled her eyes. "Poor Peter, the outcast."

"It's true, and this would be the iron-clad proof for them that I'm bad for you." Rose shook her head. He took a sip of water. He wanted to reach for the bottle of rye under the sink but didn't. "I talked to someone on faculty and he told me about a clinic in Buffalo. It'll cost a bit but there's no questions asked."

"Buffalo? Damn it, Peter, why would I want to go there?"

"Because no-one will find out."

"But what kind of a place is it? I'd feel much safer here at the General."

"I know, sweetheart, but we just can't. I'm sure this clinic will be fine and we can come home the same day." He laid his hand on hers. "And we can pretend that nothing happened."

They fell silent. The fridge cycled off and the only sound came from the dripping kitchen faucet. Rose slid her hand from under Peter's and sat up straight in her chair, staring into the living room. Her chin quivered. Peter tried to touch her arm but she pulled it away. Tears rolled down her cheeks and fell on her sweater. She folded forward onto her arms, and he hesitantly laid a hand on her back. She began to sob, silently at first, then loud as it came up from deep inside her. She blindly reached for his hand and squeezed with a strength he had never felt from her before. He shifted his chair alongside hers and leaned his head on her shoulder while she cried.

"I wish we were staying the night in the hotel by the clinic," Rose said as the bus left Buffalo. "I don't feel up for this trip."

"The sooner we're home the better." Peter's stomach ached from anxiety. He could smell the acrid odour of his own nervous perspiration. "Then we're there in case your parents call and besides, the operation already cost a lot."

"I've got terrible cramps."

Peter shook out two of the painkillers the clinic gave them. "These'll help. Lie across my lap and I'll rub your back. It's not a long ride."

"I'm worried about all this blood," she said as she crawled into bed. "Don't you think it's abnormal?"

"I don't think so." He willed his hand to stop shaking as he dabbed her forehead with a cool cloth. "Remember what they said at the clinic. You should expect bleeding for a few days."

"But this is so much."

"It is a lot. We'll see how you are in the morning. Maybe a good night's sleep is all you need. Do you want a couple more pills?"

"I'll have one." She grimaced as she sat up to sip water. Peter helped her back down and tucked the blanket under her chin. "I wish I could call my father. He's always looked after me."

Her face was pale on the pillow, her long hair dull. "I'll look after you now." He kissed her on the forehead. "You'll feel better in the morning, guaranteed."

He closed the bedroom door behind him and leaned his head against it. His heart pounded in his ears as he listened for any sound from Rose, then went into the kitchen and took the bottle of rye from under the sink. He watched his hand shake as he poured a glass half full.

The roses he bought for her days before were drooping, a few petals lying on the Formica surface. His note to her leaned against the wall, held up by the saltshaker. He drank the whiskey, swallowing down his feelings as it burned down his throat, then went to the hall for his book-bag and sat at the table to study.

He brought her toast and tea the next morning.

"Are you feeling better?"

Her eyes were half open. "Maybe. I'm not sure. I had to change pads twice in the night. They were soaked through."

"I didn't hear you get up."

"You were dead to the world."

He put the tray on her bedside table and sat on the edge of the bed.

"Has the bleeding stopped, or slowed down?"

"Slowed, probably. I don't think it's stopped."

He put the back of his hand on her forehead. "You feel a bit warm."

"Only a bit. I think I'm fine. You've got an exam today, don't you?"

"I can miss it. I think maybe I should stay with you today."

Rose shook her head. "No. Go write your exam. I can look after myself today."

"But you've lost a lot of blood. I should stay."

"Peter, go. I don't really want you around right now. I need some space."

Her jaw was set, her eyes red. Peter felt empty.

"Are you sure there's nothing I can do?"

Rose shook her head. He stood up and looked out the window through a gap in the curtains. Hard pellets of snow blew past bare branches. He turned back to Rose.

"I'm sorry." He felt the words coming from someplace new inside him.

"I know, Peter. Close the door behind you."

At four thirty he entered the apartment building and climbed the two flights to their floor. He heard the phone ringing as he came down the corridor, searching in his pockets for his key. As he unlocked the door, Mrs. Jenkins's door opened.

"Your phone's been ringing steady all afternoon since they came for her. I haven't had a moment's peace."

"Since who came for her?"

"The ambulance people, of course." She looked pleased to be the first to deliver bad news. Peter pushed open the door and went in while she kept talking. "Took her on a stretcher. She looked pretty bad, I'd say." He let the door slam behind him.

The phone had stopped ringing but he picked it up anyway and listened to the dial tone for a moment, then put it gently back on its cradle. The lights were off, but the curtains were open and the streetlights on St. George let him see around the apartment. He lost sense of time passing, of breathing. The bedroom door stood open and he felt like he was moving underwater as he went into the room.

The sheets and blankets were on the floor in the shadows. The tray with untouched toast and tea sat where he'd left it on her bedside table. A swath of streetlight fell across the bed. He was shocked when he saw the size of the stain it revealed, in the spot where Rose had been lying in the morning. The nightdress she was wearing when he kissed her good-bye was on the floor near the door. He picked it up and felt the sticky damp that covered its back side.

He went to the kitchen to see if there was a message on the table. Only the roses, with more of the petals dropped. Nothing else changed from when he had sat there the night before.

The bathroom light was on and it shone under the closed door. He pushed it open and saw towels lying in the tub, smeared dark with blood. The tile floor was dotted with dark spots, and as he turned he saw a trail of them leading back to the bedroom.

The strength went from his legs. Jesus, how could I have let this happen, he asked the empty room as he fell back against the wall and slid to the floor, barely able to breathe. His eyes wandered around the room and stopped at the framed print on the wall behind the couch. He always said its name to himself whenever he looked at it and he heard the words now. *The Wild River.* J.E.H. MacDonald. The silent sound repeated in his mind as he took in the reds, greens and oranges of the hill, the two pines tilting through the foreground, the barest glimpse of blue water calm before the rapids, two streams of foam tumbling past an island of rock and heading somewhere.

The phone rang again. He struggled to his feet, crossed the living room and reached for it with his hand shaking.

"Hello... Mum. I... I just walked in the door. I had an exam... I can see, there's blood everywhere. How is she? Is she all right?... I'll be there as fast as I can."

He hung up. He wasn't sure he could walk or even keep standing, but he forced himself to move, to go to the hall and put on his coat and stumble out of the apartment. He walked unsteadily along the corridor, through the fire doors and down the stairs. When he got to the sidewalk he started running down St. George, pushing his way through the stream of people heading up from the university to the subway entrance. He was sweating and breathless when he reached Bloor Street where he waved down a cab.

Peter's father met him when he entered the Intensive Care Unit. The severe look on his face made him afraid.

"Come with me," he ordered, and led Peter to an empty office and closed the door.

"Rose's condition is grave. I want you to tell me what has happened to her."

"I'm... I'm not sure," Peter stammered. "I saw the blood in the apartment. Maybe it was a miscarriage. She's been pregnant for a while. We were waiting to tell you until..."

His father's hand came up to stop him. "That's enough. Rose has told her father about the abortion and how advanced her pregnancy was. I wanted to see if you were prepared to tell me the truth."

Peter wanted to look away but he was held by his father's eyes.

"Making her pregnant yet being unwilling to accept parenthood, choosing a very risky late-term abortion as a way to deal with your problem, going to a clinic across the border on the sly to avoid telling your parents. And now lying to me to try and cover up what you've done." He shook his head in disgust. "You disappoint me in every way, Peter." He turned towards the door.

"What exactly is her condition?" Peter asked, his voice weak and shaking.

"Extremely serious. It appears that the abortionist didn't remove all the fetal tissue and she's hemorrhaged as a result. She's been given blood, but her clotting factors have become diluted. She continues to bleed." He turned to face Peter. "If she had been treated sooner she wouldn't have lost so much blood," he said angrily. "How could you have left her alone in the apartment in her condition? How could you have been so irresponsible?"

"She told me she'd be alright. I had an important exam to write."

"And that was more important than your wife's well-being."

"That's all that's ever been important to you." Peter's voice rose. "My becoming a doctor. What else from me have you ever cared about?" He stood with his hands clenched, glaring at his father. "Your marks aren't good enough, Peter. You have to go to medical school, Peter."

"It's what you said you wanted," his father replied.

"I just wanted to be like you." Peter wanted to shout the words, but they came out strangled.

They stood looking at each other. Sounds from the hospital world came through the door. Peter wished he could close his eyes and lean into his father, be held by him. "I know I screwed up. It was one mistake after another. Getting pregnant, going to Buffalo, leaving her alone. I was going to write the exam then come home and take care of her."

His father paused. Peter heard him sigh. "What's done is done." The voice was sad, soft. Peter turned back to him.

"Does Mum know what happened?"

"No and it should stay that way. Her miscarriages affected her so deeply that to hear that this is the result of an abortion …"

"I know Dad," Peter interrupted. "I want to go see Rose now."

His father nodded. Tears filled his eyes and he dried them with his handkerchief. "I'll get you a gown."

From behind the nurses' station he took a gown and helped Peter put it on, then led him to Rose's room. He looked intently at his son, as if committing his face to memory before saying goodbye, before opening the door to let Peter step through.

Rose's father stood at the foot of her bed, making notes in a chart. He glanced up when Peter entered the room, looking at him coldly before turning back to the chart. A nurse removed an empty bag from an I.V. pole, replacing it with one full of a clear solution. A half-full bag of blood also hung from the pole. Tubes from both snaked under the covers. A heart monitor by the bed beeped in time with each upward spike on the screen. Peter knew the beeps were coming too fast, the spikes on the screen too close together. The nurse leaned over the bed tending to Rose, blocking his view of her.

Dr. Linwood finished his notes and put the chart in its holder. "I'm stepping out for a few minutes," he said to the nurse. "I'll be in the waiting room with my wife."

He stopped in front of Peter on his way to the door. "I always feared you wouldn't take care of my daughter." He gave Peter a look of contempt, then pulled open the door and left the room.

The nurse put a blood pressure cuff around Rose's arm. Peter's insides trembled as he took a few wobbly steps toward the bed. The nurse made a note on the chart, then turned to Peter.

"You're her husband?"

Peter tried to answer but he couldn't seem to form a word. He nodded instead.

"I'll give you a couple of minutes with her. She's very weak, so don't expect her to talk."

The nurse left. His knees shaking, he moved a chair to the side of the bed, sat down and hesitantly put a hand on her arm.

"Rose, sweetheart." His voice was a dry whisper. "It's me."

She rolled her head towards him. He was shocked by how she looked. As pale as the sheets, lips cracked, eyes dull. Had she looked like this in the morning? Was he so blind as not to have seen? She whispered something.

"Don't talk," he said. "Save your strength to get better."

"I had to call," she said, the words barely making it past her lips. "To Dad." Her eyelids slid closed. "Don't be angry at me."

"No, never. You did the right thing."

She opened her eyes again. Peter watched tears gather and spill out. They rolled over her cheekbones and down onto the pillow. "I always thought we'd have a baby."

Peter felt like he couldn't breathe, his chest and throat like they no longer existed.

"We'll have one, I promise. We'll make a family once you're better."

He took her hand in both of his and leaned his head onto them. His mind spun and he let himself believe he was in a dream. He felt out of his body, somewhere up high in a corner of the room, when an alarm sounded in the heart monitor, jolting him upright. He looked at the screen and saw the lines spiking downward. The door crashed open and the nurse came in.

"Move," she ordered, shouldering her way to the bedside.

Peter looked at the monitor and saw the spikes were gone. The line was irregular, up and down without a pattern. He stared at it unbelieving until the nurse pressed a button on the wall and spoke into a grille beside the bed. "Code blue. Room eight three three." She turned to Peter. "You have to leave."

Peter stared at Rose. He couldn't move.

"Now," she commanded.

He stumbled backwards, taking a final look at Rose before opening the door. He collided with Dr. Linwood as he rushed in to see to his daughter.

TWENTY-ONE

Photo portraits of Stikine's general managers graced the walls of the second floor of the Administration Building. Thomas Miller, manager for five years, sat in thoughtful profile, his thick neck looking confined in a shirt and tie. Peter studied the weathered face, the eyes that seemed clear and certain, so like his father's eyes. He turned from the portrait and checked his watch again, wondering if he had the day wrong, when Iggy came up the stairs. He looked blankly at Peter.

"Stevens?"

"Yes," Peter said, surprised, then his hand came up to touch the side of his face. "I shaved."

"Oh, I see." Iggy walked towards his office and Peter followed. "What brings you here?"

"The safety tour. You told me to be here this morning."

Iggy paused for a moment, then unlocked his office. "Of course. Come in."

He sat behind his desk and arranged a few papers. Peter took in how grey his hair was. He looked as if he'd had very little sleep.

"The accident the other day," Peter said. "Is everything done?"

"Yes. The report should be typed by now and the body's on its way to the airport." He rubbed his hands over his face and through his hair. "I spoke with his mother in Cape Breton. She had another son killed in a coal mine out there a few years back." He shook his head. "I can't imagine how she must feel."

Peter looked out the window at the grey sky, sadness filling him. "Could I have her address?" he asked.

"Well, normally it's not permitted, but I don't see the harm in you writing to her."

"No, not to her. George had a son. I want to write a letter to him."

"That's kind of you, Stevens."

"He needs to know that his father loved him and thought about him all the time. He's only eight. He needs to know that."

"Yes, I'm sure he does"

"Is Claude Savard still in the infirmary?" Peter asked.

"Yes, he'll be there another day or two. No serious injuries apparently, but it was pretty hard on him hanging up there for that long."

"I wonder if he'll go back to work here?"

Iggy shrugged. "He'll get his airfare back to Edmonton if he leaves."

"Will he get any compensation for the accident?"

"Not unless there's some permanent injury that keeps him from working."

"Jesus, don't you think he deserves something for what he went through?"

"If he deserves something according to the Workmen's Comp regulations, he'll get it." Iggy shuffled papers on his desk. "If not, there's nothing I can do about it. I don't make the rules."

Peter shook his head. "That's not fair." Iggy didn't respond, just kept looking through papers. A half minute passed. "So what about the safety tour?" Peter said. "Are we getting it done today?"

Iggy looked at his watch. "Right, yes." He flinched as the phone rang on the corner of his desk. He let it ring again before picking it up.

"Iggy Benedetti. Yes. Would you hold on a second please." He covered the receiver with his hand.

"This is private. Give me a minute alone."

Peter waited in the corridor for fifteen minutes, then listened at Iggy's door. No voice, no movement. He knocked gently but heard no response. He opened the door a crack and saw him at his desk with his head in his hands.

"Hello? Sir? Are you okay?"

Iggy looked up. His face was even paler than before. Peter took a hesitant step into the office.

"Close the door," Iggy said, then swivelled in his chair towards the window. He pulled tissues from a box, wiped his eyes and blew his nose.

"My wife is ill. She has a lung problem."

"I'm sorry." Peter waited for Iggy to say more, but he didn't. "What's the diagnosis?"

"They're not a hundred percent sure. There are possibilities..." Iggy's voice trailed off as if he ran out of air.

"Such as..."

Iggy didn't answer.

"Is it asbestos related?"

Iggy seemed in a trance. "It's just not possible. The asbestos here isn't supposed to be harmful."

"That's just Company bullshit," Peter said angrily. "Didn't you look at those studies I gave you?"

"They always told us those studies were biased."

"You mean you've seen those reports before?"

Iggy took a deep breath and let it out slowly. "Like I said, we were told they weren't to be believed."

"What the hell else would the Company tell you?" Peter was shaking as he looked at Iggy. "And you just went along with that lie and fed it to your wife and everyone who came to work here."

"She didn't work here." Iggy's voice was pleading. "She never set foot in the Mill or Rock Reject. Her exposure would've been nothing at all."

"For christsakes, the dust is everywhere, and you don't need much exposure to it to get sick."

Iggy shook his head, his face a picture of misery. "This job has gotten us what we've wanted. I'll retire and we'll spend our time at the cottage. That's been our dream, and now what?" He looked up at a knock on the door. "Come in."

Susan stepped into the office carrying a file folder. She smiled when Peter turned to her, but the smile fell away when she saw the anger on his face.

"Here's the accident report and two Xerox copies."

"Thank you Susan." Iggy's voice was weak.

She turned towards the door. Peter tried to catch her eyes, to work up a smile, but she didn't look his way and left the room.

Iggy held the report in his hands.

"So who gets the blame in there?" Peter said. "Have you been the good Company man? Let Moffat off the hook and blamed George for his own death so the Workmen's Comp premiums won't go up? Christ, only the victims are responsible around here."

"Carl Moffat isn't off the hook. He's meeting with Miller and the personnel manager this afternoon, and this will go on his record. And for your bloody information I've made recommendations about supervision that I intend to see put in place. Someone got killed and it shouldn't have happened. Is it blood you're after now? An eye for an eye?"

"No, goddamn it." Peter flung out his arms in frustration. "Just blame. Someone's guilty. Blame them. Punish them."

"I suppose you think I'm to blame that my wife's sick."

"Yes," Peter said angrily.

Iggy stood up quickly. His chair banged into the wall behind him. "I've had enough of this." He planted his fists on his desk and leaned forward. "I'm asking you for your father's help for my wife. If you can't give me that, then get the hell out of here."

Peter looked into Iggy's eyes. He saw himself with his father in the hospital, with Rose dying in a bed down the hall. He felt again the gaping hole in his chest that he felt that day.

"I'm sorry," he said, shaking his head. "I've got no right to say those things. I'll write to my father."

Iggy straightened and went to the window. His hand went to the back of his neck and he rolled his head, trying to loosen his tight muscles. "Do you think he can help her?"

"He might. He'd for sure know what was possible, and he'd need to see all her information. X-rays. Specialists reports. Does the doctor here have all that?"

"No. She's been seeing a doctor in Watson Lake. The Company might have access to files in the Infirmary here and we don't want word of this to get around."

"Why not?"

"Because they'd find a reason to fire me then. It wouldn't look so good to have the safety supervisor's wife get asbestosis."

"I can't believe they'd do that."

Iggy shrugged. "I don't trust that they wouldn't."

"You could take them to court."

"Maybe that's what happens where you come from."

Peter felt his ears flush hot. He looked down at his hands. "Can you get me copies of all the documents of her case?"

Iggy nodded. "Lynn can drive up there tomorrow and get them." He went back to the desk, picked up the accident report and offered it to Peter. "Do you want to have a look at this before it gets sent to Workmen's Compensation?"

Peter took it and looked at the cover page. Company letterhead on top: Stikine Asbestos Corporation. Report of Fatal Accident, March 23, 1975. He looked at Iggy.

"Does it need a Union signature?"

"Not unless the Union challenges it."

Peter looked to the window again. Patches of pale blue were pushing through the clouds. "Is there anything in it that would affect payments to George's family?"

"No." Iggy's voice seemed far away. "I made sure of that."

Peter handed the report back to Iggy. "I trust what you've written."

Iggy put the papers into the file and looked at Peter. "And the blame you wanted?"

Peter shrugged. "I suppose there's been enough misery already. Besides, the way Carl Moffat coughs, I think he's going to need all the help he can get."

Peter waited at the bottom of the stairs while Iggy gathered his materials for the safety tour. He hoped he might see Susan, might get a chance to tell her how he felt. He saw her come out of an office down a hallway and he raised his arm, cleared his throat, but she didn't look his way before vanishing through another door. Iggy came down the stairs from his office.

"Let's try to be quick with the tour, Stevens."

"You're sure you want to do it today?"

"I want it done. I don't want something else hanging over my head."

TWENTY-TWO

The turnout for the March Union meeting was small. "With the new contract, nobody's going to give a shit," Alex Bruce had told Peter. "We can tear through the agenda and get out of there pretty quick."

Peter sat at the end of the table at the front of the half-full gymnasium in the Rec Centre, nervously waiting to give his report. A group of new hires sat near the front, listening intently as Alex spoke. Other members in the room seemed to be paying little attention, perhaps too tired from battling the relentless cold. Dan Grandison sat with three other native men in the back row.

Alex ended his executive report by giving the bargaining committee a pat on the back for the gains made in the new contract, then called on Peter to give the safety and health report. Peter opened a file folder that contained his notes and stood up, gripping the folder tight to quiet his shaking hands.

"We've had two deaths here recently, and neither should have happened." Those who had been dozing in their chairs suddenly came alert and looked at him. "Obviously there are risks in mining, and everyone needs to take responsibility for making sure we finish our shifts without getting hurt, but the biggest hazard in this place isn't what killed Dave McGuinness or George MacDonald. It's the dust, and it's a ticking time bomb in our lungs that can kill anyone of us sometime down the road."

"What the hell are you basing that on?" Spencer rose from his seat in the second row. "That kind of talk can shut a place down."

"Well maybe that's what needs to happen." Peter felt lightheaded as he carried on. "Maybe that's what has to happen to get the Company's attention."

"Wait a goddamn minute." Alex was on his feet, glaring at Peter. "You can't go advocating a work stoppage over this."

"Alex is right. Where's the proof?"

"There are studies that show a clear link between our asbestos and cancers and other lung diseases," Peter said. "And if our health isn't worth fighting for, then what is?"

"Our jobs are, for christsakes. If you're so worried about the dust, then you can wear a goddamn mask."

"I do," Peter replied. "And so should everyone who works in the Mill or Rock Reject or anywhere else where there's fibre. But who's going to wear one when you're in your bunkhouse or living in the Reserve?" He glanced at the men at the back of the room.

"The Reserve?" Spencer said derisively. "What's this got to do with them?"

"I've been out there," Peter said defiantly. "There's dust all over their land. It's in their homes. Their children play in it and we should take responsibility for stopping the pollution."

"If they're so concerned, they can move. And you can move with them, for that matter. I'm happy to put up with some dust that probably won't harm me a bit."

Alex Bruce shouted for order. "Everybody calm down." He looked at Peter. "And I mean everybody. It seems that Stevens here has some new information about health that nobody's heard before, so before we get excited we need to find out if it's all correct. A lot of these studies aren't worth the paper their printed on."

"These are from scientific journals."

Alex glared at Peter. "Like I say, we need to take time and assess these claims. There's too much at stake to go off half cocked."

"There's too much at stake to do nothing about the dust. People are getting seriously ill in town and in the Reserve. They may even be dying."

They stared at each other for a moment, then Alex raised a hand to Peter to stop the discussion. He turned to face the room.

"Let's nobody get excited. I'll contact the Union head office and see if they can clarify this for us, and we'll let everyone know what they have to say. And maybe like Stevens says, if anyone's working in a dusty area, you can get a mask to wear. I think that should take care of any possible problems." He gathered his papers into a file folder. "I think that covers everything, so the meeting is adjourned."

There was a dull roar of discussion in the room as people got up from their chairs and headed to the doors, directing looks of concern or anger towards Peter as they left.

"In my office, tomorrow morning," Alex said to Peter as he shoved his file into a briefcase.

Peter reached into his backpack and took out copies of the asbestos reports that his father had sent him. "You should read these, Alex. That's all I'm saying."

Alex looked at Peter for a moment, then took the papers and put them into his coat pocket. "Tomorrow morning," he repeated, then limped to the door.

Peter watched him leave, and turned to see the three new employees standing near the table, waiting for his attention.

"We've only been here a week," one said. There was something of a wild look to his face. "We're up in Rock Reject and after what you've said I wonder what we need to do to protect ourselves."

Peter ran a hand through his hair. "I should say this to myself as much as to you, but get out of there as soon as you can." The three men smiled. "Until then, get masks," he continued, "and don't work for long stretches of time. Sucking air through the filters strains the lungs, especially when there's so much dust in the air. Take lots of breaks." He stood up and put on his coat. "And do get another job. Rock Reject is hell on earth."

The three men looked at each other. "I'd say that's pretty accurate," one said. Peter nodded and left the room.

Outside the Rec Centre he looked up at the sky. The cold air burned through his nostrils and down his throat. The aurora pulsed above, shimmering southward, alive above the black mountains. Dan Grandison and his friends stood by a pickup, also watching the sky.

Peter went over to them.

"Beautiful, isn't it?" he said.

Dan turned to Peter and offered his hand. "You're going after the dust. That's good."

"I'm not sure how much good it'll do, but maybe something will come of it."

Dan turned back to the sky. "I've read how the old people in the Nordic countries thought that the aurora happened when the gods were angry. I think they would be pretty angry at what's gone on in this valley."

TWENTY-THREE

On his way to the Union office in the morning Peter checked his mailbox in the post office. Inside was a thick envelope addressed in his father's handwriting. He stood at the window in the weak sunshine reading the note that was attached to numerous photocopied pages.

Peter,

I'm pleased by your request on behalf of your colleague's wife. It has been my hope that the tragedy of Rose would transform you into someone who will be devoted to others. It appears that you are heading in that direction.

I have enclosed outlines of the latest treatment options for asbestosis. You will see that there is no treatment method that can reverse the existing damage to the lungs. However, further deterioration can be prevented and symptoms can be alleviated with proper treatment. I would be happy to examine her and recommend treatment if she were to come to Toronto.

Your mother is well and sends her love.

Sincerely,

Your Father (Dad)

Peter looked at his watch. Alex was expecting him in the Union office, but he was anxious to put the information in Iggy's hands. He left the post office and went to the Administration Building.

Susan was on the phone at the reception desk and as Peter approached he saw that she had cut her hair. She finished the call and turned to him.

"Your braid is gone," he said.

Her hand went to the back of her neck. "Yes. It was time for a change. Isn't that what you said?"

His hand went to the side of his face, fingers sliding over three days' stubble. "I'd better shave again before my change gets undone. It looks good on you, the short hair."

She smiled. Peter's mind tumbled with things to say but nothing came out.

"I'm pretty busy. Is there anything you wanted?"

"Oh, sorry. I wanted to see Iggy for a minute."

"He's in a meeting with Miller and Carl Moffat, but it might not last much longer. If you can wait a bit you might catch him then."

"Right. I will, yes."

Susan turned to her work. Peter remained by the desk, watching the back of her neck, the movement of her hands. She glanced up at him.

"Go sit down, Peter. I can't work with you standing there."

He flushed with embarrassment, "Oh, sorry," and went to the end of the reception area to wait.

A door opened down the corridor and Carl Moffat emerged. He walked past Peter and out of the building, a look of anger on his flushed face. A moment later Iggy appeared and Peter stood up, holding the papers from his father.

"Do you have a few minutes?" he asked. "I have some … ideas I'd like to run past you."

Iggy glanced back to see Miller coming out of his office and towards them. "I can't this morning," he said. "I'm busy with meetings." He wrote on the edge of a page on his clipboard, tore it off and folded it twice. "Here's a time when I'll be available." He handed the paper to Peter, then turned to the stairs and went up to the second floor.

On the steps outside the building Peter opened Iggy's note. It was an address, followed by "7 p.m. tonight."

He stood on the edge of the road, facing south and the sun that had now inched over the crest of the mountains, feeling its warmth on his face. He turned to the north and the white wall of mountain on the opposite side of the valley, brilliant in the late winter light. He followed the crest, sharp against the blue sky, along to where its edge was broken by the excavation of the mine pit. Buckets of asbestos ore, tiny in the distance, floated out of the bottom of Rock Reject and drifted down the slope on the tramline. A truck's air horn honked behind him and he stepped up onto a muddy melting snowbank to get out of the way of a semi, fully loaded with bags of pure asbestos. It rumbled out of town and Peter wondered where the fibre was going and how many lives would be shortened by it.

Alex was sorting through papers on his desk when Peter knocked on his open door.

"How about getting us both a coffee? My goddamn leg is killing me today."

Peter nodded and went to the sink. "Do you take creamer?" he called out as he poured the coffee.

"Black. That creamer shit'll kill you. Nothing but chemicals."

Peter paused and shrugged at the irony, then carried the mugs into the small office. They sat across the desk from each other, drinking in silence. A heavy vehicle drove past, shaking the trailer with its vibrations. Alex put his mug on the desk and leaned forward on his elbows. His complexion looked pale and unhealthy in the overhead florescent light.

"Listen, Stevens. I know you probably think I'm a real sell-out, that I just go for the money in the contract and ignore the other stuff. See, you're a smart kid, got lots of education, got high ideals. It's easy for you to want to rock the boat and demand they cover the tailings pile and clean up the Mill and Rock Reject so you can eat off the floor because it wouldn't matter a goddamn to you if the Company said screw you all and closed down the whole fucking operation because of what it would cost. You've probably got a well-off family back home and being here is just play for you. Now me, I'm just a working slob and a practical union guy and I got a lot at stake being here."

"So you're telling me to shut up?"

"I'm telling you to play ball. Team ball. You're a rookie. A union isn't about some guy firing off on his own agenda. I didn't appreciate what you said in the meeting about shutting things down here. If things are going to change on the health front, there's gotta be a strategy."

"Strategy? But all you've ever said to me is that health doesn't matter, that people only care about their paycheques."

Alex leaned back in his chair. He nodded towards the file folder on the desk. "I read those reports you gave me last night. They're pretty convincing."

Peter nodded.

Alex reached for his coffee mug, swirled it and drank what was left. He looked out the small dirty window. "You needed to be pretty tough, growing up where I did. Limping around like a cripple."

"And fighting for the health issues isn't tough."

Alex shrugged. "It's not dollars and cents. A lot of the guys working here are young, they think they'll live forever, never get sick."

"Is that what you think?"

"I'm not young, Stevens. And like I said, I've had to be tough. You've likely got no idea what it's like to be poor, or to lose something you care about."

"Alex, you don't know the first goddamn thing about me or where I come from."

"Fair enough, I'm a judgmental bastard."

"Or what I've been through, for christsakes."

Alex raised his hands in surrender. "Okay, Christ Almighty. So I don't like where I *think* you come from." He leaned back and looked at Peter for a moment. "But I'll put that aside because I think that you're probably right. We need to make health a priority." He opened a side drawer in the desk and took out a mickey bottle of rye, poured a splash into his mug then offered the bottle to Peter, who hesitated a moment, then took it and poured some in with the rest of his coffee. Alex raised his mug.

"To controlling the dust."

Peter raised his. "And keeping the place open."

He left the Union office at noon but wasn't hungry and could think of no place he wanted to be. He wandered away from town, past the Administration Building and down a slushy service road he hadn't been on before that led to the town's large satellite dish. From inside a concrete hut beside it he could hear the audio of the noontime television show the dish was receiving. He listened for a minute to a discussion about land claims that natives were making in British Columbia, then continued along the narrow road through a stand of spruce to where boulders had been pushed into a pile alongside the river, and found a flat one to sit on.

The river was wider here than upriver at the bridge. About seventy-five feet, he thought. In the middle the ice was shifting, breaking, heaving up in jagged sections and slowly moving downstream. At the edge of the bank the ice had pulled back and a patch of clear water reflected the sun. He sat for half an hour, breathing in the clear air and letting the shimmering light play on his face until the sun slid behind a mountain peak, leaving him in its cold shadow.

TWENTY-FOUR

He hadn't known that the streets in town had names, but as Peter walked along the slushy road after dinner he saw small, weathered signs attached to the power poles. The third street was Cassiar, and he turned right. Halfway down he saw Iggy's white pickup in front of a neat-looking home and he went up the walk.

The house was a pre-fab like all the rest. The exterior looked like logs laid lengthwise, smooth and varnished and overlapping at the corners. Curtains were pulled tight across the picture window in the front. The door was a bright green.

Iggy answered and welcomed Peter inside. "Thanks for coming by, Stevens. Take off your boots and come into the kitchen."

While unlacing his Kodiaks, he looked into the living room at the wall-to-wall carpet, the coffee table with books piled neatly at the edge, lampshades with plastic dust protectors. Glass shelves were mounted in a corner of the room, holding carved figures that were lit from above. Jade, Peter thought. He put his boots on a tray next to two pairs sitting neatly in line, took the envelope from his coat pocket and went through to the kitchen.

"Stevens, this is my wife Lynn."

She half rose from her chair at the end of a dinette table, smiled and shook Peter's hand, then sat down again. She looked older than he remembered, from when he'd seen her outside Iggy's office. Her face was lean then; it seemed almost gaunt now under a short haircut.

"It's good to meet you," she said, her voice tired. "Iggy has told me about you. Have a seat, please." Her hand slid over to her husband's and gave it a squeeze. "Why don't you pour him a cup of tea?"

"Or a beer instead?" Iggy asked.

"Tea's fine." Peter glanced around the spotless kitchen. He thought of his mother's kitchen, three times this size, and how cold and distant he felt the last time he was in it. He felt warm and comfortable sitting here.

Beside the fridge an open doorway showed a room with a workbench and carving materials. "Are those your pieces on the shelves in the living room?"

"Yes," Lynn said. "It's what I love to do. Are you interested in jade?"

"I've only seen a few pieces before. Dianne—Bob O'Neil's wife out in Crystal Creek—I've seen a few of her carvings."

"She's very good. I taught her some basic techniques a year or so back and now she's doing wonderful work." Lynn paused for a moment to catch her breath, then went into the workroom and took a carving from the bench. "Here's something I just finished yesterday."

She placed the piece in front of Peter. Three inches across, six inches high, open through the centre, it twisted and looped back on itself. The veins of the stone snaked through and around the shape of the carving. He picked it up and felt its smoothness.

"It's beautiful. Is the shape symbolic of anything?"

"No, it just emerged like this. I've been playing with shapes that are open, which is a real challenge. On this one I mostly let the veins of the stone dictate the shape."

Peter rotated the carving slowly between his fingers. "Have you ever seen sculptures by Henry Moore?"

"No, but I've seen books about his work."

"In the Art Gallery of Ontario there's a room of full of the casts he made for his bronze sculptures. This piece of yours reminds me of them because the whole feel of it changes as you look at it from different angles."

"Isn't life like that," Lynn said with a twisted smile.

"My wife the philosopher," Iggy said as he put cups of tea on the table.

"But it's true," she said. "Look at us. Everything about our life here is changed because of my health."

"Except being able to afford to leave," he said as he sat down.

"We managed alright when we left Vancouver."

"We were younger then." Iggy's eyes looked strained. He rubbed his forehead with his fingertips.

"True. But we'll manage again."

Peter sipped his tea and put the cup down. "You're both from Vancouver?"

"That's right," Lynn said. "I was born there, but Iggy came when he was little."

"From Italy. Milan. I was all of three when we came to Canada."

"How did you meet?"

Lynn looked at Iggy. "Talk about starting over," she smiled.

"It's true," Iggy said, taking her hand. "I was working for B.C. Forest Products downtown and in comes this beautiful woman to work there. A few months later I'm completely in love with her. The problem was that I was already married to a nice Italian woman and we had two kids." Iggy smiled at his wife. "Everything changed for me after we met."

"We had to leave Vancouver," Lynn said. "So we went to Trail where Iggy worked for Cominco in the smelter. Then for a few years at Tumbler Ridge in the coal mine before coming here for the last, how many years now?"

"Eleven. And this was supposed to be it until retirement, and now we just don't know."

They sat without speaking for a minute, the wheeze in Lynn's breathing audible in the still kitchen.

"This is the treatment information my father sent," Peter said, taking the papers out of their envelope and laying them on the table. "But I think the most important thing is for you to go to Toronto and have him examine you. He'll be able to determine the exact extent of the disease and then you can go from there. In the meantime, you should probably do all you can to avoid any more exposure to the dust."

"We've wondered if Iggy's been bringing it into the house on his clothes."

"That's right," Iggy said. "The Union people change in the Mine Dry, but management wear their work clothes right into the house."

"And you go all over the Mine and Mill on the safety inspections," Peter said.

Iggy took Lynn's hand. "This goddamn place," he muttered.

"Well, here's our chance to go to Toronto," Lynn said. "It'll be our vacation. We'll go see that room of Henry Moore sculptures and maybe they'll help us see things differently."

"The only thing I want to see is you healthy again," Iggy said, placing his hand on hers.

At the door, Iggy offered his hand. "Lynn and I appreciate what you've done. But please remember to keep it to yourself."

Peter nodded. "You can trust me." The words echoed in his head as he left the house and walked along the road. They sounded strange to him. He hoped they were true.

TWENTY-FIVE

The doctor leafed through the copies of cancer studies that Peter had just given him. Peter waited, his eyes roaming the desk and settling on a small photo frame standing to one side, two children in a plastic splash pool grinning gap-toothed for the camera. In the background were fences, suburban homes and deciduous trees, a scene from a world far removed from Stikine. The doctor's chair creaked loudly as he closed the file folder and leaned back.

"Nothing that I see here surprises me. Can I keep the file for a while and go over it more closely when I have the time?"

"I made that copy for you. I was hoping that we could get you involved with the Union's push for some real dust control."

The doctor shook his head. "I have to stay unofficial. The Company's my employer and it's in my contract. If I went public over any issue I'd be fired as fast as the last doctor."

"What happened? Did he say things about the dust?"

The doctor eyed Peter for a moment. "You haven't heard this from me, but he sent a letter to Indian Affairs in Ottawa about the dust in the Reserve. He was backing up the petitions from the Band, and when the Company saw his name on the letter, he was gone."

"When did this happen?"

"About three years ago. The Company started promising to clean things up, said they were allocating money to do it…" He sighed and shook his head. "You can see for yourself where things stand."

Peter nodded. "Well, hopefully some real change is coming. Are you sure you won't consider standing up on the issue? It would put a lot of weight behind it, and it must scare the Company to have their own doctors speaking out. If they come after you, we can make an even bigger stink about it."

The doctor shook his head. "I'm not a community spokesman. And I'm not a martyr either. I treat the people who work here, and that includes those from the Reserve. And if it means anything to you I've sent information on asbestos disease to the leaders in the Reserve."

"Can you send these studies to them as well?"

"Yes, I will."

They looked at each other and Peter nodded at the photo on the desk.

"Nice looking kids."

The doctor turned to the photo. Peter watched his face, saw his eyes change and his mouth soften into a smile. "Yes they are." His voice seemed far away. "They're wonderful kids."

Peter stood to leave, pausing halfway to the door. "I know of at least one person here with asbestosis."

The doctor turned in his chair to look out at the dirty snow piled up outside the window. "There's more than one, I can tell you that."

TWENTY-SIX

Peter climbed the steps of the trailer and opened the door to an uproar inside the Union office. The table was crowded with members of the executive and shop stewards from various departments, and a few looked angrily at Peter as he stepped into the room and hung up his coat.

"There's a fucking wildcat strike in the Mine, Stevens," said a bear-like sheet metal worker from the mechanical shop. "And it's over the goddamn dust shit you've been stirring up."

Peter took a chair at the end of the table. "What're you talking about?"

Alex came out of his office. "Some labourers in Rock Reject. The day shift foreman found them sitting drinking coffee in the Mine office just after nine. They told him that they were allowed to take breaks every hour because of the dust. Foreman tells them to get their asses back shovelling. They said they had the backing of the Union health official and to go screw himself." He stared hard at Peter for a moment before continuing. "So these yahoos go stand in front of Rock Reject to keep the trucks from dumping ore, and convince them to shut down over health violations. No trucks, no mining."

"Goddamn truck drivers'll shut down over anything," the sheet metal worker said.

"This is very fucked up." Bukowski slapped his hand on the table. "Sure it's miserable fucking work in Reject, but where did this take a break every hour bullshit come from?" He looked down the table at Peter, who sat and said nothing. "I take your silence as an admission."

"I don't want to waste time talking about how we got here," Alex said. "We have to decide where we want to take this. We need to see it as an opportunity."

"An illegal walkout is an opportunity?" Bukowski said, shaking his head. "That's quite a stretch, Alex."

"Why not?" Peter said. "We've got the Company's attention. Now's the time to make them live up to all the promises they've made in the past to clean up the place."

"Or at least to get them to stop the bullshit and make some new promises that they'll keep," Alex added.

Excited, Peter leaned over the table. "So let's get clear on what our demands are going to be."

"Slow down, Stevens," Alex said. "We're not in a big rush here. The Company's going to wait and see how this plays out today and tomorrow before calling us in to talk."

The sheet metal worker folded his arms and leaned back in his chair. "That's for sure. We'll see if the afternoon shift is as anxious to lose their pay as the day shift was. If they go in to work, there goes your opportunity."

"*Our* opportunity," Peter said. "We're all living in this shit together."

His heart pounding, Peter entered the Mine Dry at ten to four, before his shift was to go up to the Mine. Some of the miners were dressed for work, others not. All were huddled in groups talking about the wildcat strike. The window into the management office was open with De Vleit inside, watching what was happening. The man-haul bus pulled up outside.

"This strike makes no sense to me." Spencer stepped to the front of the group. "It was started by some idiots and should never have been supported in the first place. I'm going in to work and put an end to this bullshit."

A few men muttered agreement and made movements towards the door. Peter stepped into their path.

"Jesus Christ, Spencer, I thought you were a Union man. You come to all the meetings. And here you won't give up a day's pay to back a fight for improvements on health."

Spencer looked at Peter with disdain. "If I thought that this was the right way to do things I'd be in support of it. But for now, you can get out of my way."

Peter stood his ground. "Goddamn it, this is wrong. There's a strike on and we can't just let it collapse without gaining anything. We have to keep this going and get something real from the Company."

"He's right," someone said from the back of the crowd. "I'm going to stand with the day shift. It's about fucking time they did something about the dust."

The men in the crowd looked at each other and began nodding in agreement. Spencer gave Peter a condescending smile. "Well done, Rock Reject. You earn your solidarity badge today. Now excuse me, I'm going to work." He shouldered his way past Peter and went alone out the door.

Peter watched Spencer climb onto the bus, then turned to the room to see the men from his shift changing out of their mining clothes. He smiled and touched the arms of a few that passed him on their way out the door.

De Vleit watched from the inner office. "I hope you've enjoyed your time here, Stevens."

TWENTY-SEVEN

In the Union office the next morning, Peter and Chris Murton, the vice-president, were discussing the strike when Alex came out of his office.

"Call just came from management. They've got a couple of senior people flying up from Vancouver and they'll be ready to meet with us at two o'clock."

"So let's start listing our demands," Peter said.

Alex nodded. "The health stuff is your department, Stevens. What do you want to see happen?"

Peter took a file folder from his backpack and pulled out a sheet of paper. "I did this up last night but didn't get a chance to make duplicates. I've put down the obvious ones at the top, dust suppression in the Mill and Rock Reject, and increased break times for people digging out all that crap in Rock Reject. I've also included having all employees perform a lung function test, so that there's a basis for determining if someone's lungs are harmed by working here."

"That's good," Chris said. "Otherwise it would probably take an autopsy to prove that asbestos has harmed you. It'd be a bit late by then."

Alex nodded in agreement. "I say we go for a Union-management committee on dust control. That way we can make sure the ball keeps rolling on the issue."

"Great idea," Peter said. "And we can't forget the big issue of the tailings pile and how the dust blows off it from the stack piler."

Alex shook his head. "I say no to that. We're not going to push that issue now."

"But what better opportunity will we get? Work is shut down and the Company's sending in their bigshots. They're scared."

"They're not scared, Stevens. This is an illegal strike and they hold the cards here. We need to put reasonable demands on the table and dealing with the tailings pile goes too far."

"So the health of everyone in the town and down the valley doesn't matter. That's going too far, in your mind."

"That's what I said. We'll get what we can now, the things they've already promised and done fuck all about 'till now. The other stuff will have to wait until the contract expires. Maybe then we can get help from the Department of the Environment on the tailings business. But for now, we keep it simple."

Chris Murton cleared his throat. "So, is that it?"

Peter sat back in his chair and folded his arms. "Okay Alex. Whatever you say."

"Except of course for the standard demand in a wildcat," Chris said. "That nobody gets disciplined for any of the actions."

"That's right," Alex said as he gathered his papers and stood up. "No disciplines, no firings. We meet at the Administration Building at two." He limped into his office and emerged a moment later with his coat and briefcase, and left the building without another word. Chris stood up and nodded to Peter. "See you then, Stevens.

Peter nodded and managed a smile. He felt the trailer shake as the door closed, then sat listening to the tick of the electric heaters, the hum of the bar fridge. He looked around the dismal room, at the notices taped to the dirty panelled walls, the velvet tiger staring with its nicotine-yellow eyes, a calendar with photographs of mining equipment tacked above the sink full of dirty coffee cups. He got up and paced the room, an agitation growing inside him, tightening around his chest, a feeling without a cause he could name.

He took his empty coffee cup to the sink and filled it with hot water. He felt dizzy, like his legs might buckle under him, and he gripped the edge of the counter for support and closed his eyes to catch his breath. He opened them to stare unseeing at the calendar in front of him until a photo of a D9 bulldozer came into focus. He had lost track of the date, his time had become measured by the hours in Rock Reject and by the rotations of his shifts from days to afternoons to nights. His gaze slid down the calendar to the days of the months of March, where someone had put a neat X across each day past, each day closer to something. His breathing stopped as he saw today's date, as he realized that the day before marked one year since Rose's death.

He fought with his memory, pushing against images of her at the end and searching for those of her smile. A sadness that was almost unbearable flowed through him as he saw her skating on the frozen pond in High Park, spinning, her arms and hair flung out to the sides. Happy. We were happy, and if I hadn't…

He cut himself off, brought himself back to the room, to Rock Reject, to the strike. He went into the back office and from his wallet he took the slip of paper with Theresa's phone number in the Reserve.

"Theresa, it's Peter Stevens. I thought you might like to know about a situation here that your people may be able to take advantage of."

TWENTY-EIGHT

Sleet plastered Peter's hair and ran down his neck as he entered the Administration Building at a quarter to two. Susan was at the reception desk. She laughed as he shook the wet off the shoulders and back of his coat.

"You look like an old wet dog."

He smiled and imagined sitting with her in her room, drinking tea. He wanted to tell her about the anniversary of Rose's death, about how the weather was the same today as it was then, about his phone call to Theresa, but instead he smiled and shrugged, and she reached into a cabinet under her desk and produced a roll of paper towels.

"This will get the worst of it out of your hair," she said.

"Thanks. It's miserable out there." He wiped his head and neck and handed back the roll. "Did the bigshots make it in from Vancouver?"

Susan nodded. "They're meeting with Miller now." She turned to see if anyone was nearby, then leaned towards Peter. "Things are really tense," she said in a whisper. "Miller's not what I'd call happy."

The front door opened and she bent to her work. Peter turned to see Alex and Chris come in out of the weather, and he went to join them.

"You can provide the details, Stevens," Alex said as he took off his coat. "But remember what we said about the tailings."

"Whatever you want. I'll follow your lead."

The door to the conference room opened. Miller came out and went to Susan's desk. "Any message from Iggy?"

"Nothing yet. But he knows about the meeting, and I'll send him in as soon as he arrives."

Miller's face was tense. He ran a hand through his grey hair and beckoned the Union men to follow him into the room.

At the far end of the long table were the two Company men from Vancouver. Miller took a seat next to them, but turned his body away. Simon De Vleit and Carl Moffat were also at the table. Peter followed Alex and Chris and took a chair next to them. He was trembling as he placed his notes on the table. He folded his hands in his lap to hide his nervousness.

"Good afternoon gentlemen." The man at the head of the table appeared calm. His accent was English, but softened, Peter thought, by his time in Canada. "I'm Marshall Whitmore, the vice president of Canadian operations for Pan-American Asbestos. To my right is Gerry McMillan. He's the head of our labour relations department."

McMillan nodded. His three-day beard looked carefully trimmed, as if he always wore a three-day beard. Whitmore leaned forward and looked at Alex.

"Needless to say I'm not happy to be here. We signed an extremely generous contract with the Union just a few months ago, and now the place is shut down for what seems to me to be trivial reasons. I am sure you know that we will not hesitate to seek an injunction against this illegal walkout, and we will proceed with that this afternoon if we can't resolve this situation here and now." He paused and took a sip of water. "Now I understand that a few of your members, apparently acting on the advice of a Union officer, decided to re-write the rules regarding hours of work. They decided they could take breaks whenever they bloody well felt like it. I ask you, gentlemen, how can we run a mine when people feel they can do whatever they want?"

"Rock Reject is a hell-hole," Peter said, trying to keep his voice calm.

"And you're paid fucking good money to work in there," De Vleit growled.

"As if that's all that matters," Chris said.

"Mr. De Vleit's point is valid," Whitmore said. "I want to know the Union's justification for this action."

"We want this thing settled as soon as possible, just like you do," Alex said. "But it's time the Company lived up to the promises you've made about controlling the dust."

"Dust control projects for the Mill and Rock Reject both have the green light," Whitmore said.

"You've been saying that for years," Chris said, "and it's time to stop the bullshit. When is this going to happen?"

"Implementation has been slowed due to world prices for the commodity," Whitmore said. He gave a sideways look towards Miller. "And due also to your extraordinarily generous contract settlement."

The door opened and Iggy came in. He gave a terse apology for being late and took a chair beside Carl Moffat.

"Prices for asbestos?" Alex said incredulously. "We all know that you can get whatever price you goddamn well want for Stikine asbestos. There's nowhere else that has fibre anywhere near as long as here."

"The amount of high-grade product coming from Stikine is dropping," Whitmore said. "In fact all production is down."

"So you're punishing the Union for bargaining hard?" Chris said. "You pull back on money that would keep us all from getting cancer and asbestosis?"

"Whoa, hold on," Gerry McMillan said. "Who's talking about cancer? This walkout is about some pussies who can't work for more than an hour without taking a break."

"No," Peter said. "This is about the long-term health of everyone here. The whole community. We need to have everyone's lung function tested to establish baseline data. Then it'll be clear that it's the dust that makes people sick."

Whitmore looked at Peter. "I would have thought, Mr. Stevens, that when you were hired on here, recently I imagine, that you would have been told exactly what is mined here." He nodded towards Iggy. "Surely Mr. Benedetti explained to you that chrysotile asbestos is very different from the other, very dangerous types and that there is little cause for concern for anyone living and working here."

Peter glanced at Iggy, who sat with his arms folded, his mouth drawn in tight.

"How can you say that?" Peter said. "There is a clear link between chrysotile and these diseases."

"There is hard, scientific evidence from McGill University that backs me up, that's why I can say that," Whitmore said, a hard edge to his voice. "And I'm not about to debate it with you."

"Goddamn it. Let's get to the issue," De Vleit said. "Why do those guys think they're entitled to a schedule like that?"

"Because it's a strain on the lungs," Peter said. "You can't do that kind of heavy work steadily in those conditions, breathing through a dust mask with the filters clogged with dust or frozen up or both. It's not healthy."

"This isn't a goddamn health spa," McMillan said, toying with an expensive looking fountain pen.

"That's pretty easy for you to say," Alex said. "I don't see any dirt on your hands."

"Or fibre stuck in your lungs," Chris added.

McMillan let go of his pen and folded his arms across his chest.

"Alright," Whitmore said sharply. "I want this sorted out. I don't think it's unreasonable that the men digging in Rock Reject get two additional breaks each shift to clean their masks and get fresh air. It's your jurisdiction, Simon, what do you say to that?"

De Vleit shrugged. "If they would actually work the rest of the time instead of fucking the dog, we'd probably be further ahead."

Whitmore looked at Miller. "Any problems with this, Tom?"

"Would it matter if I did?" Miller replied. Whitmore gave him a sideways glance, then turned to the Union men.

"So, will you get this place back working with that guarantee?"

"No discipline, no loss of pay for anyone," Chris said.

"No discipline, but absolutely loss of pay for the time missed."

"And we want a say," Alex said. "We want a committee to oversee the changes that need to be made and we want equal representation from the Union on it."

Whitmore shook his head. "You can't be serious."

"Goddamn right we are. There's gotta be assurances around health. This is about more than rest breaks in Rock Reject."

"Very well then," Whitmore said. "This meeting is over." He pointed a finger at Alex. "And make no mistake, we will get an injunction and we will seek heavy penalties if this fucking wildcat isn't resolved very soon. You will be contacted when we are prepared to continue."

The Union men stood up to leave. Peter looked at Whitmore. "Don't you know that there are people with asbestos disease in this valley? People who have never set foot in Rock Reject or the Mill. That's the truth about your Mine." He glanced at Iggy, saw the grim look on his face, then turned and left the room.

TWENTY-NINE

Peter left the cookhouse after dinner and walked into a wind blowing heavy, wet snow. He had in mind a hot shower and the quiet of his bunkhouse room, but light from the window in the president's office of the Union trailer drew him up the wooden steps and inside.

It was dark in the main room, except for the small red light of the coffee maker by the sink and a narrow rectangle of yellow light that fell on the dirty linoleum under the door to the president's office. Peter crossed the room and shut off the coffee maker, pouring the hours-old dregs into the sink, wincing at the bitter, burnt smell. A chair creaked in the president's office. Peter listened for voices but heard only the sound of wind against the trailer. He went to the door and knocked gently.

"Come." Alex's voice sounded weary. Peter went in.

A mickey bottle of rye was on the desk, a cigarette burned in an ashtray. Peter took a chair. "I didn't know you smoked."

Alex stubbed out the smoke. "I don't, really. Just now and again, when things get to me." He took a drink of whiskey from a glass and offered the bottle to Peter, who shook his head. The wind shook the trailer.

"Weather's a bitch this time of the year," Alex said. "I'll take forty below any day."

"Is that what's getting to you?"

"Part of it. Got a call from Whitmore an hour ago. They want us there at nine tomorrow. And he told me that they've done a big shake up. Miller's out."

Peter nodded. "I was wondering about that today, the way he was acting. Will De Vleit be taking his job?"

"Seems so, and that burns my ass. I can't stand that bastard." He poured another drink into his glass and took a sip.

"He's got a lot of contempt for the Union," Peter said.

"It's more than that," Alex said. "It's the fucking racism that comes out of him. Little things he says just get under my skin."

"He's hardly alone with those attitudes here. I've heard it from a lot of guys."

"It gets to me more coming from him. Maybe knowing where he comes from, all the apartheid business there." His voice trailed off and he stared at the cigarette package that he toyed with. He took another sip of whiskey and let out a deep breath.

"My birth mother was Cree. From Manitoba. I never knew until I was thirty, when I decided I wanted to find out where I came from. I made all the calls and tracked her down and found out she lived on a reserve five hundred miles north of Winnipeg. There wasn't a god-damn road into that place. I had to fly in." He shook his head. "I was used to living in rooming houses that weren't pretty, but the conditions my mother's people had to live in…" He stared at the desk, his mouth twisted and his teeth scraping across his lower lip.

Peter hesitated, unsure about the question he was about to ask. "So why have you been so opposed to helping with the dust problems on the Reserve?"

"Pretty simple, I guess. I've been ashamed of where I come from." He took a cigarette from the package and lit it. "I know it's pretty fucked up, but I thought that if I didn't support them then nobody would suspect that I was Indian."

"And you still don't support them. We could have pushed the company about the tailings pile."

Alex nodded. "That's true, we could've put that on the table, but it would have been thrown back in our faces. Maybe I'm wrong, but I think we have to take this one step at a time, and if they'll start some real clean-up in the Mill and Rock Reject and make us part of a joint committee on environment issues, then that's a good step for now."

Peter took a deep breath and let the air fall out of him. He felt drained, like he could lie on the floor and sleep for days. "Maybe I will have a drink," he said.

Alex reached for a coffee mug from the top of a file cabinet and poured whiskey into it. Peter let it slowly burn down his throat. They sat with their drinks, the only sound the ticking of the electric heater in the room and the wind outside.

"Are you in touch with your birth mother?" Peter asked.

Alex looked down into his drink. "She died of tuberculosis a year ago."

THIRTY

With the Mine and Mill shut down Stikine slept in silence. The weather system that had brought the snow was pushed aside by high pressure from the southwest, and Peter woke from a dreamless sleep with sun shining into his bunkhouse room. He lay for a while, dazed and collecting his thoughts and thought of Rose, sitting by the window of their apartment playing her guitar with spring sun lighting her hair. He held on to the memory, clinging to the image and the sweetness it brought him, knowing it could be pushed aside in a heartbeat by his sorrow.

The Union team met in front of the Administration Building.

"Obviously we're not in a strong position," Alex said. "The Company will get an injunction if we stay out and I don't see the point of defying it."

"There'd be big time fines if we did," Chris said.

"That's right," Alex continued, "and I can't see the membership wanting to fight against the Company and the courts over this. Let's see what we can negotiate in there, but in the end we'll likely have to go with what they offer."

Peter followed the men up the steps. At the door he stopped and turned. The massive tailings pile loomed behind the Mill, dwarfing the building's six-storey height, but glowing innocent white in the morning sun, entombed by snow and unblemished by any new tailings with the Mill shut down. The air above was crystal clear, free of the haze of dust that usually hovered in the valley. The scene was almost serene, matching his mood, and he imagined for a moment going back down the steps and wandering into the wilderness. He took a last breath and went inside.

Alex and Chris stood by Susan's desk. Raised voices came from the conference room and a moment later the door opened and Carl Moffat came out. He walked past the desk with a grim look on his face and slammed his way out of the building. Simon De Vleit appeared in the doorway in his wake.

"Let's get this business settled," he said to Alex, his voice sharp, then he turned back into the room.

Peter rolled his eyes at Susan as he passed her desk, and she nodded in agreement.

De Vleit sat beside Marshall Whitmore, his arms folded across his chest. Miller was in a chair farther down the table, beside Iggy. Whitmore shuffled papers in front of him.

"Gentlemen," he nodded towards the Union men. "I hope you have come in an agreeable frame of mind and that we can get this operation moving again today. The Company stands by the commitments made yesterday, regarding the scheduling of work in Rock Reject. We are also pleased to tell you that work will begin on dust suppression there and in the Mill by mid-June. And we agree that we can add a lung function test as part of all new hires' medical exam."

"What about everyone who's already here?" Chris interjected. "Why just the new hires?"

"We're not the Department of Public Health, for christsakes," Gerry McMillan said. "We're not going to spend that kind of money to monitor such a low-risk situation."

"You're still sticking to that lie," Peter said.

"What about the joint committee to oversee the changes?" Alex asked.

Whitmore shook his head. "We're not prepared to give over authority in these matters to a committee."

"No joint committee is going to run this mine," De Vleit said. "I'm running this mine."

Miller glanced at De Vleit, his lip curled. Whitmore cleared his throat. "That is an issue that we will address shortly. At this moment, however, what I want to hear from the Union is that their members will be back on the job for the afternoon shift."

Peter and Chris looked to Alex, who opened his folded hands on the table. "Given the promises you've made, and we want to see them in writing, we will recommend that the afternoon shift go in."

"But there better be action on the dust by June like you promise," Chris said. "Or you can be sure you'll be flying back up here to deal with another wildcat."

"And you can be sure there'll be a different response to an illegal walkout next time," De Vleit said. "This mine is going to produce, I promise you that."

"Thank you, Simon," Whitmore said. "As the Union knows, Mr. De Vleit will be taking over the position of general manager from Tom, who has served the Company well for many years now and who is being offered a transfer to another of the Company's operations."

"Cut the crap, Whitmore," Miller said. "You can't call being offered a brake-lining plant in outback Australia a transfer. I'm fired."

Whitmore shrugged. "Call it what you like, Tom. We gave you a relocation option, you refused. That's not firing in my book."

Miller folded his arms across his chest and shook his head. Whitmore turned from him to the Union men.

"And you should also know that Carl Moffat is taking early retirement and his position will be advertised immediately."

"He's being paid to go away and keep his mouth shut, that's what." All the heads at the table turned to Iggy. A surprised silence hung in the room.

"Carl Moffat has been a loyal employee for almost twenty years and he's being rewarded," Whitmore said, his tone persuasive, but uncertain.

Iggy straightened in his seat and looked at Whitmore, his jaw set. "He's sick. He's sick from working all those years in the goddamn dust and you're afraid that he might go to the Compensation Board. It's cheaper to just pay him to go away and sign some deal so he won't say anything about it."

Whitmore leaned towards McMillan and said something into his ear. McMillan pulled a file folder from his briefcase, sifted through it and handed Whitmore a sheet of paper. He looked at it and handed it back. He folded his hands together on the table and looked at Iggy.

"You've been with the Company quite a few years now, Mr. Benedetti, and..."

"You're goddamn right," Iggy interrupted. "And how many people have I told there's no health risk working here?"

"You've been provided with objective scientific information," Whitmore said, his voice raising.

"Selectively compiled by Company scientists," Peter said.

Whitmore gave Peter a brief glance then turned his attention back to Iggy. "What's of greater concern to me, Mr. Benedetti, are the deaths and injuries that have been occurring here under your watch as safety supervisor. These have brought about greatly increased costs for Workmen's Compensation premiums and we are not happy about this."

Iggy's eyes and his voice lowered. "Neither am I. Those men died needlessly. But this place needs a hell of a lot more maintenance than we can do with the budget you give us."

"Your budget is sufficient," McMillan said. "The problem is with the attitude of the workforce, and that has to start with you."

"I have to agree, Gerry," Whitmore said. He looked down the table at Alex. "This is not a discussion for this meeting, gentlemen. We will adjourn and get this operation producing asbestos again."

"Is it true that Carl's sick?" Alex asked.

"Yes," Iggy said. "He told me last night."

"That's enough, Mr. Benedetti," Whitmore said angrily.

"Enough of the truth?" Iggy replied.

"Let me remind you that your contract expires next month," McMillan said.

"And I won't be renewing it. I'm not going to stand in this room and tell any more young new hires that there's nothing to worry about here. That this dust doesn't cause disease."

"There's nothing you can prove," Whitmore said.

"Tell that to my wife." Iggy banged his fists on the table. "She has asbestosis. So if you want to let me go and avoid the embarrassment of another diseased person in town, let's see what you've got to offer. "

Whitmore and McMillan looked at each other. Miller and De Vleit looked at Iggy who sat staring at his hands, his jaw muscles working hard.

"Iggy, I'm…" Tom Miller shook his head. "I'm so sorry. Are you certain of this?"

Iggy nodded. He took a handkerchief from his pocket and dabbed at his eyes, then blew his nose.

"This is troubling news," Whitmore said, taking control of the meeting. "And I want you to know that the Company will assist you and your wife in whatever way we can." He paused for a moment and looked at Alex. "You gentlemen may go and notify your members to be at work for four o'clock."

There was a knock on the door and Susan entered carrying a folded piece of paper. She handed it to Miller and left the room. Miller read the note and handed it to De Vleit.

"Welcome to the job, Simon. You may enjoy looking after this. It'll take you back to your South African days."

De Vleit read the note, then crumpled it into a ball. He turned to Whitmore.

"Goddamn Indians have put up a blockade on the road into town."

"What the hell for?" Whitmore said. "And Christ, why now?"

"The note didn't say."

"I would think it's about the dust pollution in the Reserve," Peter said. "From the tailings pile. And here they've got an opportunity to talk to someone higher up the Company ladder about it."

"How do you know this, Stevens?" De Vleit demanded. "Do you have anything to do with this?"

Peter shook his head. "I'm just guessing, but it seems pretty obvious. There's more dust there than where the Benedettis live. And we know that Lynn didn't get asbestosis from working in the Mill."

"Enough of your speech-making, Mr. Stevens," Whitmore said. "Simon, get the RCMP on the phone. I want this situation cleared up." He gathered his papers and left the room. McMillan hurriedly packed his briefcase and followed behind. De Vleit stood and started towards the door, then paused and put a hand on Iggy's shoulder for a moment, then left the room.

Miller, Iggy and the three Union men sat at the table. A phone rang at the reception desk, truck doors slammed closed and an engine started. Iggy slowly stood up and left.

THIRTY-ONE

Peter followed Alex out of the conference room. He hesitated in the reception area, wanting a word with Susan but she was on the phone and Alex was holding open the door for him.

"Chris is heading back to the office to start notifying the membership," Alex said. "But I want to go out to the blockade. Come with me."

Alex started his truck but didn't put it in gear. They sat looking towards the Mill and the tailings pile. "I noticed you weren't surprised when Iggy said that about Lynn," he said. "You knew about it?"

Peter nodded. "I got information for them from my father."

"Your father's a doctor?"

"That's right. He's a specialist in lung disease."

"Like I said before. You're a rich kid."

"Christ, get off it Alex. I'm no better than you. And I don't want to disown where I come from."

"Like I did?"

Peter shrugged. "People do what they need to do." He zipped up his coat and buried his hands in his pockets. Alex turned up the heater in the truck.

"What's it like here in the summer?" Peter asked.

"Beautiful. Warm. Days so long you lose track of time. I'm not one for fishing like a lot of guys here, but it's nice just to be in that sun on your days off." He put the truck in gear and started out of the parking lot. "You figure on being here when it warms up?"

Peter looked out the side window. Clouds scudded above the trees, opening for glimpses of blue sky. He shook his head. "No. I've breathed in enough dust here. I'm going to head out."

"That's what I figured." A hint of criticism in Alex's voice made Peter ashamed. He tried to imagine staying, doing what he could to make conditions better in Stikine, but his mind was a blank. There was nothing beyond this day.

Alex stopped at the main road and waited as a big front-end loader rumbled past them towards the highway. Towards the blockade, Peter thought. To rip it apart. It disappeared from sight around the Administration Building, but Alex continued to wait.

"What you said about people doing what they need to do. You're the only person I've ever told about my mother. How fucked up is that?" Alex shook his head as if in disgust with himself, then turned onto the road to follow behind the loader.

Around a bend was the blockade, a pile of long, thick logs that stretched across the road. The front-end loader stopped behind a few pickups and the RCMP cruiser. Twenty or more people were on the other side of the barrier, some directly behind it, others around a bonfire in the middle of the road, a hundred feet back. A large tent was near the fire—behind it pickups and a logging truck. Two RCMP officers flanked De Vleit and Whitmore at the edge of the barrier. Alex parked his truck on the side of the road opposite the loader.

"I hope this doesn't get ugly," Peter said.

"I doubt it. If it was just De Vleit I think he'd have a dozer going through there by now, but with Whitmore here he has to cool it." Alex opened his door and stepped out. Peter followed him.

Theresa and her brother Dan stood across the barricade, shoulder to shoulder with others, their arms folded defiantly. Two people with cameras and one with a pen and notebook watched from behind.

De Vleit's arm made a sweeping gesture at the barricade and back towards the loader that was idling behind them, ready to push the logs aside. Whitmore stepped in front of him and raised a hand of caution. De Vleit shouted for the protesters to get the hell off the road immediately, and Whitmore's hand came up onto his chest, firmly pushing him away from the barricade. De Vleit shook him off, then retreated to his pickup.

"This could take a while," Alex said.

"I hope they get what they're after," Peter replied.

Alex watched the people gathered by the bonfire. "It's been good having you on the team," he said. "I'm sorry to lose you."

"I feel badly about leaving. There's so much to do here."

Alex shook his head. "The fight doesn't depend on you, Stevens. It just goes on." He took his hand from his coat pocket and offered it to Peter, who was puzzled as he accepted the handshake.

"You've done your part," Alex said, then turned and walked to the barricade. He climbed awkwardly onto the logs, Dan Grandison offering him a hand down on the other side. Alex spoke while Dan listened and nodded, then they shook hands and went to the fire to join the others.

Peter stood in the middle of the road, feeling a calm come over him that he hadn't known in a long time. He watched a few minutes longer, then turned and walked back to town.

It was just before noon when he reached the steps of the Administration Building. He sat and looked north across the forested valley. A breeze dislodged a clump of snow from the top of a spruce tree, causing a cascade down the branches. Lower ones, freed of the weight, sprang up, throwing snow in the air. The mountain was a wall of white, topped with blue sky. The wide stairs vibrated with footsteps and he turned to see Susan standing on the step above him.

"Waiting for someone?"

"Waiting for you."

She sat down beside him. "Did you go see the blockade?"

"I went out with Alex. It looks like it's a stand-off for the moment." He paused, realizing that emotion was rising in his throat. "Alex went over the barricade to the other side."

Susan looked at him with surprise. "You're kidding. Alex Bruce? Dave always said he was only about the money."

Peter shook his head. "I think he's looking for some truth now. I can tell you more later, but I was wondering if you'd like to go for a walk."

She hesitated a moment, then nodded. "Sure, lunch can wait. Any destination in mind?"

"I know a place."

They walked a hundred yards and he turned them down the service road to where the satellite dish pointed to the sky.

"I didn't know this was here," she said.

"It's neat. You can hear the audio part of the tv signal."

They moved closer to the cement-block hut beside the dish and listened. The midday news was on, talking about a planeload of orphaned Vietnamese children that had arrived in Vancouver to be adopted by Canadian families. They had been flown away from Saigon as North Vietnamese troops were taking the city.

"God, those poor children," Susan said. "To have lost everything and then suddenly they're in a strange land."

"I can almost relate," he replied. "I felt like I had lost everything when I came here in the fall."

"But you didn't lose your home like they did. You can go back if you want."

"You're right. And I think I can go back now."

Susan turned to look at him and their eyes met for a moment, then he pointed through the trees toward the river. "There's a great spot to sit just over there."

The road was unplowed past the dish and they pushed through a foot of unbroken snow to the pile of boulders by the river's edge, where they swept clean a spot to sit. The river was in full break-up, its surface a mass of shattered pans of snow-covered ice tipped at all angles, snapping and moaning as it slowly turned and ground its way downstream.

"I'll miss this," Peter said. "Being able to walk into a forest and sit by a river. Seeing mountains every time I step out of the bunkhouse."

"How soon will you be leaving?"

"In a couple of days, I guess. Assuming of course that the roadblock comes down. I want to go out to Crystal Creek to see Bob and Dianne, and I've got an invitation to dinner in the Reserve."

Susan scooped a snowball together and threw it across the river into a tree. It sent up a cloud of tiny flecks of snow which slowly settled onto the grinding river of ice. "I've been thinking that my time is up here, too."

246

Peter nodded. The cloud cover opened and he felt the warmth of the sun on his face.

"So you're going back to Toronto?"

"Yes. And you? Winnipeg?"

"I can't see it. I don't think I could start something new there."

"I know what you mean. I've wondered if Toronto will be so much of Rose for me that I'll be stuck in the past."

"But perhaps you'll be different, Peter. You've gone through a hard year, and I'm sure it's changed you."

"I hope so. I can't be like I was, but I don't want to forget, either." He looked down at his hands in his lap. "What do you see yourself doing next?"

"I've been thinking about going back to school. Getting a social work degree, maybe in Vancouver. Or…" Her sentence trailed off. A crow flew up the river, sleek in the sunlight, and landed on a treetop. Another flew past and soared high, catching a breeze and hovering in mid-air for a moment before plunging down to a branch farther up the river.

"Or?"

"Or Toronto."

Peter glanced at her. Her face was flushed.

"Toronto would be a great place for you." His voice felt uncertain.

"But I wouldn't want you to think…"

"Don't worry. It's a big city." He felt that the words came out wrong. He wanted to say something more, something encouraging, but the right words weren't there.

"What are the things you need to straighten out back home?" she asked, easing the tension he felt.

"Medical school, for one, to see if they'll let me back in. With a lungful of asbestos maybe I can specialize in respiratory disease. Follow in my father's footsteps."

"Would that make him happy?"

Peter shrugged. "It would probably make me happy. As for him being happy with me, I guess that's another thing I want to straighten out."

They fell into silence, watching the moving mass of broken ice before them. Peter felt the familiar ache in his chest, and wanted to lean against her, to take her hand in his, but couldn't bring himself to do it.

Instead, he pushed himself up and stood atop the rock beside Susan and stretched his arms out wide.

"Now hear this, mountains. I solemnly pledge myself to consecrate my life to the service of humanity."

"My goodness," Susan laughed. "Where did that come from?"

"It's from the Physician's Oath. I'll need to declare it later on, but this seems like a good moment to make a statement."

"It makes me think of the line in the Company's brochure where they call asbestos the Magic Mineral, whose virtues are in the service of mankind."

"The service of mankind." He looked across the river, at the dense spruce forest rising up the slope, breathing deeply of the air that flowed down from the peaks. "Primum non nocere," he said quietly.

"Meaning?"

Peter felt his tears spilling from the corners of his eyes. "First, do no harm."

ACKNOWLEDGEMENTS

Writing my first novel has not been a solitary exercise, and I am indebted to many individuals who have supported me in the process of writing *Rock Reject*.

I am grateful for the inspiration and thoughtful critique I received from Jill Ker-Conway. Readers Brenda McGilvray, Raymond Larkin, Merle Lister, and Linda Pellowe gave valuable feedback, as did the wonderful writing group led by Annie Jacobson, who sadly died in 2005. Lynn Riley and Elizabeth Allemang provided expertise on medical issues. Herb Daum is the Webmaster of the award-winning website www.cassiar.ca which is a great source of photographs and asbestos-related information.

I wish to thank those who have established the Beacon Award competition: Anne Bishop, Steve Hart, Jan Morrell, Beverley Rach, Errol Sharpe and Gloria Wesley. Their efforts have created a tremendous opportunity for writers of fiction with a social justice theme. I am honoured to be the first recipient of the Beacon Award, and I urge writers and those who wish to support the award to visit the website at beaconaward.ca for information.

I am deeply grateful to Beverley Rach and Errol Sharpe of Roseway Publishing, without whom *Rock Reject* would perhaps live only inside my computer, and to my editor Sandra McIntyre, whose outstanding work encouraged me to push the manuscript further.

And finally, to my wife Jane Finlay-Young, who inspired me to begin writing, and who has helped to shape and deepen the novel throughout its development. Without you, and your encouragement and support, Rock Reject would merely be a place where I once worked, many years ago.

More than 100,000 people die each year
from lung disease caused by occupational exposure to asbestos.